Dedication

To J.A.T. 1981

Keep young and beautiful
It's your duty to be beautiful
Keep young and beautiful
If you want to be loved

— "Keep Young and Beautiful"
by Harry Warren and Al Dubin

Dear Diary:

This party is going to be the death of me. I am running around like a Red Bull and vodka in a china shop. I have no one to blame but myself. You see, the thing about giving fab parties is that everyone expects them to be just that. Legendary. Perfection. Divine. The tough part is living up to the hype that you yourself created. Usually Jason will at least make a guest appearance, a token gesture before he disappears saying "Oh honey, this is your turf. Your parties are always great, just handle it." But see, it's our party. Our twentieth anniversary of unwedded bliss and it can't just be another party. It has to be EPIC. And now that marriage is legal for us I want to pop the question in front of all of our friends. So you see, dearest of diaries, with an eleven o'clock number like that, not just any old perfect party will do. This is history in the making...

Moving men are carting tables, ginormous flower arrangements and crystal cacti from one place to another as I keep changing my mind. I've gone through three of the top party planners in New York and have flown in some vamp, who I'm thinking is Joan Crawford reincarnated (seriously, I do not know) from Palm Springs. "It needs a woman's touch," I am told in a basso profundo voice by La Joan who is trying to sell me on a 'desert of diamonds' theme but nothing seems right. I am going to be judged on this frigging party, not Jason. Me. The boy who hit the jackpot. And it's wrong. All of it is just wrong. But how do I make it right? Tell me, Jason, I'll do anything.

The day did not start well. There in his jewelry tray, the black lacquered one with "te amo" written in gold in the center, it was the first luxe gift I ever gave him, are his watch, his bracelet, his earring, …his plastic hotel key? In the immortal words of, oh pick a diva, any diva, "What the fuck?!

When I asked Jason about it, gently asked, casually asked, he stumbled. Just for a moment. Live with a man for twenty years and no blink gets past you. He hemmed.

"Oh that," he hawed. "Lorraine was having trouble with Chris. She had me get her a room in my name so if he started calling around he couldn't track her down."

"She could have stayed here," I say.

"Honey, you don't even like Lorraine." True, but when you live in a triplex penthouse apartment it seems to me you should be able to have the odd house guest, and trust me, Lorraine is odd, without them being underfoot. I know if I pursue the matter I'll just come across as lame, so I drop it and go about getting ready for our day. We'll hit the gym with our his and his trainers, go shopping, he'll call his broker and then it's off to lunch, something mostly liquid, then dress for drinks, meet friends and finally off to an event where we will be photographed and envied.

Jason emerges from his dressing room in a suit. For the gym.

"Who died?" I ask.

"Our investment banker needs to meet with me today. I thought I told you."

You know you're in trouble when he can't even bring himself to lie well anymore. I play along.

"Yeah, you did. I forgot. I'll go with you."

"You'll be bored," he adds a little too quickly. "And you shouldn't skip the gym." He wiggles his eyebrows at me and smiles. "Someone's developing a Special K pinch." I hit him playfully and we laugh. I think I'll buy him a "just because" present when I go shopping. We kiss and he leaves. He always looks his best in a suit. For a man who never had to work a day in his life, he was born for business wear.

I look at myself in the mirror. I can pinch, at best, half an inch, if that. As I do a full 360 to see the level of damage that half an inch has inflicted, I hear a sound from Jason's dressing room, and there on a shelf is a phone, vibrating. It's not his phone, at least not one I would know. You need a code to open it and of course I don't have the code. The vibrating phone goes still in my hand. I put it back, making sure to wipe my fingerprints off it. Like Jason has a fore-senics crew on retainer or something. Why does he need a mystery phone? Who does he need to call that I shouldn't know about? I sit on our bed and make a call of my own.

"Hey Lorraine," I say in a voice that screams "smiley" faces, "it's Javi. It's been too long. You and I need to do lunch."

I pick an obscenely well lit restaurant. It's like we're two marijuana plants under a grow light. All the easier to see her face twitch. And it does. Lorraine lies worse than Jason. He at least kept his cool, Lorraine is openly sweating.

"So how are things with you and Chris?"

"I think we've stabilized." She says as she dabs her upper lip as her food goes uneaten.

Which I take to mean that Jason will be shopping for another alibi. Lorraine is not an eater. In all the years I have vaguely known her the only thing I've ever seen her put in her mouth, besides alcohol and cigarettes, are tic tacs: the woman lives off breath mints. I've brought her a fancy-schmancy cigarette lighter which she fawns over. The chit chat is strained reminding us why we don't really see each other outside of Jason. I pay for lunch, I insist. We air kiss and just as Lorraine was about to make the pitch perfect exit I break with protocol, the never spoken, cast in stone agree-ment that has always existed between us, and grab her hand. She knows something. To ask her point blank would tell her that I know that Jason is seeing someone and it would get back to him and I would automatically lose, cause by knowing I would have to take some action. Do something. I also have to say something. I just can't hold this jittery woman's hand as she half sits half stands. I gently try to tug her down and she, just as gently rises.

"Look at the time," she exclaims, even though neither one of us are wearing watches. She sees the fear/shame/pleading in my eyes and for the first time ever she lets down her considerable guard.

"Darling, survivors survive." And with that she's out the door.

I'm a few blocks away from our investment banker, I could just pop over and take Jason out for drinks, instead I call. Yes, it's the coward's way out, but do I really want to be there when I'm told-

"Hi, this is Javi, is Jason still there?"

This is followed by the pause that does not refresh. The poor assistant hasn't been given his lines. He's smart enough to know he should lie, just not how. Was Jason ever there at all? Did he just leave?

"I...uh...uh..."

"Oh I'm sorry," I say, letting him off the hook and probably saving his job, "I think that's him trying to call me." I hear the grateful exhalation on the other end as I hang up. The kid's probably thinking he dodged a bullet. I wonder if this is his first job, how old he is, is he in love? I'm pretty sure I saw him once at our Christmas party. He looked so out of place. I think of the generic hotel key of this morning and decide to cold call the top three boutique hotels in the city. That key and Jason must be somewhere. I get (un)lucky my second call in.

"I'll connect you with Mr. Wilcox's suite."

The sane part of me wants/needs/has to hang up, uh huh, like that part has ever held any real sway over me. People have meetings in hotels all the time, I lie to myself. There is an eternity and then a "Hello?"

It's not Jason's voice. It's younger, almost sweet actually.

"Hello?" he repeats. I hear Jason's voice in the background. "Who is it, baby?"

And because when in free fall your brain decides to save itself, if not you, I blurt out "Housekeeping. You need towels?"

"No," and I hear him giggle. Kill me. No, really, kill me. "We're good." The giggler says and hangs up.

I close my eyes tightly and am deafened by the sound of my own breathing; the hollowness of it. And just like that I know I'm not enough for the man I love. What I want to do more than anything is grab him by the lapels and scream at him, "You respect me!!!! You respect us!!" but that is not an option. Early in our relationship, I even forget for what, I got so angry over something and had me a full out hissy fit. It wasn't even at him but Jason was beside himself. What could have creased the perfect brow of his perfect boy? And then. it changed. Jason got mad at me for being mad. It didn't matter what I was mad about, it was trivial, unimportant and how dare I be mad? Wasn't I just the luckiest person in the world? I felt terrible. Guilty over the fact that I had been angry. So I never was again. Not in front of Jason, not in front of anyone. But here's the thing, you keep tapping down something, pushing it back, denying it and it sort of disappears. Right now I'm angry at Jason, so angry, but I don't know how to be angry anymore so I scream/whisper at myself, "You fucked it all up! You idiot! You nothing!" "Who is it, Baby?" I keep hearing Jason ask. And here I thought I was baby.

Cue the Alice Through the Looking Glass moment. I am brought out of my self flagellation when I turn a bit too abruptly and walk through a huge sheet of glass two of the manly men movers were gingerly carrying from point A to point B. The whole thing happened as if in slow motion. I hear gasps but in the moment itself it's almost eerily beautiful. Like ice on trees or walking through rain drops that were falling so slowly you could count the individual raindrops. The glass shards, small, large, all sharp and shiny seem to float all around me. I'm about to be sliced to death and I think to myself "Wow, death by cuisineart, what a really odd way to die. Didn't see that one coming." It's strange, grisly and peaceful all at the same time. It's true what they say; in the nano second before you die your life or a montage of your life's greatest hits, pass before your eyes. So quickly and selectively but with enough hidden little triggers to render you zen like before you're officially dead. And all my memories, every single one of them, were about Jason. As if I didn't even exist before him. Jason's first shy smile at me, our first kiss, the first time we held hands-

The moment of perfect silence is broken by a high pitched scream by one of the hirsute movers. I blink and all the broken glass is at my feet. No cuts, no scratches on me. As people grab me, make sure I'm not cut and kiss me, who the hell are these people! (no a better question would be who the hell am I?) zombie like I just say "I'm fine. Really. No, really. I gotta go," and as I walk out I hear someone say, "Did you see that? The rich? Man, they are so fucking lucky."

And so between hyperventilating and the need to projectile vomit I find myself at Vavoom, a gay bar I've never been to, but right now an oasis in this diamondless desert. I have no idea how long I've been here or how many drinks I've had, all I know is that I'm at the come hither urinal, just a peeing away. It's one of those automatic flush things, so your hands can occupy themselves elsewhere I assume. I look at myself in the gold flecked mirror that faces me and not for the first time, I see myself, but not my eyes, like I'm out of focus or something. This is not the cocktails talking. I stick my tongue out, wiggle my eyebrows, but I'm not there, somehow

I'm not really a part of my reflection. Then it happens. My urinal flushes. Hello? It's supposed to sense my presence. I'm standing right in front of the thing, penis in hand, so why the flush job? Okay, clearly I'm not here, and I wasn't there when the glass sliced the air around me but left me intact. So where am I? Will I at least have the common courtesy to send myself a postcard? "Having a wonderful time! Where the fuck are you?" I go back to the bar, and no, no and no. Someone has taken my seat. I left a half filled martini on that bar top, the acknowledged signal for "drinker on board." Now there is a cherub parked on the bar stool that is mine. "Excuse me, hello, that's my seat. My drink was there."

The golden youth (Christ! is no one carding anybody in this hellhole?!) looks me up and down and returns to his conversation with his equally nubile date. I do the only thing I can think of, I whip out my ebony Amex and slap it (ow) hard on the bar top. The bartender, as if lured by its limitless line of credit, magically appears.

"I'm still here!" I Elaine Stritch him.

"So sorry, my fault," the broad smiling bartender says.

"I'm here!" I repeat in a shouted whisper, feeling incredibly stupid immediately afterwards, then angry at myself for feeling stupid. I squeeze my lips together to keep myself from saying anything else.

The bartender puts another drink in front of me, "On the house, sir!" And boy do I feel old. I buy drinks for the guy who took my seat and for his friend, making a big flourish as I sign my name on the tab, leaving the bartender a thousand dollar tip.

notice me.

The bartender barely nods his thanks and moves on to his next customer.

Notice Me.

And the guy at my stool, with his friend, had they played

their cards right I would have been the bestest friend they ever had.

Please Notice Me.

I leave the bar with this feeling that I can't shake; that my warranty is almost up. That I'm about to be going, going, gone. There's a cab stopped at the light and I just get in. The driver is on his cell and ignores me. I tap on the partition and he holds up his hand in a silencing gesture, and the apple cart is finally tipped, the camel has received its last straw. Like a spoiled child I start banging on the partition, screaming, "Notice me! You notice me!!!"

"You crazy or something, mother fucker?!" the cabbie screams back at me.

I apologize all over the place and hurriedly get out and speed walk away as he continues his open and shut case against my sanity.

Walking home calms me down, a bit. I pass some lovely shops and know I could have anything I want in them. No fooling. Emporium Armani? "I'd like everything on this floor. Please." Always add the please, it makes you less, what? shallow? acquisitive? bored? Extravagance is not my birthright. I partnered up. Way the hell up. I remember the first time Jason took me shopping. He was more excited for me than I was. I'd be asking how much things were (none of these stores have price tags. It is beneath them.) and he's like "You like it? It's yours!" I started crying, happy and scared, cause this was so fucking alien to me. He would dress me up like his own Puerto Rican Ken doll and all the sales help would ooh and ahh, and if you, dearest of Diaries, bring up the shopping sequence in Pretty Woman it'll be book burning time for you. But you know, it may be hard to believe, but shopping gets old after a while. You see something shiny and new and you have to have it, but then it gets replaced by something shinier and newer and on and on and world without end, amen.

So what do I do now? This ghost, this translucent man that I've become. I must be lonely, I'm calling my parents. I get my father and tell him I'm running errands. I ask him if he wants anything. He never does.

"No, I don't need anything."

"Not need. Want. Do you want anything?" I am suddenly jonesing to buy something, anything and thus return to the land of the living. The thing about calling my parents is I never have to ask to speak to my Moms, cause even if my father answers the phone it is still her conversation. And I'm not even on speaker phone! She's talking over my father, me, the planet.

"La bendicion," I say, and they answer as they always do, "Que Dios me lo proteja (may God protect you)"

I walk into an ultra chi chi antique shop. They are closing, but upon seeing me smile, pop open the champagne and practically carry me inside. I pick an obscenely expensive chinoiserie, a ridiculous word in any language, for my best friend, uh … Roberto! From back in the days before Jason. Now I see him at our Xmas party and always give him the best gift I can find. I wonder how it will go with Roberto's decor. I've never actually seen his apartment. I must have someone find Roberto's number and reconnect. It's been too long. As I leave, everyone at the store makes a big deal over me, and I hate to admit it, but I feel better. They noticed me. So, did I, Javier Rivera, exist before Jason Wilcox? I go home to an empty Shangri-La and look in the one place I've always been ever since I got my very first one in Woolworth's. My diaries.

Dear Diary:

Today's the day!!! My very first audition! Ever!!! Wish me luck. I'm sooo scared. Big red circle on my calendar, big old knot in the pit of my stomach. Rain had always been real lucky for me so the fact that it's raining is good, right? Right?...

Moms leaned out our sixth floor walk up and told me and the neighborhood that I needed to take an umbrella. She was fully made up, every hair in place and wearing her pink robe with black feathers. She stuck out like a sore thumb. We both did.

"Mira muchacho, llevate una sombrilla, esta lloviendo!"

"Throw me one!"

If she thought I was going to climb back up to our apartment before an audition, she was crazy.

At sixteen I started taking ballet classes. A little late, true, but they were free and I was taller than the girls and I could lift them so I was a find. Moms threw down an umbrella, the one covered in flowers.

"Don't lose it!"

I opened it and hoped it came equipped with a "kick me," sign. My parents thought I was going to school and indeed that was the direction I was heading in; but this day was gonna be different, this day, oh shit, I saw some of my classmates/torturers and tried to hide as much of me as possible under the neon flowered umbrella.

"Adios loca!"

"Quitate del medio, maricon."

I pretended I didn't hear them or see them. That worked on the outside, but on the inside, bueno, not so much. I prayed my Moms had ducked back in and thank God she had. I walked to the subway with the catcalls still raining down on me hot and heavy, wow, someone had their Wheaties! And then someone decided to add the "fua" sound. A person, if we can indeed call them that, says "fua" every time you take a step. It means you're wiggling your ass when you walk. So the sound is "fua, fua, fua." If you stop, they stop, you start up again, they start up again. Strangers even join in, I'm not kidding you. People stand apart from you, no one wants to miss a "fua." And if I tried to ignore it, it didn't matter, they just kept at it. Until my cheeks were burning so much I wished they would just beat me up and get it over with. Girls have even joined in. I tried to butch up my walk which only made it worse. And this happened every day, every fucking day of my life. We got to the subway and while they headed further into the Bronx, I left it. I headed to the Manhattan bound side. Their train arrived first and they all got in some final name calling but they're gone. At last. My breath and facial color returned to normal and I got on my train. Someday, I thought, maybe not today, probably not tomorrow, I'll get on this train and I'll never come back.

It was around this time, even as it sat safely hidden away in my room, that I started talking to my diary as I tried to block out the rest of the world. Notice I said, Diary and not Myself. Talking to myself, well, that's just crazy, talking to a Diary who I could imagine as the keeper of all my thoughts and secrets, who didn't judge, who just nodded and would occasionally say, "Hmm, I see," that got me through every-thing. Sure, you're supposed to outgrow your imaginary friends, but my Diary kept me sane and more importantly let me think the unthinkable, that I would one day be the man I was always intended to be. Just live through this, Javi, cause there is a light at the end of the tunnel. There has to be.

I got lost looking for the audition studio. I made number 68, which meant that after they'd seen everybody from equity and sixty seven non equity people before me, they'd see me. If there's still time. And if they hadn't picked everyone they needed. I took out the notice in Showbiz and read it again, why I don't know, cause I'd memorized it.

"Young Male Hispanic Dancer"

That could be me. I sat on the floor and watched and imitated. I saw somebody stretch, I stretched. Everybody seemed to know everybody else and these guys, when they walked, lemme tell you, it was like a "fua" festival. Somebody smiled at me and I looked down, hoping they didn't see that I really didn't belong there, cause God help me, I never ever wanted to leave this place. Everybody's life is a musical, maybe this is where mine was going to start!

Dear Diary!!!!!

I got it!!! I am a dancer in a Broadway show called, "FUEGO!" I love the entire world!!! Thank you thank you thank you baby Jesus!!!! I'm doin' a novena starting tonight! ...

I lucked out. I had the looks they wanted, if not the skills and they kept me pretty much in the background until my one solo bit. Front and center I did a full rotation jump. I'd be walking right at you and all of a sudden I'd get airborne, like I was gonna tumble at you, only I'd land on my feet and keep walking. I had seen somebody do it in a movie once and I taught myself how. Took weeks, hell, probably months and I was too young and stupid to know I could have broken my neck so I kept trying till I got it.

When I auditioned for the show I was easily the weakest dancer; I had only just started taking classes, so just as they were about to cut me from the line up, I did the flip. Uncalled for and unexpected. It was followed by total silence. The dance captain looked me up and down and said "Do that again." I did. Somebody behind me muttered "bitch," but hey I was in. And the first thing, the very first thing I did was drop out of school. My parents, the school counselor, God himself could not make me go back.

Dear Diary:

Rehearsals are going good. They put my flip in the big opening number and after that I think they're going put it in the finale, that's like the end of the show before the curtain calls. I don't know about how anything is supposed to be done. So many of the people from FUEGO know each other from other shows. I asked one of them, I still can't remember their names, if we were gonna go out of town to preview, like when they show it in the movies, and he looks at me like I'm retarded or something and tells me, "Oh please, we're lucky this piece of shit is opening at all!" I don't think that's very loyal. Roberto says they're just bitter theatre queens. Roberto is so funny!!!...

Dear Diary:

They tell me I got to wear my costume in both acts, even though the story takes place over a couple of weeks. I wanted to ask the director about that but I didn't want him to yell at me too, so I just decided that my character is poor. I gave him a name, too, cause right now he's "the boy who does the flip." I've decided my character's name is Augustin Adams. Classy, right?! Maybe I should make that my show business name, what do you think? Once the show opens and I'm making me some good money I wanna get an apartment in the city,

*roommates with Roberto. I'm gonna learn how to drive. And I
wanna start dating!!!! I can't wait to fall in love...*

Dear Diary:
I just noticed this guy who's been coming to our show...

At this point I put my diary down and pour myself another
drink. I refuse to go into this part of my past without an alco-
holic chaperone. I was so green, so trusting and Jason, well,
Jason was so perfect. I look up and see a picture of him, and
toast him, "Hey, remember me? You came to see my show...."

Dear Diary:
*Our reviews were only a little betterer than "Got Tu Go
Disco" but this guy, he's coming every fucking night. He's
gorgeous too. I asked Ruben (another dancer and I HATE
him!) who he was and he told me, "Girl" and why do they
call me girl, I'm not a girl!, "he's just an usher. Ignore him."
Well, that explains it, I mean every night, and every performance a different seat and always up front. I think he's scoping
somebody out, but who? Then one night, after my flip, when I
landed, we were totally eyeballing each other. he had found the
seat. Every show after that, including matinees, hello, fucking
matinees!, he was there and I would flip and land in his eyes...*

It took two weeks before he talked to me. Met me at
the stage door. No Pops, like in the movies, just an evil old
short woman with a flash light she used like a club. Jason

was outside. Didn't say anything, just looked at me till I said "Hey."

I was still seventeen.

After every show he was there, outside the stage door, kinda shy and sweet like. We talked a little and then I would go out to a bar. Until one night I finally asked him, "Aren't you hungry?" So I took him out for some Chinese Cuban, which he'd never had, but loved right away. I didn't let him pay, cause hey, I asked him out and if he's an usher he was probably not making as much as me anyway. We finally held hands when he walked me to the subway, and even though some fucker yelled out "Faggots!" I didn't care. I liked him so much.

Dear Diary:

The first time I see the limo I thought, oh look at him, that's so cute, he's gone and done himself a rental, but then I find out, no, this shit is his. The driver, in full uniform okay?!!! opens the door for us and as I'm sitting there Jason drops it on my stupefied lap. He's rich. Not well off, not wealthy, rich.

"Hey, I'm rich too!" I tell him how much I make "and that's after they take out all my deductions! So tell me, why you ushering?"

Jason looks at me and smiles so big, he takes my chin in his hand and kisses me.

Now, I know you're supposed to close your eyes when you kiss, cause that's how the movie stars do it, but I can't and he can't and we start giggling while we're kissing.

We drive around, me oohing and ahhing, cause somehow everything looks different from the back of a limo. Jason is just smiling at me. At some point he falls asleep, he said he was so nervous about telling me he didn't even sleep last night, so he's there with his head on my shoulder (like the song!) and a little drool runs out of his mouth on to my shirt. I think I just fell in love...

I put my diary down and look around. I'm in my office, surrounded by pictures of myself, or I should say of us. Us being fabulous, with celebrities, royalty, in places that defy logic. Pop up books of colorful memories, candid shots that have been mounted and framed like my hunting trophies. Look what I did! Look who I am! But what did I do and who am I? My eyes come to rest on my favorite picture. The one that makes me smile every time I see it. It's a picture of Hillary Clinton, and no I'm not in it. Neither is Jason. It's a picture of four presidents, Carter, Bush, Clinton and Bush and their first ladies. Hillary (oh look, now we're BFF's), Mrs. Clinton had just run for the New York Senate and won. The photo was taken a day or two afterwards. Now, I'm assuming she was locked into this presidential photo op win or lose, but she won. And the total joy smile on her face is so - alive, so there, so present. Hey, Hillary, how'd you do it? How did you get your own life, I ask her. She's still smiling. Mama's got herself a job!

...Well, I have a job, too. I call the questionable party planner and leave a message.

"Change in venue, we're doing it here; the theme is the past. Twenty years worth of memories. You can use anything you need," then add in my best Tim Gunn, "Make it work." This party will prove to Jason, my understudy and the world, that mine still is the name billed above the title!

When Jason comes home I am on the floor of our room, full martini shaker, two glasses and surrounded by every Valentine's day card he has ever given me.

"What's this?" he asks cautiously.

I pick up the card nearest me, don't even bother opening it and smile, "Belize. 2003."

There is a small hesitation on his part, or am I imagining it, but he smiles and sits on the floor next to me.

"And this one." He just shows me the front of it, but that's all I need.

"1999. London."

"You've memorized them?"

"Hey, it's our history."

He pours the martinis as I recite from memory the year and location of every card. It's easy. I treasure each and every one of them. That night we made love and spooned and as he drifted off to sleep, I dare to say, "I love you, Jason."

"....me too."

And his half hearted answer was how, after the day's earlier miraculous miss, my heart, my heart was finally shredded to pieces. Help me, Mrs. C, how did you do it? How did you take a public humiliation of such front page magnitude and rise rise rise? Cause I'm sure it's not just Lorraine who is Jason's secret keeper. How many people are laughing at me behind their imported Swiss lace dinner napkins? This should fire me up and it does, but what it doesn't do is help me pull the trigger on my rage. Why didn't I ever learn to throw a punch, to fight instead of just being quiet and hoping that all that is hurtful and painful will pass?

"....Jason?"

He doesn't hear me.

"Jason," I repeat, in a more 'yes, my balls have dropped' voice.

"Yeah?" he answers, totally nuanceless. My fear that if I bring it out in the open he'll be forced to tell me what I don't want to hear, silences me until I finally say, "You and me should go away together. Someplace we haven't been to.

I don't know. Someplace. It's our anniversary. Twenty years."

"I know," he whispers in a tone that is weighted down with everything and nothing. Thinking that shattering glass means I can shatter silence, I throw down. It's all I got, and it comes from the heart.

"We should get married."

Saying it in the dark, while we both stare at the ceiling, offers me none of the safety net I thought/hoped it would. I have used the last bit of self control/self respect I have by not adding 'please'. Yeah, that's my triumph, I proposed to the man I love, but I stopped myself from begging. When did New York become so quiet? When did every sound in the universe disappear? I reach over to turn on the light but he takes my hand and kisses it. And that's how we ultimately fall asleep, two men who have been in love for twenty years, holding hands. I don't know if nothing was resolved or if everything was.

Dear Diary:

He's gone before I even wake up. I stay in bed as long as I can, but the sound of my Ms. Party Planner and her merry men mean I have to get up and deal with the party. As the weakest man in the world I don't know what else to do. You think you hate me, Diary, you think I'm nothing more than a pathetic weakling? You have no idea the slime I throw on myself, the hatred I feel at me for not knowing how to say, "No! This is unacceptable!"…

Midday, Jason appears, like some sort of golden mirage. He comes into the eye of the party planning storm and casually puts his arm around my shoulder as I walk him through what has been planned so far. He nods, smiles, introduces himself to everyone as we walk around, and his arm never leaves my shoulder. He must be able to hear my heart, beating like a drum machine through my chest, I can. He looks at me and there is the shy smile I first remember. I am so afraid of destroying the fragility of this moment that as much as I just want to be alone with him we stay right where we are. He tells me how great everything looks and kisses my cheek and it's better than romantic, it's ownership. It's us. Again. Maybe my cowardice saved me. Maybe I was right all along. Be quiet and all will return to normal.

Dear Diary:

All systems go for our anniversary party/coronation. We just have to survive tonight and get out of town, anywhere, first thing tomorrow. Fingers are crossed!...

It is shoulder to shoulder guests, most of them men, all of them certifiably fabulous. I am certain he has invited "baby" to the party, don't ask me why. Maybe to compare us side by side? To get his friends opinions? I tell Jason to mingle while I hold court, but really it's just so I can follow him throughout the party. I want to see who he spends too much time talking to, or who he very specifically ignores. People keep stopping me to wish me happy anniversary and I just air kiss them and keep my eye on my prize. Okay, Jason is good. No lingering glances, touches or cheek kisses. I lose Jason in the crowd, coño, where is he? A cater waiter exchanges my empty appletini for a full one, and I'm off. He calls out a "happy anniversary" to me and I give him a half smile and hurry after Jason. I can't look at any young guy here without thinking, "is it him? is that the one?" The party is in full swing and I finally find Jason upstairs in our room, alone with his head in his hands.

"Hey honey," I whisper to him, "the party's downstairs."

He looks up and he's crying. Tears streaming down his beautiful face.

"I don't want to ruin it for you. This is your day.," he says. "Our day," I correct him. All I need to do is tell him, "let's put this all behind us, I forgive you." Instead I say the stupidest thing any human being can say.

"As long as you're honest with me, everything will be okay."

He looks at me and says it.

"I'm in love with somebody else and I want to be with him. I have to be with him."

And I die. There's just no other way to put it. I die.

I never made it back down to the party. They cut the cake, piled up the presents and left while I polished off a bottle of vodka with my puffy eyes swollen shut. No, Jason won't tell me who "it" is and his friends are useless and suddenly unavailable for lunch, and by lunch I mean cocktails.

You give twenty years to a man, you think you're safe. Not so fast my homohoney. I could dig in my heels and refuse to leave or I could be all noble and Norma Shearer like and get out, knowing that he'll love me even more in the last reel. Guess which one dummy did?

I take no money from him (I know, world class idiot) but I had lived off him for so long I wanted him to realize that it wasn't about the money, I really loved him. Love him. So, having no money, no job, no skills, I did what anybody would do; I move in with my parents.

After eleven years, Jason had finally won them over and they live in the brownstone Jason had bought for them on my 30th birthday. I remember Jason handing them the keys and thanking them for having me, the love of his life. Shit, even my parents had to accept the building after that line. My Moms walked the entire building in total silence, which if you knew her would scare the crap out of you. It was the pocket doors from the dining room into the kitchen of the main floor that finally got a reaction from her. She nodded her head and said, "okei." She and Jason sort of got along after that, not like best friends or anything, thank God, cause that would have been weird, but she no longer scrunched up her face whenever she mispronounced his name after that. My parents kept an apartment for themselves and rented out the others. That became their income. My Pops quit his job in maintenance and planted a vegetable garden in the back. I think it was the first time I saw my Pops really smile.

Dear Diary:

Today I arrive at my parents with nothing with me but my personal belongings. No credit cards, no money. I want Jason to know it's him that's important, not his bankroll. Of course I do have a few bags and trunks. Forty two to be exact. Hey, I'm not gay for nothing...

The driver piles up my bags around me. My Pops takes them down to the basement, two by two, cause that's where the only empty apartment is, and that's to be my new home. I'm kinda shell shocked. Seeing all my clothes, over twenty years of couture, defining me, surrounding me, can do that to a guy.

I grab two bags from the remaining pile and follow my Pops downstairs. My Moms calls out that she'll watch the bags still left. "Hey, leave that alone. Those belong to my loser eson. The one who landed a billionaire and couldn't hold on to him!"

Ah, my Moms. My relationship with her has always been what our lady of Ms. Oprah would call "complex" and what I would say was "quitate tu, pa' ponerme yo" (get out of the way, so I can replace you with me). She always knew how I should be living my life, never hesitated to share it and when it turned out that I was right about something and she was wrong, she'd swear - hand to heart on her very life and that of her own mother- that my being right had come from a suggestion she had given me. So living with my parents in the same apartment was not an option. Living in the basement apartment originally meant for a super and kind of unrentable because of the fluorescent lights and half windows that make it look like Guantanamo Bay Club Med, living here is a better option than upstairs with the Spider Woman and Gentle Ben. My Moms and me under the same roof? Uh, no. My Pops is a quiet man, only I think cause after a while he stopped trying to get a word in edgewise.

I have to duck my head to enter the basement doorway. I had only seen it once, when Jason and me and my parents did a walk through and he handed them the keys to the building. Man, I loved him so much that day. I just hung back and took it all in. When we left, my parents waving us off, proud homeowners standing on their very own stoop, recipients of the American dream, I started crying so hard that Jason had the driver pull over. It was, as the saying goes, the happiest day of my life.

The apartment is, well come on, it's a fucking basement apartment. I had just left a triplex penthouse. My Pops clears his throat and tells me how they cleaned it up. There's furniture pieces here and there that other tenants have left behind. And my never ending suitcases help fill it up so it doesn't look so pathetically empty.

"No, it's fine, Pops. It really is." I nod and ooh and ahh.

He's happy. We're interrupted by a loud thud, thud, thud. "Somebody put sneakers in the dryer again!" and Pops is off. It seems my little nest is right next to the laundry room. What bliss.

Dinner with my parents was an obligation I couldn't get out of. Or as my Moms put it:

"Nene, ju have no food in jour fridge yet and by the way how are ju gonna buy groceries when ju don't have a yob yet." My Moms needs no oxygen when she's on a roll.

I, dutifully go upstairs for dinner and my Moms has made all my favorites. My Pops has made me a Cuba Libre and Moms has put out the Ritz crackers with Cheese Whiz as an appetizer along with the little Vienna sausages that come in a can. I'm suddenly thirteen again and my taste buds drop their acquired high faluting airs and embrace the much missed high processed salty goodness. I am so grateful that my parents always have their radio and television going at the same time, it means that conversation is not mandatory and any big personal reveals can't outlast the commercial breaks, so as long as I nod and say "okay" every so often, I'm fine.

We get to the main course, which I should have thought of before gorging myself on lower level food, and we're all seated at the table. That's when the empty place setting next to me sets me off. I can't help myself and I begin to cry. And like the numskull, idiot, loser I am, I try to power through. Like my parents won't notice me crying as I continue to shovel the food in.

"Javi..." my Pops says gently. My Moms, wanting to say something, but invariably going the drill sergeant tough love route, says "Que feo se ve un hombre llorando." (Nothing uglier than a crying man). In this case I have to agree with her. So I pretend I'm not crying and they pretend I'm not crying and we continue our meal. Not one of our more comfortable ones, but also not the worst one we've shared.

After tonight's tear fueled meal, Pops makes me a Cuba Libre for the road, the short walk back to my basement apartment. Moms waits until he's watching La Condesa (a gossipy political puppet, and no, I'm not kidding) before she switches out my drink for a pitcher. She doesn't say a word, just a "sssh" gesture as I sneak out.

Later on I start unpacking and turn on the TV. My father had rigged the cable and Robin Byrd's Men for Men comes on. I look at all the beefcake gyrating and I wonder could Jason have left me for somebody like that? Coño, she's been airing these same guys since the Inquisition. Vladimir Correa looks so young. Was I ever that young? The next day I stay in bed, between the hangover, the crying jags and my own little pity party, it's quite a full day, thank you very much. My Pops comes down to check on me but I just tell him I vant to be alone. Suddenly I'm Swedish. I wait until I hear his sigh and his footsteps fade before I go back to what I've been doing for three days, reading my old diaries, trying to find the Javier Rivera that Jason fell in love with. I'm in there. I know I am.

Dear Diary:
I wanna do it already!!!!!! Today's my eighteenth birthday. Jason gave me a bracelet, he couldn't even look me in the eyes, and told me he loved me. He is breathing really loud. I tell him I love him, too, cause I did. He says,
"No, you're in love with being in love." And I told him, "No, asshole, I'm in love with you!"...

I threw myself at him in the limo. And we didn't come up for air until we hit the penthouse suite of the Plaza Hotel. I almost died. I knew he had money, but I had no idea what rich really meant. Being the sane and considerate person he was, he was trying to walk me through what it meant to be rich in his world. "They're renovating my place. I hope this is okay." Baby, it was more than okay

The bitches back stage were all sure he would dump me once I put out, but the opposite happened. He wanted me with him 24/7. He wanted me to sleep over. I reminded him I still live with my parents. What was I supposed to tell them, huh? He was patient, but persistent, like a dog with my bone, but when the renovation on his place was finally done he asked me to move in with him.

"He must have a lesbian gene in him." Ruben, the chorus boy from hell, sneered.

I had no idea what that meant. I didn't care. I loved him. So I had a Bacardi straight up, and I told my parents everything. My Pops, oddly enough, took it pretty good. I mean, he's a Puerto Rican Pops. I half expected him to kill Jason, then me. But no, he just nodded sadly. My Moms, she was another story. Hell no! No. No period. She would not accept it. Case closed. Jason brought flowers, gifts. She was always polite, but cold. Like those thin lipped people who say "love the sinner, hate the sin." Only in my Moms case I didn't even think it was about religion. She just thought I would change. Like I'd start wearing a dress or something. When I told her I wouldn't, her eyes went dead on me. "Ju are breaking jour Pops' heart," she said. This stopped me for a beat, cause I realized I probably was, but I was in love and I knew Jason's the one. So at 18 and 7 months I moved in with Jason.

I was swallowed whole by gay society. Jason was one of their Gods and that made me a demigod. I didn't talk right, dress right, hell breathe right, but suddenly everything I did was "charming, simply charming." People started calling us, JasonandJavier, all one word, or Jas and Javi. That was us!!!

Just as I'm done relieving and reliving myself I enter my

living room to see my Moms standing there with a plate of food. How could I have thought she wouldn't have an extra key? Cutting to the chase, she opens with, "Three days! Three days, cabroncito, and ju look like eshit."

She takes over the unpacking and I eat. I firmly believe that in another life my Moms was a mute, or not allowed to talk because she more than makes up for it in this life. On the plus side, all you have to do is nod every so often, that's all she needs. My problems somehow become her problems, her memories, her life and she's off! I go to take a shower, come out and she's still talking. I finally snap.

"Moms, it's my life that sucks, not yours. Mine! So can we talk about me for half a second?!"

"Well, honey, of course jour life is in the toilet. Ju never want to follow my advice."

And as she turns to go, she delivers her zinger.

"If I had landed a Yason Wilcox, ju'd better believe I estill have him."

And she's out the door, her work here clearly done.

Dear Diary:

So I don't think Roberto likes Jason. Every time I tell him to come out with us he's always making up some lameo excuse. Why can't he just be happy for me? That's what best friends are supposed to do, right? I mean we still go to the bars and clubbing, but every time he sees Jason I can tell he don't like him. Tonight we were at the Sound Factory, best dance club!!!! and this really good song comes on and I had to pull Roberto up to dance with us. What's up with that? Tomorrow is Roberto's birthday and I'm gonna spend it just with him...

I see I taped the cringe worthy Polaroid to prove that we did just that. No, really, who dressed us? I took him to Fiorucci's and bought him this really cool (for then) jacket and when I went to pay he asked me, "who's paying for this, you or Jason?" We had our first fight that day, right there at the cash register. He had been my everything before Jason. The first program I got for "FUEGO" I didn't give to my parents, I gave to Roberto. Suddenly it hits me, before Jason broke my heart, Roberto did.

Dear Diary:

I blame the Solid Gold dancers for my demented desire to be a dancer. Them and Rita Hayworth. She was so beautiful and graceful and Latina (okay, half Latina, hey, Spain counts) that I would dream of dancing with her. Whenever I see a movie of hers is on TV during the day, I make up an illness to stay home so I can watch it. And I read everything I can on her. Did you know she was married to some guy called Orson Welles and that she was so intimidated by his friends that when they were all at a party she wouldn't get up from the sofa cause she thought that everybody would just stare at her. Ms. Rita, of course they gonna stare. You were head exploding beautiful...

Jason found out about my obsession with La Hayworth and bought copies of all her movies so that I could see them in the comfort of his mini (and there ain't no mini about it) theatre. But it's strange, you know. It wasn't the same thing, me sitting in the lap of luxury as opposed to me under an old ratty bedspread, popping Cheetos and watching them in my underwear.

Yeah well, opulence wasn't just for breakfast anymore.

Not in Jason's world. He had decided to host an informal little get together to introduce me to his friends. It was three and a half months and I guess the man was coming up for air. He took me to get my hair cut - $500.00! had he never heard of Cuts For Less? and shopping for a dressy casual ensemble. I use to know them as a shirt and pants, but in this world they are an ensemble. At one point he followed me into the dressing room to "check the fit" ahem ahem and practically did me right there. I swear the man is the horniest person I ever met. We made out in the car on the way back, on the elevator. He couldn't keep his hands off me and I liked it. I mean, I was all into him, but Jason transcended brazen. Security cameras be damned. The man was a walking Barry White record.

Once home, the hors d'ouevres (food) is set up, we dressed and the first guest is "announced." Yes, announced; and they just keep a coming. I had invited Roberto and sweet baby Jesus, am I glad when he showed up, cause I had already screwed it up. Apparently, instead of air kissing people I'd been laying a big old wet one on them. Jason gently corrected me and I thought, first mistake. How many do I get? Someone named Kearn arrives, looked me up and down, and I swear to God, smirked. I grabbed Roberto and steered him to a corner. He was my life preserver. The only way I could get through this thing is clinging on to him for dear life. But Roberto had his own worries.

"I thought you said dressy casual."

"You're fine," I whispered back, complimenting him on the crease in his jeans. Roberto's not having it. To be fair I've had a little more time to acclimate to the luxe life, I just threw Roberto into the deep end and screamed "swim, mother fucker, swim!" I kept getting pulled away to be introduced to someone or other and my friend was left trying to look like he belonged here. I recognized that look. I saw it every single day when Jason's not around and I had to ask somebody how to turn on the TV. Heroic Roberto tried to tough it out but he suddenly developed a flu and said he had to leave.

"No! Please don't!" I was not above begging tonight. I can't do this alone. I kept telling Roberto how great he looked, but I knew he felt like our parents plastic slip covered living room furniture placed in the lobby of the Hilton Hotel. I tried to hold on to my best friend's hand but I felt it slip away as I was lifted on my pedestal beside Jason.

"I'll call you," he told me as he zipped up his Members Only jacket and headed to the elevator. Roberto's discomfort had only made clearer to me how thin the air is up here. I found a spot on a settee (small stupid sofa) and rooted myself on it. Jason, sweet sweet Jason, had made the whole thing a buffet, no doubt thinking the more informal it was the more fun (and less threatening) for me it would be. But as everybody moved around, getting food, talking to people, refilling their drinks, I, shades of Rita, stayed firmly planted in place. I was afraid. Who was I to be in this room with all these fabulous people? Jason winked at me from across the room and I prayed that the sounds of the party would drown out the sound of my grumbling stomach. Roberto got on the elevator and we stared at each other for a moment, we both nodded and smiled, but it's like we both knew that we're now traveling in different galaxies. In the semi seconds it took for the doors to close on him I thought of the two boys we were not so long ago. Him assassinating Shakespearean monologues and me trying to imitate dances I had seen on TV. We were just boys with dreams we hoped would be enough to take us out of sissyboy hell. I got out, why couldn't I bring my friend with me? I looked around the room and took in my new peeps and I just just knew there was not a Roberto in the bunch.

I suddenly hear something at my door, someone's there. They don't knock, just slip an envelope underneath. I look through the peephole and see my Pops quickly disappear up the stairs. Inside the envelope is fifty dollars and a little note "mi'hijo, go out and enjoy yourself." Yes, it's come to this. My Pops is footing the bill for my return to the gay scene. Nadir, table of one, that's Nadir table of one. Okay, so I can't go to one of the bars in the gayborhood cause I don't want to run into anyone Jason and I might know. Worse, what if I run into Jason and my replacement? I ain't no Meryl Streep papito, I would crumble like a house of cards. But I have vaguely heard of a bar nearby, walking distance. Who knew? When I grew up all the gay boys would have to commute. Apparently not now. We're here, we're queer, we're local locas. This is the difference to my folks living in the Heights opposed to the Bronx where I grew up. Just a couple of subway stops away, but a world away from the place that was my battlefield for so long.

Having more than a few fashion options at my disposal, I will armor myself with the perfect outfit. Let the outside do all the work while the inside remains MIA. Get through this, Javi, or stay in this basement apartment for the rest of your life.

It's still on the early side, but the bar I've chosen for my debutante re-debut, The Red Castle, is packed. I order my appletini and look around. Couples, singles, women laughing hysterically at some bitchy comment said by their gay boys. I'm too old for this. I should be home, oh that's right I don't have a home. Vintage Yolandita/Ednita is playing in the background, and even though it's a dance mix it's still about that evil man who done did them wrong. I lose myself in my drink. Holding onto the stem of the glass as if it were my best friend and therefore I wasn't alone, no, I was with someone. Someone who found me attractive, smart and funny and knew enough to never leave my side.

And that's when I notice Roberto!! Only my very best

friend in the whole entire world! Pudgy, sweet, glasses. "Roberto!"

I run over to the other side of the bar and embrace him.

"Omigod, Roberto! I have been missing you so much!"

"Oh look, it's Javi."

I notice his less than enthusiastic reception but that's probably cause Roberto, he hates Rob okay, Roberto was never much into PDA's. I take the stool next to him.

"I am so fucking happy to see you, it's been like forever and ay, another martini, you?"

"I'm good. And it's Rob now."

"Oh. Well, you're more than good." I sing out, "You're simply the best!" No smile, no nothing. "Okay, so I've just had the worst couple of weeks of my life. I broke up with Jason, no, I know, I know, but he no longer prizes the prize that is me, so he must be taught a lesson, don't you think? So I'm bacheloring it and looking at career options and you are like a gift from the gods, see when I decided to make my move I knew it was the best thing for me and running into you proves it!"

"Does it hurt less the faster you talk?"

Okay, direct hit.

"I, me, I, me, those are the only two words you know." snaps Roberto. Sorry, Rob.

"I was never jealous that you fell in love or that you had that glam life, but I was angry mariconcito, that in that triplex heart of yours with the 180 degree skyline views, there wasn't a corner for me and our friendship."

Okay, maybe a little one sided, no?

"Rob/Roberto, you were jealous that I fell in love, and I couldn't help that. You left me. You walked out on me when all I wanted to do was stay friends. I would call you and you wouldn't return my calls. You left me. You were the one who ended it, not me." When the words leave my mouth I realize I'm talking to both Jason and Rob/ Roberto/whatever he wants me to call him, and I'm about to lose it. I make to bolt out, but he grabs my forearm.

"Sit."

I've yet to cry in this particular bar and I would like to keep it that way.

"Ask me about me."

I sit back down. Roberto/Rob's face has regained some of it's softness.

"How are you?" I humbly ask.

"I'm a 39 year old tubby actor, losing his hair, temping more than I'm acting and I'm still unattached." We share a small laugh. "And I'm still doing better than you are right now," he adds.

"Missed you," I say, totally from the heart.

"Shut up," he teases. "You still have most of your hair. Speaking of which you better land somebody before you start spray painting your scalp brown. I'm just saying."

"Was I really such a bad friend?"

"You used to invite me to your posh Christmas parties and then ignore me."

"I gave you gifts!" it sounds weak, even as it's leaving my mouth.

"No, the butler handed them out. You were too busy playing Perle Mesta."

"…they were nice gifts." I half heartedly mumble.

"No, Javi, they were spectacular gifts. I'm not gonna lie, I don't do that anymore, those gifts were insane. I paid my rent with them."

"So can we be friends again?"

"Buy a girl a drink at least."

I suddenly realize that after my last round and tipping like I was still the me of yore, I don't have enough money for this most basic of social transactions.

"I…."

"I'll cover you. I didn't fall from Mount Olympus so I still earn my money."

"I didn't fall. I left."

"You didn't leave. You were dumped." He softens. "No more lies, remember?"

"That's great for you, but not for me."

"Have you seen him?" he asks.

"Who?"

"The kid Jason dumped you for."

"What do you mean kid? Is he a minor? Is Jason a predator? Can I expose him? I'm kidding."

Rob calls Victor, the bartender, over.

A word about Victor. He is not for the faint of heart. He is the consummate cockteaser, gorgeous and wears as little as legally permitted. His name is spelled out in varsity letters on his red spandex short shorts across his perfect ass.

"Rob! When are you gonna marry me and take me away from all of this?"

"It's on my todo list, Victor. This is Javi. My good friend."

I exhale.

"We need a couple of Hawaiian Punchtinis and some info."

"You remembered!" I almost shout. "I haven't had one of those in so long!"

Victor begins preparing the drinks. He is poetry in motion. Lewd, filthy, obscene poetry, but hey, poetry.

"So you're the dumpee? Dang, that's rough." Victor says without judgment.

"You've seen the kid, right?" Rob asks, as if he was doing a guest shot on Law and Order.

"Yeah, I was working a benefit at the Met. Usually don't like those fully dressed things, but hey, it was closing in on my nephew's birthday."

"Focus, Victor. What did the guy with Jason Wilcox look like?"

Victor pours, studies me for a moment, then drops:

"Like you, only twenty years ago."

I grab the drinks, yes both of them, sloppily down them and run out, almost knocking over a drag queen making her grand entrance.

"Bitch! I will cut you!"

I get outside and I can't breathe. Hell, I can barely stand. I sit on the curb. Rob joins me and surreptitiously passes me a drink.

"Nurse this one. You'll need it." It gets worse. "He was a cater waiter," Rob adds.

Oh God.

"At one of the parties you guys gave last year. On Valentine's Day."

"How do you...." my question dangles in the air.

"I had Victor ask."

"So you were like enjoying all of this? I was like your fucking entertainment?"

"No, I just wanted to know what my friend was up against. Come on, let's go back inside."

"I can't face Victor."

"Please. That loca has seen more drama than Bette Davis. We'll order a pizza and share it at the bar. I'm buying."

Back inside, the drag queen "Lorena," hisses at me, but other than that, people ignore me. We sit again. Victor approaches me with a fresh Hawaiian Punchtini.

"I can sugar coat it or I can give it to you straight," Victor says.

Rob counters with, "Mira loca, the only thing you ever gave straight was vodka."

"That was neat, not straight."

"Whatever."

Bringing us back to my drama I hear myself ask in a voice that sounds oddly like Greer Garson in When Ladies Meet, "Does the kid have a name?"

"Eric Colon," Victor says, as gently as possible.

"Once you've had Rican, you won't go a seekin."

I kill Rob with my eyes.

"Eric's a sweet kid, sorry, that's what I hear from everybody." Victor adds. "He's about twenty, kinda shy, kinda of a mystery. This is the hard part." Victor warns, "Take a big swallow."

I gulp half the drink.

"Everybody is saying that Jason was the one who did all the chasing. Eric knew about you and didn't want to have anything to do with him."

The saint.

"He scored himself a Jason Wilcox." Victor says in a kind of awe filled voice.

"You'll kindly refer to him as that worm!" I snap.

"Just wore him down. He's moving Eric in."

And as Lorena hits the stage and launches into Whitney's "It's Not Right, But It's Okay," I know that now I have officially crossed over into hell.

I lay in bed all night unable to sleep. Not the alcohol, not the exhaustion from the constant crying, nothing can usher me into dreamland. Every time I read an old diary entry I am reminded of my paradise lost and how completely and stupidly guileless I was. And I must take full responsibility for that. If indeed I was armorless, defenseless, it was a choice I made, cause it would make me more what? Desirable? A catch? When did ignorance become an aphrodisiac?

Dear Diary:

I am going jogging today, cause I can't afford a fucking gym membership! But I'm not bitter, or angry or fuck fuck fuck Could Jason possibly have bought the little skank a membership to our gym...

Jogging gives me a chance to look at the old neighborhood. The building my parents own is just a couple of blocks from where I grew up. It's one block into Manhattan from the Bronx. Siberian Manhattan, but Manhattan. There are enough people who speak Spanish that when the whites move in they learn the language just to be able to haggle with the local shopkeepers who have no respect for you unless you bitch and moan about the prices. Someone stops me thrusting a pamphlet at me. Have they never heard of runner's etiquette?

"We're having a meeting at the Center," cute guy informs me.

"Excuse me, running."

"One of our gay brothers was assaulted right on this corner and the cops did nothing."

"Okay, first, not my brother, and what makes you think I'm gay?"

"Purple running tights?"

"I haven't fully unpacked."

"The fact that you even own them."

I tell him I'm apolitical.

"No one's apolitical, they're just selfish."

I hand him back the pamphlet and start off.

"The meeting's tomorrow at 8pm. Do you even know where the center is?"

Later, Rob is at my cozy nook, visualize it bitch diary, helping me set up one of the clothes racks my Pops got me ("mucho cheap!") so I can finally finish unpacking.

"You didn't bring anything with you but clothes?"

"They just seemed more personal."

"You have other stuff that's yours, right? I mean, twenty years. We'll rent a car and I'll help you get it."

"If I do, then it's really over."

"If you don't, puta boy gets to use it."

We are having Goya nectar cocktails. Just add rum.

"Hold that up," I tell Rob, who holds up a D&G black pirate shirt. "That would look nice on you. Keep it."

"No sangano, I'm clothing, not couture."

"Try it on."

Rob does, finding the price tag still on it.

"You haven't even worn it yet and- are you kidding me?!! For a shirt?!!"

"It was part of their collection. I just got the whole thing, it was easier than picking and choosing."

"See, that's why I hate you. You could sell this stuff. Paging Ebay!"

"No, I could never sell them, they're my babies."

"You just gave me one."

"Cause you're special, cabron. Do you know where the Center is?"

"You've never been to the Center?"

"We raised money for it once, so I must have been."

Thanks to Rob's directions, delivered as sarcastically as possible, I'm back again tonight at 8pm. Whole lotta people. I scan about for "the" guy, when-

"Hey Purple Tights! Didn't think you'd make it."

"I have a name."

"Yeah, but I don't feel comfortable calling you Nice Ass. My name is Joel." He pronounces it Joe-L.

We hardly have a chance to size each other up when the rally starts. People talk, drone on really. I nod my head, sign a couple of petitions and honestly, I do see the gravity of the situation, but I am bored senseless.

"If a police officer doesn't treat you with the full respect you deserve, you have a duty, an obligation to report them."

I sneak a look at my watch and wish I had sat by the door. I use to be able to pledge some large amount, people would ooh and ahh and I would say "Let's celebrate, cocktails all around!" and everybody would laugh. Did they really find it funny or was it just checkbook laughter?

"Bored much?" asks Joel.

"Senseless," I whisper and smile.

"So what are you gonna do?"

"I could probably make a couple of phone calls to some people who will still take them. Can't donate money, and I'm not much of a joiner."

"Baby steps."

Even though we're surrounded by bars, when we get out I invite him uptown to the Red Castle, where Victor has foolishly opened a tab for me. On the way I find out that Joel has worked his way through just about every gay organization in the city. When he gets burned out at one he just joins another. He's half Dominican and half Rican and has cat green eyes, a great smile and just wants to be friends. And he himself has a very nice ass. Well, it's true, but that doesn't mean I'ma tap it, just admire it.

At the bar Rob greets me.

"You just missed Lorena, you lucky loca."

Joel launches into a political rant on drag queens, pro or con, I zone out. Victor taps the sign over his head. "Absolutely No Politics Allowed."

"And it's in my handwriting, so I mean it."

Joel relaxes, we all do. And for some reason I look around and feel content. No, almost happy for the first time in a while. I'm listening to Rob describe his last temping job with full body gestures, Victor is leaning back, the bar light hitting his package just so, hey, gotta keep those tips a coming and Joel, well he looks like he belongs here. And I'm like far away, but sort of smiling.

Dear Diary:

Moms paid a visit today. Pay is the operative word here…

"Honey, no offense, but ju need a yob."

After two weeks my Moms thought we should discuss my financial situation which was, hello, non existent.

"I esaw on Cristina," (Cuban Oprah) "how kids after they're adults will move back in with their parents and mooch and leach and esponge off them forever."

"Gee, mami, what do you really think?"

"I'm yust esaying."

"You want me to pay rent?" Does my voice sound as whiny to her as it does to me?

"I think ju'll feel better about jurself if ju do." And with that, both she and her doobie-do leave what I'm hoping will be my rent controlled hovel.

What was I cut out for?

"Well, ten years ago you could have hustled," offers Rob.

Joel looked me up and down and said "Make that five years ago."

"Victor," I plead, "in the name of all that's holy, keep them coming."

Victor sidles up to me, all half lidded eyes and husky voice and whispers, "Papito, we got to talk about your tab."

Fuck the rent. My bar tab is in jeopardy, okay, now I need a yob!

Dear Diary:

It's late when I get back but Pops is sitting on his impeccably kept front stoop waiting for me. And yep, he reads me...

"You have to get over it, Javi, I'm saying this with love, you need to think of your future."

Does he think I don't want to?

"Your heart has been broken, it bled, but now you need to look forward, not back. You know what, you need to throw a party!" How can you not love this man? His reasoning is simple. "Every day you stay in your apartment until that bar opens."

"Pops, it's called the Red Castle."

"Then you go there until it closes. Everyday, back and forth. What kind of life is that? You need to reconnect. I'm your father and I'll always be here, but you need a social circle of friends, of people who will move you forward. You have friends with power. Invite them. Friends help each other. That's what they do."

I, for the life of me, can't imagine any of the JasonandJavier crowd in my basement apartment. But then my Pops, as is his way, breaks my heart, by slipping my two one hundred dollar bills. This is not chump change to him. He is making a sacrifice for me and I know it.

"Here, let me pay for your party. Ssshh. It's an investment in your future." My Pops says and smiles. As I recount this touching tableau to the Red Castlers, Victor says, "Two hundred will just about cover your tab."

"Please, Victor," I beg, "I've got a plan that could really make this party pay off for me."

"Okay," Victor sighs, "I'll just try to hold off the owner a little longer."

"Oh puta, just blow him like you always do!"

"Shut up!" and Victor smacks Rob on the back of his

head for his accuracy.

"Look, my friends with Jason probably think I just slunk off somewhere to die."

"You did," offers Rob.

"But I'll give a party, a mother fucking kind of party. I use to host fab parties, *the* parties, and I'll invite everyone and they'll all be so curious they'll come even if it's just to rate it, they'll come. And I, in all my glory, will push myself as a party planner or something equally fitting."

"Pimp?"

"Ho?"

"We covered that. Ten years too late."

"Five!," I snap. "Victor will wear as little as possible and tend bar, Rob, you'll wear as much as possible and cater waiter and Joel promises to refrain from any political rant. It's a go!!"

Dear Diary:

I rally! No really. For awhile the adrenaline is pumping, baby, pumping, until I discover how much everything will cost. But Victor offers to help with the booze (wonder where he's getting that?!) and Joel says I'll just have to find a way to stretch two hundred bucks. Which even in my positive thinking mode sounds ridiculous...

Rob told me about some place that has discounts (I hate that word) on paper goods, "Heap Cheap Pete's!" and putting on the least couture outfit I have I headed out there. The old me was really trying to resurface. I was strutting back, fabulousity reborn, shopping bags in hand, when I saw THE car. I of course recognized the license plate. I froze. The driver opened the passenger door and out stepped Jason. So gorgeous. Wind hitting his hair just so. I couldn't help it. I took off my sunglasses and just stared at him.

Then I heard the laugh from inside of the car. Boyish, yet full. Jason smiled, like he used to do with me. And the tramp stepped out.

I was …unprepared.

It's like I was cloned. Back then. Back when we first met. Long, dark curly hair, 28 inch waist (hey! A guy's gotta eat!) tight pants, hell, tight everything. Eyes only for Jason. And Jason, he was worse than in love. He's smitten.

The kid stepped into the building in front of them and in the split second before he did I knew Jason was going to turn and see me. I dropped the plastic bags and stepped away from them. What would I be doing carrying plastic bags?!

"Javi?"

His smile was sincere. I put my sunglasses back on and threatened myself with an acid body scrub if I shed tear one in front of him.

"Hey," I say, sounding as casual as I can.

"What are you-"

"Just running errands."

We both hesitated, good, it's mutual. Then we went in for the quick peck on the cheek. "You look good."

"You too."

It doesn't matter who said what, we're both lying.

"I hear you're having a party."

"Wow, it's a nationwide hookup, huh."

"Word gets around."

"Of course you're invited."

"Nine pm, Tuesday."

"Dang, have the soothsayers already predicted what I'm gonna wear?"

"No. Just that you'll look great, as usual." Jason says sincerely.

Breath don't fail me now.

"So, yeah, come on by if you want. A lot of our friends should be there. ...And bring him." I find myself adding. God, I am so well mannered and shit. Out of the corner of my eye I saw the kid at the building's glass door, wondering what's happened to his man. I wish I had wondered. "Gotta run. Soirees don't happen by themselves, you know."

We kissed each other goodbye, I hope HE saw that, and I headed off, empty-handed in more ways than one, but I'd be damned if the kid's first image of me was gonna be me swinging four plastic shopping bags down Canal Street.

Dear Diary:

It's the day of my party and I have begged, borrowed or coerced every piece of stemware, china and flatware (paper, what was I thinking?!) that I could. My Moms has promised not to spend the entire night by the window and my Pops has put up two kitchen chairs in front of the building as a reserved drop off area for the limos. Hope is a thing in feathers called my father...

Rob called, he is running late. A call back! He's been living on the outskirts of show business for over twenty years but the idea of a call back, even for a small role, excites him. How does he keep that dream alive? I must ask him sometime.

Joel arrived early to help me set up.

"How many people you expecting?"

"I invited everyone I know, which means half will try to

come which really means a quarter will actually show up, but some of them will bring dates so now we're up to a third."

"How many people RSVP'd?"

"I never put RSVP on my invites. People who want to come will come. We always had enough of everything. Our parties are always SRO."

"Yeah, but you ain't 'we' and you ain't 'our' anymore."

Joel was helping me set up music. Secretly I knew what will happen. People would come, just to be able to rate it the next day. I have to work the perfect game face tonight.

"Isn't it fabulous that I get a second shot at life!"

"I feel so young, so energized!"

"Don't you wish you were living in your parents basement, too!" Okay, that last one needs work.

We are moving clothes racks around. When I ask Joel for a hand, he places it on my nether regions. Where it stays.

"Let's do it right here," he hisses, "sloppy and sweaty."

I look at Joel as if he's crazy.

"My parents are upstairs! They come down every couple of minutes to see if I need anything! I'm giving a fucking party in a couple of hours!"

And with that he pulls my shirt over my head and I lunge for his mouth. Omigod, how long has it been since I had sex? We were like a circus act, whirling around the room removing each other's clothing and licking, kissing, exploring every part of each other's bodies. Joel reaches for his pants and pulls out, I swear, like fifteen condoms, okay, I'm guessing he's done this before. I can't breathe. No, really. It's as if desire, a need for sex, for sex sex sex has taken over my central nervous system. He spanks me, I spank him back. He blows me and I throw my head so far back I can almost see my own ass.

"Damn, you're a loud one!" he says.

I thought about the last time I had sex with Jason.

Perfunctory. Like his heart and his dick were already else-where. I snap. I become violent. Really going after him. Joel becomes violent, too. What the hell is he angry at? Then it became sweet, gentle, back to violent. I came when he first fucks me and again when I fuck him. Joel and I struggle to top each other, to bottom each other. So this is what the first sex after a break up feels like. We were down seven condoms when I heard my pops' voice coming down the stairs.

"Javi, where do you want the ice?"

Rob arrived with my Pops as Joel beat a hasty tasty retreat. Rob eyeballs me and knows immediately. "Puta, you just had sex!" he whispers. "You are one giant hickey! Tell me, am I standing on the spot where the deed was done?"

"If you're anywhere in this basement you're standing in it."

Rob starts to fan himself as my father drops off the ice and, cluelessly left.

Rob and I high five each other and I put on the most open collar shirt I can find. News of my hickey should reach Jason within seconds of my first guest's arrival.

Victor arrives and sets up. He has tried on thirty two versions of the same spandex shorts. He also insists that he never be under direct lighting. Hey, a boy's gotta know his limitations.

Oprah, yeah it all comes back to her, has said that before a party you should toast yourself. To the joyful event about to come. So Rob, Victor and me all raise a glass. I keep looking at the door, expecting Joel to walk back in, but as it turns out I won't see him again for weeks.

He is not the only no show. As ice melted, music droned and we awkwardly stared and made small talk with one another, it becomes clear no one was coming. No. One. My banishment was complete. It is one minute past midnight. Cinderella, she be dead.

Well, not quite. At what, 12:01 and ten seconds, just

to make it dramatic, headlights slow down in front of my window. Victor snaps to, pulling his shorts further up his crack and Rob like a madman starts hiding food.

"What the fuck are you doing?" I practically scream at him.

"Here's your story and you're sticking to it," Rob says, "everybody's been here. It was always supposed to end before midnight and it was a fucking free for all!"

"But they all know each other!" I stammer.

"They'll just assume everyone came but them and they won't want to admit it. Now, yawn and get the door, bitch!"

Who knew Rob had a top gene?

I open the door, trying to look like I've just had the time of my life, but it's not a guest. It's, Randall, Jason's driver. Holding a large, obviously expensive, floral arrangement.

"Sorry I got here so late, but I couldn't remember where it was," Randall apologizes.

"Yeah, well sometimes I wish I could forget, too." Randall hands me the flowers, nods and leaves.

Victor, who was in full shimmy modes, asks, "Wait, wasn't he rich?"

I read the card.

"Wishing you the best time. Sorry we couldn't make it, signed Jason and Eric." Oh look, It can spell it's own name.

Cher's "Believe" comes on in the background. Rob takes the card from me and reads it. I am among the walking dead. He nods to Victor to turn off the music, but that beautiful, magical man does just the opposite. He blares it louder than ever and begins to dance, gyrate around us. And while he is perfection in every physical aspect, the man cannot sing. But bray he does! And loud!

"Do you believe in life after love!"

Soon Rob joins in, jumping around dancing, whipping off his shirt and screaming:

"Hey, Javi, how'd you like to have these love handles!"

And in spite of myself I dance with my two friends. Maybe you can't dance your way to happiness, but hey you gotta believe, right?

Dear Diary:

Kearn has been in the doghouse with Jason since the little smirk incident with me. To win his way back into Jason's good graces, he has decided to host our six month anniversary party. Wait. Six months? I'm supposed to count out our anniversaries in 6 month increments? What the hell is the life expectancy of a gay couple? Jason acquiesces (says yes, sometimes it's like I'm watching my life on PBS) and Kearn goes into overdrive to dissoffend me...

I would rather had stayed home, and when you see what Jason called home you would have too, but being in the first throes of love I squeaked out a "Cool!"

"And for tonight, I'll pick out something for you to wear and you can do the same for me." Jason said. He had given me my first ever credit card, which he insisted I use but I wasn't gonna buy him a gift with his own money, hell no, so I broke out the money I've managed to save and got him a sweater and some slacks. I'd been shopping with Jason so I kinda knew what he liked, but his present wiped me out financially. No mas dinero until my next paycheck came through; but hey, I had a good job. And even though "FUEGO" got some shitty reviews everybody's hoping for a couple of Tony nominations and we'd be fine. We'd breeze into the second season no problem.

We did our performance that night to a packed house. I did my flip and there was Jason wearing the outfit I gave him, same seat as usual. After the curtain call I ran back to my shared dressing room, and by shared I mean five nasty pieces of work and me. There was the gift, wrapped so pretty that it could have been the be cover of "Presents Weekly." A couple of the guys couldn't help themselves and oohed and ahhed. The others made snide little comments like "paid in full" or "services rendered" that I pretended not to hear. I once tried going at it with one of them and it was not pretty. Their tongues are razor sharp and they didn't care if you wound up bleeding and curled up in a fetal position they would just keep going.

I carefully unwrapped my present, taking my time. I knew these skanks were pretending not to look, but they were dying. I pulled out my outfit and... oh no. Jason what have you done? Okay, lemme call it. It's lederhosen. Hey, I saw Sound of Music, I know what lederhosen is. My outfit, and it's out there, was silver lame shorts with suspenders, a gauzy gray tuxedo shirt, black bow tie and cummerbund and a black bolero jacket. Oh, and silver high tops. No really, silver.

"What? No change maker?" Ruben sneered. He's had it out for me from day one. I was mortified, but I would not give them the satisfaction to show it. I would not. I dressed, said goodnight and left as if dressing like a Reynolds wrap little slut is something I did everyday. I was angry and confused. I mean really, what the fuck, Jason. **You** couldn't afford long pants? As confused as I may have been it all changed when I saw how Jason looked at me. I was, apparently, the last Coca Cola in the desert and Jason was dying of thirst. In the car I kept hoping he'd just rip this costume off me and I wouldn't have to wear it, but no such luck. We arrived at Kearn's, where a sit down for 60 of Kearn's nearest and dearest, wait, that man has nearest and dearest? awaited us. I was so self conscious but everyone was super kind to me, the older guys especially. One of them sat me on his knee and he laughed, and everybody laughed and I laughed too, but I felt weird. This guy, I'll call him Santa, too many names to try to remember, got more touchy feely the drunker he got and I saw Jason getting jealous, which was kinda cool. There were some other young guys there, wearing super expensive looking clothes (and long pants!). They nodded in my direction, smiled and said nothing. At dinner, the talk turned to theatre and someone asked me what my favorite Shakespeare play is and I said, "The one I read was pretty good. Midsummer-" The rest of my answer was drowned out by laughter, but unlike my dressing room mates, no one looked snarky about it. Jason blew me a kiss from across the table and I suddenly felt like a baby seal balancing a ball on my nose.

The young guys at the table nodded to each other and smiled, and that besides the search and grope mission Santa went on looking for his napkin in my general crotch area (Oh yes he did!) was dinner.

Cordials (and what the hell are they?) were served in the gallery and while Kearn cornered Jason, I found myself surrounded by the youth brigade. Before I could even say "Hi." Blond number one gave me a smile that had yet to reach his eyes and said, "Well played."

Blond number two joined in, "Very."

Me? Not a clue, so I just said my name, "Javi. And you are?"

"Oh honey, we're the Brats. Welcome."

That was it. No names, no nothing.

"The Spoiled Brats, we've been upgraded," a redhead added.

I looked like what I am. Confused.

"Honey, it's what you are," and it was back to Blond Two, "we're kept boys."

"I have a job," I stammered, and one of them, and really

at this point, who cares which, nodded in Jason's direction and said, "And a damn fine one, too!"

"I got a job," I repeated, cause maybe the first time didn't take. "I make my own money, I pay my own way."

The Redhead's eyebrows descended from their permanent arch and he took my hand. "Javi, those shorts you're almost wearing cost $2,500, the shirt is $4,000, the jacket $6,000 and shoes and accessories bring it up to $21,500. Retail."

My jaw was on an extended visit to my knees. It cost that much to look this cheap!!!!

"Well, this was a gift, but I gave him what he's wearing. I paid for it." This last sentence came out in a broken whisper.

"Good for you," Redhead said, apparently giving up the ghost of trying to school me.

Blond One leaned in and left me with, "We're all for sale. Just don't sell yourself cheap is all."

All I wanted to do was vomit the expensive mega meal I just had. I searched for Jason, I want to leave. Now! Before I could reach him, Santa made one last attempt at making me his ho ho ho.

"Get offa me!" I hissed.

I found the bathroom and ran cold water on my wrists and looked at myself. Why would Jason dress me like this? What the fuck was he thinking? I pulled myself as together as I could in time to see Jason handing his old pal, Santa, another drink. Santa's laughing it up but there was a steel in Jason's eyes I'd never seen before. Then it happens, one drink too many, Santa lurched and knocked over what surely must be a multi million dollar sculpture and it smashed to pieces on the floor. Collective gasps. I stared at Jason in total disbelief, and he, Dios mio, winked at me. Kearn gave Santa the heave ho and we stayed for a little while longer but Kearn was in a tizzy, so we left. Jason noticed my silence and finally said, "I didn't like him touching you. That's all. Don't worry, I'll make it up to Kearn, I'll buy him something wonderful."

"Not everything is for sale, you know," I shot out, way too quickly.

"You okay? You're not mad about the sculpture, are you?"

"Why did you get me this outfit?"

"Are you kidding?! You look great. Hot. Sexy."

We kissed, cause the man did say the magic words, "hot," "sexy."

"I make my own money."

"I know," Jason smiled, "I'm wearing the outfit you bought me."

"I pay my own way."

"Sure, but when "FUEGO closes ... "

"It's not gonna close."

"Javi, sure it is. You read the reviews."

"We had a full house tonight."

And Jason had to explain to me, the professional dancer, what papering a house meant.

"They were all freebies?" I asked, sadder than I ever thought I could be.

"Most of them. The show won't last much longer, Javi. But it'll be okay. You're with me now and you can go to your auditions and your classes, and you've never been to Europe, have you? And Japan? There's so much I want to share with you."

Right now what we shared was another kiss.

"I'll always take care of you, Javi. Forever."

I looked at him, and I knew he meant it, and the shorts weren't that important anymore.

Dear Diary:

"So I hear your party crashed and burned!"

Ah, yes, time for my cousin Hector to reenter my life. Simply put, I don't like the man.

"And you got dumped! Left with zero! Nada, baby!"

Oh, yeah, mere dislike would just about cover it.

He and his baby making machine, Sonia, live on the top floor of my parent's building. They were all in Disney World when my world turned upside down, but apparently Moms gave them a blow by blow description of the telenovela that is my life...

"Shoot man, I'd be made in the shade had I been you."

His three kids, it is three, isn't it? it's hard to count a blur, run up and down the hallway stairs all day. And while he has never actually married Miss Poppin Fresh Sonia, she's a hard worker, always there for my Moms to commiserate on what each of their lives should have been.

But the thing I most resent about Hector is that my Pops plays dominoes with him. Four men, my Pops among them, spend the weekend playing dominoes in front of the local bodega. Years ago, when one of the guys moved away one of the other ones suggested I take his place. The scion. The natural heir. I was 17. My father didn't know I was coming out of the store, but I saw him shake his head "no" and he called out "Hector!," who happened to be next to me. And while I didn't see Hector's smirk, I felt it, as he purposely bumped into me, taking my rightful place among the geezers, and yeah, that's the real reason I hate him. My Pops chose him over me. And even with the building, the gifts, the vacations (which I think my folks took to humor me, more than any sense of enjoyment) I can't shake the feeling that they'd rather have Hector, virile, spermloaded, baby daddy as their son. Now, imagine how I would feel if I even liked to play dominoes.

Victor calls. My floral arrangement for my wake/party has been accepted by the owner of the Red Castle as payment in full of my bar tab. Oh, and I should get my ass down there pronto. Rob is suicidal. He has just been cast as the father to someone who is actually older than he is.

The reason the Red Castle can exist at all in this "family" neighborhood is that it is so fucking discreet. What happens here, stays here. You also have to know where it is, cause otherwise forget it. No sign, no windows, and it's on a side street down a flight of stairs. Maybe that's why I like it so much. I've become a basement dweller.

Rob is in his cups when I get there. I am wearing my best "sympathy" outfit. Dressing is an exact science. It is not for the weak. We must dominate it and bend it to our will. Victor holds up four fingers. I got a lot of drinking to do.

"It's cause the bastard has a full head of hair!," Rob wails. Rob never curses, hits his finger with a hammer and says "mother trucker!" so he must be in real pain.

Rob continues, "He's at least two years older than me, three even, but because he has the good luck to look like one of Charlie's Angels and I look like a Chia pet that somebody forgot to water, I'm playing his father!"

"Well, baby," I offer, "maybe they needed a really good actor for the father."

"I'm in two fucking scenes! And he's the lead! The lead, okay?!"

Obviously it isn't okay.

"And that no talent jerk, who happens to be as talented on stage as he is in bed which is to say NOT AT ALL does the best acting of his miserable life by pretending he doesn't remember me."

I run my hand up and down his back and make cooing sounds to try to comfort him. My newly reinstated tab buys us a couple of drinks..

"Turn the role down!" Victor throws his head back and proclaims. "Tell them to fuck off."

"I can't," Rob sadly adds, "I need the job."

And once he said that out loud it's like he went numb. The reality of it hit him, hit all of us.

"I'm thirty-nine and I'm chasing a dream that left the station without me. So I hold on to the ghost cause I don't know what to replace it with. What takes the place of a dream? Another dream? I haven't got one." Rob softly says. The bar is filling up, but Victor has the other bartender cover for him. Rob has stopped us all.

"I chased one thing in my life, being an actor and look at me, I've got nothing to show for it."

"Hey, you're really good," says Victor as he rubs Rob's arm. "You ever see Rob on stage?," he asks me.

"Uh, not for years, but I'm sure he is."

Rob takes me in.

"I was a bad friend, I know."

Rob shrugs, spent.

"But I remember you rehearsing a monologue for your class, years ago. On the roof. I'm doing my plies, you're emoting. And I had to stop, cause you were so good. I mean I really believed what you were saying even if I couldn't understand half of what you were saying cause it was Shakespeare. I just thought you were so good."

"I was."

"You still are."

"Every year that passes I have a little less of myself to prop that up with. Why couldn't I dreamt of being an accountant?" The background noise of the happy customers valiantly fills in the hollow that is our silence.

"You know," Victor starts tentatively, "someday they're going to ask me to work as the doorman, and when that happens I'll hang up my shorts and I'll never come back.

That's what happens to old bartenders, they become the guy you show your ID to." Victor downs my drink. We're losers! We kinda laugh about it though.

"Ay, moloca, vete al carajo!" I say.

Suddenly, Rob clutches my arm and hisses, "Isn't that your cousin Hector?"

My brain leaves our woe is us party and explodes. Now to be fair, it's hard to tell if it's Hector. I mean I've never seen him with his tongue down another guy's throat. It could be any homosexual slut into PDAs. When he finally comes up for air and turns profile so I'm not just looking at his helmet hair it's SWEET JESUS my cousin Hector!! Mister Macho, Mister still lisps and prances around when he wants to be funny, Mister never heard a gay joke he didn't like and repeat ad nauseum. "Gee, maybe he's lost," Victor offers.

"And trying to find himself in that guy's mouth?" Rob counters.

Now, Hector hasn't seen me yet. As we continue watching, the actor in Rob takes flight. "Okay, Javi, there are so many ways for you to play this scene. Big drama, throw a drink in his face-"

"Drinks aren't free, cabrona."

"Slap him and read him to filth," Rob continues, "or you could call Sonia over, invite her for a drink and just sit back and watch the fireworks."

"Patrons are responsible for all bar damage," says killjoy Victor.

It's all resolved when Hector looks up and we eyeball each other. It's weird how you can see someone's facade stay the same, but you can see their inside shatter, literally turn to dust.

The guy he's with is licking his neck now, but Hector can't take his eyes off me. How did he think I wouldn't see him here? In a pendejo way I almost feel sorry for the guy.

Then he gets up and walks towards me, I get up and meet him halfway. Oh my God, it's High Noon.

"Hola Loca," I use his favorite derogatory pet name for me when we were growing up. And my butch cousin Hector, wild eyed, leans in and throws up on me. EWWWW!

Okay, fact, nothing can clear out a gay bar faster than projectile vomit. So we both wind up running out of the bar, but for different reasons, capiche? Rob came back to my place with me and after I had burned my clothes in the sink and scrubbed myself a la Silkwood, he handed me a vodka.

"So what are you gonna do? Tell Sonia, tell his friends, tell everybody?"

"Telling my Moms would do all three. Do you know how that mamao made my life a living hell when we were growing up?"

"No, hum it."

"He would imitate the way I walked and talked. He used to make fun of the way I laugh. For years I would swallow my laughter."

"And you never suspected?" Rob asks while making the universal gesture for effeminate.

"Fuck no. You know how straight men have that annoying habit of almost pulling off an outfit then screwing it up at the last minute so they won't look gay? That was Hector. There always had to be something off just to remind you what a challenge fashion was for him."

"You have to admit he's fine."

"And he knows it."

"All you good looking people know it."

"I do not."

"I rest my case." Rob left a little past midnight. A couple of minutes later, as if he had been waiting for Rob to leave, and clearly he was, Hector is at my door. Drunk and angry/scared.

"I was just upstairs fucking my wife, okay?!"

"She's not your wife, she's your baby mama."

"That's right, and I got kids, I go to church-"

"Well, I'm sure you're on your knees a lot."

And that, dear diary was the trigger, Hector grabbed me by the neck and slammed me against the wall. Did he want to kiss me or kill me? He opts for kill. The first punch connected with my jaw and sent me flying back over the sofa. For a moment I thought of the Pitt-Jolie scene in Mr. & Mrs. Smith, but it's just a brief moment. My cousin Hector is not someone who has ever turned me on. Sure he's good looking, but his attitude really kills anything he has going on in the looks department. But I digress. The man took a flying leap to land on me, but I rolled over and he body slammed the floor and gets a nose bleed. He's holding his nose, I'm holding my chin.

"Mother fucker you crazy?!," I scream.

"You can't tell her!." Only with his head thrown back and gurgling his own blood it sounds more like, "uh an't ell er."

"Who the fuck said I was gonna?"

"Ause e on't lieve ou."

"Oh she'd believe me. And my friends were there."

Hector takes this in. Stops. Thinks.

"U ot ap in?"

I get him a napkin and a drink. He doesn't speak. No great loss there.

"Does Sonia know?"

He shakes his head, "no."

"Suspect?"

Again, no.

"Since when have you....."

He smiles, shrugs.

"Just too much sex for one person to handle."

Oh sure, that he got out loud and clear.

"You gonna tell?"

"No."

"Your friends tell?"

"No."

Satisfied, he rises to go. Looks at me, smiles. "You wanna?"

"Hell no!"

He snorts, laughs. You wanna! The very idea!

He leaves. I hear him whistling as he goes up the stairs. Coño, that guy has some cojones on him.

Dear Diary:

Just as my Moms was getting to the point of standing over me with a police baton and saying "Ju not getting any junger. A yob, sometime today." Rob came to my rescue...

We're at the bar, and Rob doesn't so much tell the story, he reenacts it. "So, I'm cater waitering at some soap opera anniversary show. I'm carrying a tray of little pigs in a blanket and pesto sauce. I haven't eaten all day, so it's one for the guest, and two for me. They're hot so I got to try to suck in air while I eat them."

"And we all know how well you suck." Victor volunteers.

"Yes, cabrona, learned it from you. So, I'm walking around and I hear someone talking smack about you."

"About who?" I ask.

"You!', he practically pushes his finger through my chest. "And pigs in a steaming hot blanket or not, I come to your defense."

"Who was it?"

"So not the point, one of the other waiters, but I jumped all over his ass. Set him straight."

"It's a good thing he respects his elders," Victor smirks. Rob doesn't miss a beat and bends one of Victor's fingers back. Painfully, very painfully.

"Okay, okay! I give!" screams Victor, allowing Rob to continue his one man show. "But then this guy, this actor from the soap, Philip, wait, here's his card, says it sounds like your friend needs a job, and I'm looking for a personal assistant."

"Ooooh, PERSONAL assistant." This time I go for one of Victor's fingers but he quickly moves his hand away.

"I haven't worked in twenty years. What the hell does he want me to do?" I ask.

"He just wants someone with social skills. I was giving him your number but he said, "No, it's okay. Here's my address, have him show up on Monday. Nine a.m.""

And just like that, I was employed! I kiss Rob and we all toast to my now safe bar tab. Hosanna! Am I lucky or what

Dear Diary:
The answer to the previous question is "or what"...

My first meeting with Philip, the devil not wearing Prada, was brief. He hands me leashes to walk the dogs (there are three of them, all bitches) and tells me to meet him at the studio. He forgets to give me the address for the studio and I forget to ask so when I finally find my way there, I'm late. I get yelled at. In front of everyone. Loud, nasty, rude. I suck it up. I get a coffee. I get yelled at. I breathe. I get yelled at. I sense a pattern.

There is no honeymoon period. He knows I need the job so he is evil incarnate. And when he's not berating, he's nosy.

In that really "it's none of your business" way. Mind you this is all the first day.

"So you're telling me you don't know how to download music into my iphone?"

I tell him, as tactfully as possible, that I had people to do that for me.

"Well, you don't anymore, now do you?" He smiles. Is work supposed to be humiliating, or is it just the way he makes it? At one point he tells me he dropped the back of his stud earring on the floor. I am on my hands and knees searching for it. I offer him mine, but no, it must be his. Sentimental value. It was a gift from his first true love. Attila the Hun had a lover?

Philip is the only WMD who has ever said that I looked older than my years. He has also suggested that a gym membership should be priority one for me and that botox is not an option but a necessity I should not live without. We usually have an audience for these tough love sessions. Some of them smirk, some of them look away in embarrassment, thankful it's not them on the receiving end. But Philip, is frustrated. You see, long ago I learned how not to blush. Weird to learn how not to do something, but I did. And as Philip's put-downs become more and more acidic I remain, to the outside eye, untouched. It's driving the man insane, which besides the pay ($25 an hour, off the books, thank you very much) is the best part of the job.

Every night I come home more and more demoralized. The man who is a good ten years older than me (I later find out, more like twenty! Mofo had a lift!) starts everyday by telling me that with my skills there's not much work for me out there in the "real" world.

"Uh, thank you?"

Today, he smiles, or what Satan would say passes for a smile and asks me to hand him the paper. The thing is two feet from him, but I reach over and get it. And folded open to the front page of the society section is a dazzling picture of Jason and Eric. I feel my cheeks start to flame. No damn it! Damn it! Fuck!!! I'm a beet.

"Aren't they a lovely couple," he coos.

He knows. The mother fucking bastard knows. I suck it up. Wait until Friday. He obviously doesn't like me. He'll fire me on Friday. He has too.

It's an odd feeling being someone's servant. Not their employee. Servant. He makes it clear with every dog dropping I have to scoop up, exactly what I am. But this, as he stresses, is what I'm good for. I think back to about ten years after Jason and I had become a super couple. I had tried to go back to dancing, signed up for a course. Actually thought that with a little brush up, I'd be back in the chorus. Uh, no. Everybody in the class was so young, and looked it. They could pick up combinations faster than I could get my tights on. And they all knew they were good and all knew I wasn't. I stopped going after a couple of days because I couldn't stand the look of tolerance on their young faces. I had barely made it into the chorus the first time; good Lord, one audition and I'd probably end up in intensive care. With a vodka drip if God is indeed merciful. I have not been out to the Castle since I started this soul sucking torture, cause I knew if I did I would drink myself into a coma; but tomorrow is Friday. Philip, I'm sure will make it memorable. He's leaving for the Pines mid afternoon, so without a doubt he'll fire my ass then and I will make a beeline to the bar that will provide my salvation.

After I walk the dogs in the morning, Philip has me carry his stair climber, I kid you not, up to the roof. The elevator stops a full flight and a half before that so I have to struggle with it the rest of the way while Philip exhausts himself by holding the door open. He wants to exercise outdoors, but jogging is too much outdoors, plus he'd be mobbed he tells me. Okay, I have yet to see the man recognized by anyone under seventy. To them, he's a sweetheart. I usually stand in the background and grit my teeth. While he's on the stepper he wants me to fan him. Fan him! I begin to visualize him taking a header off his roof and fan away with a beatific smile on my face. The day ends, finally. I've dragged down the stepper, run his errands and just about warmed the water for his enema. I am standing before him as he writes out my check. He blows on the check to dry the ink. My Moms doesn't even do that.

"See you Monday, bright and early!"

"What?!" I actually say it out loud, and in a pitch his dogs respond to.

"Monday. Bright and early." He looks at me like I'm the village idiot.

"You're not gonna fire me?" I can't help myself.

He smiles. Mona Fucking Lisa like and points me to the door.

I cash my check and go drinking.

"I'm sorry, baby, I didn't know he'd be so bad," Rob offers.

He's heinous. But, even after squaring off my newest bar tab, I still got a couple of hundred left.

"So you going back Monday?" Rob asks.

"I got to. Moms even talking about starting to charge me rent."

Shocked looks all around.

Thirty nine years old. No retirement plan, no savings and a job that will end only when he drops a safe on me.

Living on a budget is sick. I don't see how people do it. Choosing the cheapest restaurant and then ordering the cheapest thing on the menu. Brown bagging it, walking everywhere. This is why so many New Yorkers are rude, they're fucking being strangled in slow motion by their wallets.

On the plus side, Rob is seeing someone he met online. And while I'm happy for him. Rob now speaks in text. Everything is initials now. I may have to kill him.

I try to make Friday night last as long as possible. And Saturday. On Sunday morning I wake up with a headache that nothing will cure. Monday is only hours away.

I'm in week two of my nightmare job, and Philip actually smacks my hand away when I go to touch something. I look down and swallow. Even he knows he went too far, and jokes about "too bad public floggings were outlawed."

When I can, I go into the bathroom and cry. I'm a middle aged man and I'm pathetic. As I'm getting ready to leave that evening, he leans in for an apology? No, for a kiss. On the mouth.

"See you tomorrow!"

Okay, what the fuck?!

He goes back to his book and I stumble out the door directly to the Castle.

"Maybe he has the hots for you. I mean, it's unlikely, but maybe."

"Gee thanks, Victor. Thong a little tight tonight?"

"No, I mean…" Victor blushes and buys me a drink.

I am not imagining this. He kissed me. This s/m relation-ship that is now my job goes on for a couple of more days. An extremely humiliating occurrence followed by an act of intimacy that stupefies me. I hyperventilate now just about everywhere and I'm having trouble sleeping. On Thursday, after a tongue lashing that would have made Joan Collins proud, he pinches my nipple.

"Yep, he wants you." Victor, who has been pinched on just about every part of his anatomy is certain of it. Every night the guys wait for me and the latest installment of my work day. Even I have a hard time believing it, but damn it, the bastard left a bruise on my nip. I'm in the middle of showing exhibit A when Joel walks in. He kisses all of us hello, includ-ing me, as if it hadn't been over three weeks since I'd last seen him. And he's apparently developed amnesia. There isn't the slightest acknowledgment of our quickie. We fill Joel in on my travails and he smiles and shakes his head.

"I can't believe you're working for your ex's ex." Joel says.

I drop my drink, glass, jaw. "What?!"

"You didn't know?"

Rob and Victor are also children of the damning it with me.

"He's his ex? Jason's ex?"

"Yeah. When I first started at the Center, Jason who had given one of the first big checks and gotten a little plaque broke up with his lover. Philip. An actor. Strictly C."

"I didn't know Jason had someone before me."

"My job was to crop Philip out of all the pictures as per the rich donor's demand. Yeah, Jason dumped his ass. Took up with a dancer, I think," Joel adds.

Rob looks at me. "When did you meet Jason?" I don't have to do the math. I look at him and say, "I'm the dancer." And Philip. The mother fucker knows it.

Unlike the other days, I can't wait to get to work this morning. I let myself in and babycakes is in the shower when I get there.

"Hand me a towel."

I do, keeping my eyes focused on anywhere but him. He's all come hither without taking the final step. He wants me to jump his bones so he can reject me, or have me and then reject me, or God knows what, like how many more options are there? "I quit," I hear myself say.

Philip is dumbfounded. This is not the scenario he scripted for today. He barely wraps himself in a towel and offers me full medical and dental, a raise, food allowance, and I could have sworn he said blow job but he was talking awfully quickly.

"No. No thank you."

"You need this job!," he wails. "No," I say as I start to exit, "you need me to have this job."

A defeated Philip takes a deep breath and hisses "When did you find out?"

"That you were Jason's first?"

"No, that I'm allergic to nuts! You are a fucking idiot! You're useless! You're a prime reason why we need more border patrol!"

"I'm Puerto Rican. I'm a citizen-"

And that set him off. This naked man, oh yeah, cause his towel fell off somewhere after dissecting my parentage, is red faced and red everything as he tears into me. Years of wanting to let me have it and he's foaming, mad dog crazy. I let him go, like a wind up toy, until the coil finally loosens and it comes to a stop.

I deadeye him and say, "And still, he chose me over you."

Slam!

And it all came down to that. He chose me over him. Before I can make my best grand dame exit, he tops it. And me.

"And he chose Eric over you."

All of a sudden I can't get Alanis Morrisette's "Isn't It Ironic?" out of my head. Before I leave I have to ask him, "How did you survive?"

"I didn't, for the longest time. Luckily he sent me away with a hefty going away package."

Slam.

"Probably not as big as you could have gotten."

"Yeah, but I loved the man," I say, hearing the hollow in my own voice.

"And here you are picking up dog poop for a B soap opera actor." he counters.

Double slam.

"And when I was let go, I still had my looks."

Home run.

"Of course I wanted nothing more than to hurt you. Not kill you. Hurt you. I knew you were a dancer, so I was going to hire somebody to break your kneecaps, and I knew you were cute so I was gonna hire somebody to slice your face. Those fantasies kept me going. Good times. But now, I look at you, at this pathetic sad old boy, because that's what you are, you're not a man, you're an old boy, and for the first time in forever I don't think I'll need my ulcer medicine tonight."

I want to hit him. I want to hit him so bad I can taste it.

"How do you feel about Eric?"

"I don't even know him."

"I didn't ask you that, old boy. Okay, You're driving along a deserted road, Eric is jogging, no doubt keeping his pretty posterior in tiptop fuckable shape. It's just you in a car, and him running, not a soul around. Look me in the eye and tell me you wouldn't aim the car right at him."

I take his keys out of my pocket, make a big show of putting them on the table and stagger home via vodka and vermouth.

Dear Diary:
Went to have drinks with Jason and Lorraine. She scares me!!!!!!!!!!!!!! But she's Jason's best friend so gotta make nice...

I had no idea what being an "it" couple meant until breath mint Lorraine schooled me. We were in her mirrored make up room, and by mirrored I mean that the walls, ceiling and floor were like walking into an egomaniacs wet dream of a fun house. Jason and me were joining her at her place for cocktails before going out for actual cocktails, when she summoned/suggested I join her as she had herself "touched up." Now, this was no checking her lipstick moment, once we entered her den of beauty I saw the road crew she kept under lock and key whose sole purpose was to make her look like a photoshopped version of herself. While I sat on the chair next to her, and swatted away hands trying to do damage control on my still new face at the uber rich scene, she calmly informed me of my new status.

"Three months.," she said, "You've lasted three months. He's in love with you."

I burst out a smile and tried to say, "Yeah, I'm in love with him too-" but her manicured hand cut me off.

"Yes, darling, that's charming, simply charming, but you see you've moved up from lake front to ocean front property."

I didn't get it, so I just said "I'm moving in with him next week."

"With a view no less!" she breathlessly exclaimed and suddenly even her beauty brigade eyed me differently.

"All right then. You're the official "it" couple." She said this as a total pronouncement. She hath spoken. It be law. Her supremes all nodded in unison.

"I know Jason, we've been besties for years, you are the chosen one, the one who will complete him as a perfect matched set." She said this while canvassing me up and down, either trying to see what Jason saw in me or accepting it like an unlikely inevitability. I wanted her to like me so I didn't care.

"You're going to be photographed, gossiped about, people will loath you and love you, sometimes to your face, but usually they'll just want to be near you. And your P.S.? Divine."

"My what?" I dared to ask.

"Personal story. Boy from the squalor nabs the Sun King."

"Excuse me, squalor?"

"Lorraine is speaking, darling. You're going into his world now. He's giving you total access."

I wanted to say something dirty, like, "Oh honey, I've had total access!," but as she said, Lorraine is speaking.

"Mistakes will be tolerated at the beginning and then magnified. I hope you have a good learning curve. Remember everything, especially names, don't gossip or listen to gossip, but if you must gossip and it is traced back to you, deny, deny, deny. Follow Jason's lead when it comes to what parties, bars and charities to favor and dress as if life itself depended on it."

Why wasn't I writing this down?

"People will want to like you. I do. Want to anyway."

Her road crew pulled back and she studied her reflection. I mean really studied it. After a moment she pointed to what had to have been an imaginary flaw, just to keep the boys on their toes, and someone swooped in to repair it. Finally satisfied, she rose and took my hand. As we walked out I swear by all that is holy, her team applauded.

She smiled as she led me out and whispered, "And always remember, the little people can be so ….nice."

As a little person myself I wasn't sure if I should slug her or thank her, so I just nodded as we joined Jason and my future which was already in progress.

Dear Diary:
Today I spent the day at the Castle. From the opening at 2pm on. I gotta be honest with you, I'm kind of diaried out, but damn if you're not the one who knows everything and doesn't judge me, like you know that maybe there's something in me worth fighting for and more importantly, maybe it all doesn't begin and end with me. Feeling very, very mediocre today...

I sit watching the other patrons, the kind that would be outside waiting for a bar to open cause they've got no place else to go. Like me? The TV above the bar plays something from Telemundo on mute and Victor slowly comes to life, one compliment at a time. Victor is worshipped from the first drink served to the last and he will flirt with anything that draws breath and has testes. I find myself wondering how old he is. He looks perfectly perfect but I realize I don't really know much about him. He does come over every so often, checks up on me, makes dirty jokes, makes sure I pat his ass, but I always get the sense I wish I knew him better, and not in a biblical way neither. When Rob and Joel finally arrive they are surprised that I'm already manning my bar stool, and even more surprised that all I'm having is tonic water. I ask Rob about Victor. "So what's his story? Is he seeing anybody?"

"You interested?"

"No, just curious. He could have anybody," I say.

"I'm sure he has," Joel adds, and we laugh.

"He once had a lover." Rob says.

"Another Greek statue?" Okay, now we're giddy. But Rob continues. "No, Victor's boyfriend was kind of unexpected. He looked like the Pillsbury dough boy, only paler. The man had probably not seen sunlight since the first Bush administration. He never went out, he was agoraphobic, or whatever they call it. But on Victor's tenth anniversary at the Red Castle (Jesus, Maria & Jose, how old is he? I think) Luis came. And Victor, honest to God, his eyes welled up when he saw him. And he was so gentle with him, so proud. This guy who I only saw as a spandex slut showed such a different side of hisself that night. Luis only stayed for half an hour, and he sweated the entire time, but we all got a chance to meet him and Victor was the happiest I've every seen him."

"So what happened?"

"They broke up. Victor still won't talk about it. Even to me, but I think Luis left him." And I look at Victor, at the other end of the bar, and he gives me his best dazzling smile with a leer and I think, wow, even if you're perfect, you're still not safe. I go home without having had a drop of alcohol. I stay up all night. I don't cry. I don't sleep. I just stare at the ceiling above me. Jason.

Dear Diary:
I'm doing the show and everything is new to me. Previews, reviews, I had to join a union. I'm making more money than my Pops now, I give most of it to my folks. I can't even legally go to bars, but I do. Oh yeah, I got in…

Brats, Barefoot Boy, Crisco's. Oh, The Ninth Circle. I basically did the show and Roberto would wait for me and we'd go to one or the other or I'd go with some of the guys from the show. A lot of them were truly hardcore, they would drink and drug and say they were "unwinding" which made no fucking sense since they were hyper and running from one end of the bar to the other being "fabulous." I was the designated "pour them in a cab" guy. But still, it was kinda nice. I mean you were surrounded by your own kind so there was no pato this, or maricon that to worry about. At worse someone would give you shade, which by the by, I had no idea what that was. Comments intended to make you feel like less than what you are by people you don't even know who would do it to amuse their friends. It was a real eye opener, who knew there was such a thing as gay bullies? I would take my drink and nuuuurse it and just watch, like I was going to gay school. So if Roberto couldn't make it and if the other chorus boys were too busy putting on their second show of the evening, I'd just stand there. Alone and , what's the word, content. Better here than just about anywhere else in the world. Here, I belonged, even with some of the attitude and the crazy, cause here, even more than on stage, I felt cute. Wanted. Desired. These strangers could make me feel that. I didn't know how to do it on my own. I want to be snarky about the me I was; the boy who drew a heart for the letter "o" when he wrote "I want to be in love!," but I can't. He, I, was just so damn pure about love. Audible sigh.

Dear Diary
Vicki Carr tried to kill me tonight...

I didn't see it coming. I mean, I'm fine. I'm coping. I make jokes, I engage, I put one foot in front of the other so I know I'm okay, right? Sure, I drink a little more than I used to and I sleep more than I used to, but it's not like it's an escape. I'm just a tired drunk. Ha ha. But what happened tonight I didn't see coming. I'm at the Castle, a handful of party mix in my mouth, joking about how we should all try us some orajel martinis, when that nasty piece of work known as Lorena takes to the saltine sized stage for her, 'ahem', act. Now, usually I just talk through her show, as does most of the clientele who actually crave talent, but tonight, tonight Ms. Lorena has decided to lip sync her way through the legendary Vicki Carr's ode to sado masochism "It Must Be Him."
Oh hello, hello, my dear God
It must be him, but it's not him
That's when I die
Again I die
I have heard the song before. In both English and Español, but tonight the wisp of air that is my last nerve can't take it. I have to get out of here! But I can't. I'm like frozen in place, fuck it, melting in place. You know how when you're

drunk and you try to pretend you're sober? You know how pathetic that is? I am sitting there trying to swallow what feels like a barrel full of UTZ's (baked, not fried!) party mix, and my eyebrow begins to twitch. I can't stop it. And the further Lorena goes into her hysterical longing for the man who done left her the more I feel that everyone at the Red Castle knows the song was written about me. The rubber band snaps. And by that I mean my self control, dignity and composure, snapped. From that point on I must rely on the terror stricken eye witness accounts of my friends. As Lorena was rolling around the floor in grief (and no underwear!), while Ms. Carr slowly descended into tales that witness madness, I apparently jumped on the express train to crazy. Victor later told me, "Your right eye, it started twitching and you're like trying to pretend you're listening to Joel's joke but we could all see you're not there. Your head started nodding and when you finally laughed, like a beat after all of us, it was scary cause it went from laughing to crying to back to laughing."

Rob tries to hold me but I start shaking, like I'm freezing. Like I'm fucking Lucy in the episode where she locks herself in an icebox. I started making sounds that Jodie Foster only half attempted in Nell, and I can't stop. Was it anger or pain that I felt? I'm not sure. Okay, it turned into pain, cause Hector seeing the panic look on my boys' faces takes matters and my nuts into his own hand and squeezes until I out high note Vicki Carr. Ahhh!!!!!!!!

Everyone else at the Castle, who hadn't witnessed my emotional tsunami, laughs, thinking I was making fun of Lorena, who is probably planning a voodoo retaliation if her glare is to be believed. I see the look of relief in my friends eyes and as I slowly come back from wherever I went, my cousin says, "You're welcome."

It takes a few days for me to be able to sleep more than

a couple of hours. I have nightmares that I go back to that place where I fell apart and this time I can't make it back.

Dear Diary:

Joel pretends our encounter never happened so I follow suit. I have found a job, at Old Navy (how apropos) and have been there a little less than a month. And to get the job I had to shave a decade off my age...

Rob, who is no longer seeing the text man, insists I should have gone to the shops I frequented, Armani, Dolce & Gabbana, but the idea of having to wait on someone I once had at my dinner table is too demoralizing. I'm closing in on forty and have no future plans. Again, my Moms offers her sage advice.

"Nene, jou had a rich man once, ju can do it again. Get going while ju estill have jour looks. ...Well, most of them."

I can't believe I ever bought this woman a mother's day card. With a small loan from my parents, (it's an investment!), I buy a season ticket to the Met. It's de riguer for the hobs worth nobbing for, and maybe I can land another rich husband. It's a cinch they're not trawling the separates section at Old Navy.

"When does the Met season start?," Victor asks.

"I'm jumping the gun, I'm going to the last one of this season. Appletini, please."

"Not good. You've got two weeks to get yourself into shape. You're having a diet coke and Bacardi 0."

"I'm in shape. Rob, I ask you, am I in shape?"

"Yeah," answers my very best friend Rob. "But not for a

trophy boy," he adds, becoming persona non grata.

"Oh, who asked you anyway!"

"Seriously, you're competing with guys half your age," this from Victor.

"Hey! Ten years younger! Tops!" I scream.

"Who are in perfect shape." Yep, Victor is going for the jugular.

"And who couldn't have a conversation if their life depended on it." I sniff.

"And you think these rich, lonely guys want conversation?," Joel smirks.

"They want someone who is not going to embarrass them in public. Who doesn't scream "For Hire" from the moment people meet him." There, I think I've made my point.

Rob tries another tack. "Baby, I'm an actor, right? The day I get nominated for my Oscar in February means I got six weeks max to get my ass red carpet ready for the vultures that are the paparazzi. I will be dissected, torn apart and critiqued up the wahzoo."

"And I hear it hurts up there," Victor chimes in.

"So I would," continues Rob, "show up looking as flawless as I could cause I'm only gonna get one chance to make that first impression."

Silence.

"Okay, but it's not like I'm a mess or nothing."

"Oh no!" they all answer, a little too quickly for my taste.

"Just a touch up, that's all we're talking about."

So begins Boot Camp Opera.

And it's not just the physical aspect that needs to be spiffed up, I begin a marathon study course on all things opera. While I've been to a couple of them, I was never really taken with them and the last one we were at Jason slept through, so it's not like we made an effort to go back again. But all of our friends go. His. His friends go. Season tickets and the galas that go with them. We, on the other hand, would just stay home and have sex. And in the beginning, constantly. Then it began to taper off. Gushing like an open water faucet at the start only to end up just occasionally dripping, as if the well had run dry. I bet you anything that Eric is a gusher. He looks it. I've still some gushing left in me. I know it. That night watching Carmen on some high brow station at my place, it's just my little posse and me. And for some reason, maybe it was all that thinking about gushing, I can't take my eyes off Joel. I mean, it's not like we haven't had each other, we did. Once. But seeing that opera, that's all about passion, triggers it. I watch him more than I do Carmen. And when he leans in to get a beer off the coffee table, the sight of his ass almost made me jump him right there. When the others leave. I find some lame excuse for him to stay. And you know, the mother fucker was actually surprised.

"Hey, we're friends now." He barely manages to say before I pounce.

"Friends with benefits!" I practically scream as I start clawing at his clothes.

"Whoa! Ease up." He says.

But I became this different person. I literally ripped off his tee shirt and peeled off his pants. He's struggling, but not too much, like he's into it. We roll around on the floor. Me, still fully dressed, him stripped by yours truly and ready to be taken.

"Javi, knock it off!"

Does he mean it? I kinda don't care. Hell, I don't care, okay?! I gag him with the ripped tee shirt and undo my pants. I am going at warped speed but at slow motion too. He sees me skin on a rubber and at this he tries to scamper away, but I throw my full body weight on him. A couple of hard smacks on the ass, some spit, and I'm in him. He howls. Even the gag can't keep him quiet. So I wrap one arm around his arms in the back, holding them in place and my other hand goes over his gagged mouth. Gush this baby! And we fuck each other, cause as much as I'm thrusting into him, he's pushing his ass back into me. Look in the dictionary under "animalistic sex" and our picture is there. It was over way too soon. For both of us. Joel actually came first and the tensing of his body, not to mention his ass muscles, sends me over the top. We lay there panting. I let go of his arms, but that's all the movement for now. His breathing, my breathing. Who knows where one starts and the other begins. I ungag him. I don't know if I should apologize or brag. Will I be punched out, deservedly so, or be offered a post fuck drink?

"You owe me a tee shirt," Joel finally gasps.

"Yeah, I guess I do."

And that's it. Joel says he gets that I had to get rid of some of the pressure before the big opera opening. No biggie. And that, I've discovered is the thing with Joel. Sex to him is on a need it, get it, forget it basis. True to form, he will never bring up tonight again. It's not that he's embarrassed by sex, hell, I'm the one who's blushing, it's just that he thinks of the act itself as being completely disposable. As for myself, I gotta say I fucking needed that fuck. I feel like so much tension has been lifted off me. Honey, bring on that bitch Carmen!

Dear Diary:

An opening night at the Met is quite the event, as they'd be the first ones to tell you. I am wearing my custom made tux (look Moms, no love handles!) and I have polished myself up like an apple...

My hair is longer but I wisely talk myself out of a "payless super cuts!" It has taken every dime I could scrape together to be here tonight. Outside in the cab, as we are pulling up, I stop the driver, tip him way too much and stare as the limos drop off the monied few of which I was once a very proud member. Through coupling, I remind myself. And that's the only way I'll get back into that stratosphere again, through mating. I enter the hallowed hall and take a flute of the champagne (easy loca, you're on an empty stomach) and brace myself. I see a lot of people I sort of know, the kind you offer a nod to, so we both do just that. But it's the rich gays I'm worried about, that was our world and they'll be here in force tonight. My first sighting of these rare birds is Matt and Scott. I can tell by their faces, as lifted as and as botoxed as they are, that they are positively agasp to see me.

"Where have you been hiding?"

"Oh, he's back in the hood," Scott drops, quickly adding "which I hear is fabulous."

I should have snapped on him for that but I have to admit that being back among the elite has put me in a good mood. And child, the champagne doesn't hurt. The gays seem genuinely happy to see me, not ecstatic but not cold fish either. It probably helps that this was never Jason's stomping ground so it's seen as neutral territory. I am on my best behavior. A witty comment here, a witty comment there. "Five months? No, has it been that long?" I'm a new ear for their gossip. Lord knows, I'm sure I've been the source of it. I am told, in strictest confidence of course, that the new boy (Eric, okay? Eric! Why all you old witches gotta act like you don't know his name?) is dull, short, not too bright, pudgy (oh yeah, my favorite) and is pigeon toed. Life, she be good. The lights start their dimming, meaning of course that people will ignore them until the third and final dim then make a mad dash for their seats. Since all I could afford tonight was the nosebleed section I decide to wait it out in the men's room until everyone is seated. I'd rather not take that long walk up the stairs with all the gay eyes of society on me.

In the men's room I study my face under the harsh light. Not bad. For almost forty. Hell, not bad for thirty. Two. Thirty two. Or so. The music is piped into the loo so I visit a stall, do mirror work, anything, while I wait for stragglers to clear out. The bathroom is empty now. Or so I thought it was. A stall door opens and Kearn (hiss-boo) emerges.

Puta diary, you remember Kearn. He's a prick. And not the good kind. Older than the hills, but he has great carriage, a good head of hair and a mean mouth made meaner yet after a couple of cocktails. He came on to me soon after Jason and me got together. The whole hand on thigh thing. For the whole twenty years Jason and me were a couple he always treated me like a temp. Someone Jason would outgrow. And it turned out the bastard was right. He must be loving this.

"Towel please. Oh!," he says in mock horror. "I thought you were the attendant."

"Why? Didn't you bring a change of depends?" I say as sweetly as possible.

Kearn's eyes narrow. "Great way to start an evening," I think, "a bitch slap fest in the Met's toilet." Not to mention, physical confrontation being murder on couture. But no.

"So, will you join me?" Kearn says.

My shocked face says it all. What?

"I mean unless you're hot for a fellow nosebleeder in the cheap seats."

It's going to be that kind of evening, huh. I say, "Sure," and we sit in his box. One by one more opera glasses find their way up to us than they do to the two leads onstage. Kearn and me have champagne. He is the perfect gentleman. Which is not like him. Kearn has a revolving door of young men, certainly younger than me, but he drives them all away. The sweet, the surly, the bitchy all try to go mano a mano with him and perish. Jason used to say his boys came with expiration dates etched on them. At the first intermission we mingle. I'm still on the prowl for a lonely billionaire, hell, millionaire, no seas changa, but Kearn stays glued to my side.

"I never knew you liked opera."

"Yeah, well, just started." I scan the room.

"Well, you certainly picked a passionate one to start with."

Oh Jesus Cristo, please don't come on to me.

"I always suspected Jason was holding you back."

I think that actually was a compliment.

We go back to his box and somehow the old coot has ordered truffles. How? When? We sit and listen. Only once do our hands accidentally touch, when we reach for the same chocolate. He pulls back his hand. I look at him out of the corner of my eye and he is mouthing Don Jose's song of undying love to Carmen. I remind myself, I don't like Kearn. I have never liked Kearn.

Intermission.

I find myself at his side and people are talking to us as a couple. He goes out of his way to include me in the conversation. He laughs at my jokes and calls me by my full name, Javier. At the end of the opera, we rise, shout out our bravos and head out. His group decides on cocktails and a late dinner.

"Will you join us?"

Loca, think. Single rich gay men who haven't already been scarfed up are a rare commodity. But I don't wanna go. I think of my friends at the Red Castle and how much more fun I would have there than with Kearn.

"Please," he adds, "my friends owe me a dinner. Come with me and we'll break their bank."

Ah, now that's real music to my ears.

I am the youngest person at the table and I sing for my supper. I'm ON but never so much as to dominate the conversation. I remember everybody's name, laugh when I have to, listen when I have to. I puff them up. At one point I feel Kearn's hand, under the table, giving my knee a squeeze after a particularly worthy bon mot.

And then Kearn begins to drink. Heavily. He remains nice to me, but is rude to the waiters. Viciously so.

"In this country we wait to remove a plate until it is clear the diner has finished eating. Are you getting me, dummy?"

The table laughs nervously. I feel eyes on me, as if to say "He's with you. Do something!" But I'm ashamed. I feel like a geisha who's just had her make up removed by a drink tossed in her face. And the more he drinks the nastier he becomes. Lethal. Again, to everyone but me. I signal to him to calm down, lighten up, pero nada. Evil is as evil does. I've never understood why people get nasty when they drink. You can be nasty for free. Booze cost money, honey.

I rise, with every intention of clearing my throat and making a classy exit. What comes out instead is, "Fuck this shit! I'm outta here!" Next time, next time I'll be classy.

Having just enough coin for my cab ride from the Met to back home, I have to walk back to the Met in dress shoes clearly meant for riding in limos. I turn my collar up. Not too many people in the street. A light drizzle falls and feels nice and cool and forgiving. Was the real mission tonight to whore myself out? I mean, I loved Jason before I knew he was rich, but Kearn, and all the others at the opera, it was all gonna be about the money first, then maybe love.

A car slows down next to me. It's a limo and it's Kearn.

"Get in the car," he yells.

I ignore him and keep going.

"Get in the car," he pleads.

I turn, look at him, and with his crystal brandy snifter in his hand, Kearn hardens.

"Get in the car you goddamn whore!," he screams and throws his glass at me. It shatters at my feet. I look at him in shock, then rage. Complete, unfettered rage. I've been holding this back for way too long now, and today Kearn baby is your unlucky day! I lunge at the car, making a sound that can best be described as guttural. Kearn looks at me and I see fear in his face. Real, honest to God fear, and he screams at his driver, "Drive, drive, drive!" I barely open the car door when the driver burns rubber, practically dislocating my arm from it's socket. I scream in pain and grab my arm. People are looking at me, the whore, so I start walking. The pain in my arm subsides, the pain in my soul, wow, that's a keeper.

Dear Diary:
I was fired from Old Navy for my inability to fold tee shirts neatly. No really. My arm is still sore and it turns out I'm gonna need physical therapy that I cannot afford. It's Pops again to the rescue. I can't even bring myself to say, "I'll pay you back," because we both know that probably won't happen...

The boys all want to know what happened to my arm.

"Oh please, he fist fucked a republican, and you know how tight they are," Joel says this in the middle of Bed, Bath and Way Beyond. Victor, Rob and me all look at him agape. "What?" he adds. And even though we're asked to leave for laughing so hard (you had to be there) it was the perfect ending for the weekend from hell.

And wouldn't you know it, my physical therapist is a total papi chulo. Since the Kearn incident I have gained about five pounds, wait, booze and bar snacks are fattening? Who knew? Doctor Make Me McCreamy is oblivious of my crush. After a week of throwing myself at the good doctor, you know the drill, subtly touching myself, holding eye contact for that extra couple of seconds, standing as close as legally possible, (oh look who I'm telling) I've decided my medic is either hetro or involved. Certainly not that I have gained a couple of ounces.

The boys and me are doing the economy beauty day at my place (wear the avocado, don't eat it!) when Sonia, Hector's 'wife' comes a calling. Now Sonia and me have never been that close and Hector has kept his distance since trying to kill me (remember that? good times). It would be easier to like Sonia if every conversation with her didn't start with her saying "Hola, loca!." And by now, she just says it, no insult behind it, but I hate it and I tell her and she just shrugs, like "yeah, whatever." Rob calls her UMT, ultimate muffin top. The woman will not wear pants unless they are two sizes too small. I swear I think the only reason she had children was that they could help her into her bedazzled jeans.

"Junior, put down that video game and come help mami into her pants!"

It is a team effort. And her little girl, Cristina, is following in her bulging footsteps. And Sonia's taught her to greet me the same endearing way she does. So if I run into the calorie cabal on the street it's two female voices saying, "Hola Loca!" while baby Sully nurses mama's ample bazoom and Junior just rolls his eyes and stays quiet. Apuntalo, dearest Diary, I'm calling it, May 23rd, 4pm, little Junior is gonna be a sister!

But today, Sonia's usual greeting of "Hola loca" is missing, even with my aguacate covered face, instead she says one word, "booze" and I pour her a drink.

"Hector's cheating on me."

Have you ever seen three gay guys overact a denial? "Oh no!!"

"Are you crazy or something?!"

"Never!"

"With who?," that last one came from Victor, who we all deadeye.

"With some nurse ho, I think."

We all ponder this as we take in Sonia, a study in low riser jeans, thong and muffin top, and try to remain as neutral as possible except for Victor, who obviously didn't get the memo. "Go through his credit cards receipts," he offers. Our collective heads snap to him.

"I did," she wails.

"No," Victor continues, mucho to my chagrin, "create the timeline. You can totally track a man's day through his receipts."

I offer to take Victor into the kitchen to behead him, but Sonia is nodding, taking in all his sage advice.

After she leaves we all descend on Victor. "Are you crazy? You know Hector's on the downlow!" But Victor remains adamant. "She has a right to know." Dear, sweet, soon to be pimped slapped Victor.

On my next appointment I notice that my physical therapist has a hickey the size of a Volkswagen on his doctor neck. I pretend not to notice, but jeez louise, the damn thing is gay pride purple. Okay, so he's taken. That figures. I am his last appointment for the day and he's giving me the bum's rush out of the place. I see why when I walk out. His hickey donor was and is my cousin Hector. Okay, see, that's the thing about Hector. He's shameless. No really. El hijo de puta sees me and grins, like, 'hey, ain't this cool.' "No, it's not cool, asshole."

He leans in to me, "Last time I beat you up, this time I'll kill you."

I stop him with a simple, but deadly, "Sonia knows." He runs after me and I tell him everything on the elevator ride down. "So she thinks it's a woman, right?" he asks. And he's smiling.

"Hector, for now she thinks it's a woman. She's not stupid, you know." And neither is Hector. As we're walking he invests in a knock off bottle of Channel #5.

"This way, cuz, I put just a trace of it on me when I go home and Sonia will think I've been with another woman but I can honestly look her in the eye and say "no, mami, I swear on the lives of our children I haven't touched another woman.""

Hector is nothing if he's not a smooth criminal.

"Okay, first of all, don't call me papi."

"Whatever you say, papi." He smirks.

"And I'm gonna tell her. You're just being cruel to her."

"Like Jason was to you?"

This should have been the part where I slapped him.

"See, this is the thing. Jason cheated on you, for whatever reason, don't know, don't really care. The thing with Sonia is that I love her, she is the only woman in my life, the mother of my children, the whole deal, but she ain't got no dick. And every so often," he leans in now and whispers hoarsely, "I need one. You're who you are, I'm who I am. If you tell her, she'll leave me and take my little family with her. Look me in the eye and tell me I'm not a good father."

I can't.

"I promise you I play safe. And it's never anybody she knows."

"Hector, you were sucking face in the Red Castle which is in our neighborhood!"

"Oh that. Yeah, I tell her I go there to keep you company cause you crying all the time. She thinks I can straighten you out." he laughs. Hell, I laugh.

"You gonna tell her?"

"If she asks me point blank."

"She won't, you know she won't. Hey, if I didn't throw my little canitas al aire, I'd go crazy." He reasons.

"No more faggot jokes."

"I swears."

"And when Sonia calls me loca?"

"I'll laugh?"

"No, you'll tell her that my name is Javi."

"No papi, you tell her, I'm afraid of that woman. Hey, you ever suck your own dick? It's cool!"

Dear Diary:

I love farting in bed. I woke up this morning, feeling stupidly giddy, maybe I dreamt something nice, can't remember. No rush to go anywhere, just lying there as if I didn't have a final disconnect notice in the world when I just let 'er rip...

Now before, because I was like Sheila E, living the glamorous life, I had no bodily functions. None. Ningunos. I would not pass wind if world peace depended on it, okay, unlikely, but that's how tightly I could clench. I was already looked at as a party crasher by some/most of Jason's crowd, could you imagine dear Diary, if they found out this Rican used the toilet? Oh no no no no. Now lying on my futon/bed/torture rack the simple act of POP reminds me there is still a goofy boy in me. The one I kept hidden away for years.

Once Jason and me had dinner with a couple he knew since college. Peter and Paul. Funny, friendly, at least to Jason, with me it was as if they were not sure how long I had before I would sour and curdle and be replaced by the new quart of Puerto Rican love milk.

It was just the four of us after dinner, sitting around,

just talking, well they were talking I would smile and try to look like I was keeping up, but hoping that somebody for the love of all that is holy, would call it a night. Jason maneuvered me so I'm sitting on his lap, and while to him it was cute I felt like some fucking ventriloquist dummy. There was no way to gracefully get off without making a scene, so there I sat, while Jason engaged his friends in idle chatter and blew on the back of my neck as he spoke. And, stop the presses! Jason was popping a chub right under me, which made my eyebrows shoot to the top of my head, way past my forehead as I recall. Still my man went on and on about the good old college days with his chums. I decided to relieve my boredom by pressing down with my backside, as discreetly and gentlemanly as possible, hoping this would prompt Jason and his erection to hasten our getaway, when Peter, or to be fair, it could have been Paul, cut the cheese. Oh yes, I am sitting there, trying to pretend I was still breathing while I was holding my breath, waiting for someone to crack wise, or at the very least a window. Nope. Not gonna happen. They and Jason acted like nothing happened. Had I imagined it? Nobody was blushing. So, where'd the smell come from? As I tried to unravel the mystery of who, what, where, I hadn't gotten to how when one of them Ivy Leaguers did it again. Damn! Now really, no one else could smell that? Neither Peter or Paul let on that one of them was gas propelled and I knew it wasn't Jason, just by my close proximity to his nether regions. So, there it is, somebody in this gilded palace was guilty of air pollution and ain't nobody saying at the very least, "pardone-moi." And they stunk! They were like paint peelers, but apparently in a perfect world you don't acknowledge bodily functions. When we left, Jason talked all the way home about how great it was to see his buddies, and I just nodded and smiled, and tried not to gulp too greedily the air conditioned salvation the limo offered. I kept waiting for Jason to say something, cause while it was my nose, they were his friends. In my house my Moms would have hit you with the big spoon she used to serve rice, but if you're born with a silver spoon your stuff don't stink and it would have been uncouth of me to say otherwise.

Dear Diary:
Still not able to work cause of my slowly recuperating shoulder. I'm noticing a little bulge on my own once lithe torso. I can't run, bounces the shoulder, so I walk. Everywhere. For the first time I even allow myself to walk past some of the old haunts of my glory days. Stores that would pop open the champagne and salute when Jason and me would walk in...

It begins to rain, for which dear God, I am grateful. Just in case I start to bawl no one will notice. I stand under an awning, waiting for a break in the rain, when a limo slows down, stops and the window rolls down. Kearn.

"Get in."

"No thanks."

With a smile that actually looks warms and humble at the same time, he adds the magic word. "Please."

The homeless woman standing next to me hisses, "You a fool if you don't."

I get in.

As it turns out, today's Kearn will be brought to you by Manners, Contrition and Humor. Oh, look at that, he has a new law firm.

"How are you doing?"

"Fine, Kearn. And you?"

That little exchange took six blocks. In midtown Manhattan traffic. In the rain.

"I've been ....ashamed."

Okay, now the man has my attention.

"I was having such a lovely time that evening because of you, and I ruined it. Just stupidly ruined it."

I don't say a word.

"Would you have lunch with me? No drinks, I promise, no drinks."

"I'm a bit of a mess here, Kearn." Actually I think the word I'm looking for is bedraggled.

And with all sincerity Kearn says, "Oh no. When I saw you soaked under the awning, all I could think about was the first time I met you. Jason called you over and you stepped out of the pool and I thought to myself, yowza, now there's a beautiful young man."

"That was twenty years ago."

And he smiles shyly and adds the clincher, "You can't tell by me."

What can I say. The man has himself a lunch date!

Kearn is almost too sweet at lunch. I wish I could like him "that" way, but I don't And I think he wants me to. Hell, I'm sure of it. After lunch he insists on driving me back, very old school to my apartment. For a second I thought he was gonna walk me to my door. "I hope we can do this again." He says.

"We will."

And he shyly kisses me. And I let him. No tongue. And no nothing either. Zero zip.

I go to the backyard and watch my parents working in their vegetable garden Arguing, laughing. Okay, Moms is doing most of the arguing and Pops is doing most of the laughing. They've been in each others lives longer than they've been with anybody else. An eternity. A forever. They wave me over to help them, but I shake my head *no* and smile. Today, I just want to look at them.

Dear Diary:
Fuck shit coño, Sonia knows something's up....

She comes downstairs with her "Hola loca" greeting, her children are in school or preschool or juvenile detention. I am doing my weighted shoulder stretch prescribed to me by my gorgeous doctor who's banging her husband, who I wish was banging me, the doctor, NOT my cousin (you got all that?). I haven't even had my coffee yet.

"At least I didn't catch you in your manties." Sonia says. I eyeball her. "You seen my Hector?"

"A lot less than you, trust me."

She is amusing herself going through my assorted toiletries. Face creams, eye gels, masques. Once I hit 35 I too, like Cher, became obsessed with turning back time.

"No, I mean when you go out at night, do you see Hector out and about? The only place he's allowed to go is that maricon bar cause there he's safe." She takes a gob of eye gel and smears it under each eye. "You running low on this stuff."

"No, Sonia, when I'm at the maricon bar, I'm not paying attention to him and he's not paying attention to me."

"Well, duh. Hey, this shit smells like shit." She says.

"It is shit. Virgin baboon shit, great for the skin."

She drops the jar. She won't be dipping into anymore of my creams anytime soon.

"When he's not at the bar he tells me he's just hanging with his homies."

I stop myself from saying "you mean homos" and just nod.

"But that's not it. I'm not stupid you know."

I bite my tongue.

"People think when you're beautiful like me you haven't got no brain. But that's not the case with myself."

I bite my tongue harder. Draw blood.

"So I's just saying if you know anything or if you hear anything you should tell me cause if I find out you're fronting for him, it'll cost you."

I'm barely listening, trying to decide which one of them I like least. Hector or Sonia. Her cell phone rings, and yes dear Diary, what plays is the Milkshake Song.

My milkshake brings all the boys to the yard
Damn right, it's better than yours
I could teach you, but I'd have to charge

"What?!" she bellows into her phone. "Ugh. Okay. I'll be right over." She hangs up. "My sister is such a pain." She starts for the door, which I swear I will lock from now on. I mumble, "Take care." And she stops, hand on the doorknob. "When your man cheated on you, how did you find out?"

I look at her, but she is avoiding my eyes, and for the first time since I've known her she seems almost vulnerable, almost human.

"I suspected."

"Like me."

"And he told me. After I confronted him."

All I hear is shallow breathing, hers or mine, I'm not sure. Then we both cried. She gathers herself.

"Yeah, you faggots cry at everything."

Oh, yeah, that's why I don't like her.

Just before she leaves, she drops it.

"Maybe I should get pregnant again."

And hurries out. I drop the weight I was lifting for my

shoulder as I discovered that yes, you can feel sorry for someone you don't really like.

Dear Diary:

Pops got me a job painting Compai Creflo's apartment. And I'm reading the want ads everyday and going online to look for jobs. Something's gotta turn up, right? The fact that I'm not actually equipped to do anything shouldn't be a hindrance (insert Kardashian joke here), I'm a hard worker and I'm willing to learn, but I'm at, what one job placement person so tactfully put it, my mid career age. Meaning that by my age I should be if not in a corner office, at least banging someone on my way up the corporate ladder to that sacred sanctuary. My resume is of little help to me, FUEGO, Old Navy and freelance apartment painter who is slower than molasses; but I have to keep trying. I want to be self sufficient, pay my bills on time, maybe get an apartment with a sky view as opposed to ankle view. Still the same dreams I had before Jason, but not so dewy fresh. But what am I qualified for? What would people pay me for? I'm not an idiot, I have to be good for something. Everybody is. I will not give up. As scared as I get, I will not give up on me...

Dear Diary:

Happy Gay Pride!!! I'm actually going to the parade this year. In the twenty years I've been a gay man, okay I was gay since birth but I didn't know it, I have never been to the parade...

Jason and his friends would either leave town or rent a huge party boat and we'd circle the island (Manhattan, child, what's the matter with you today?!) but we would never mix with the hoi polloi. We'd have our own fun and the people on the pier would wave to us, and yet somehow I always felt I should be there in the masses. More than anything the gay pride celebration would always make me feel like I was crashing my own party. I would be with all the power gays, but that day I was soooo aware it was because I had part- nered into their clique. Oh, and the great thing was I know for a fact that after they left our mega exclusive party they'd go looking for tricks. And the same guys they'd be looking down on, they'd be swinging on their candy poles scream- ing out "Hallelujah!" Rob and me are going to meet at the parade. Joel is going to march with some political group, so I don't have to see him. I still get kinda embarrassed around him. And Victor will be dancing down Fifth Avenue on the Red Castle float. Okay, he kinda is the float, it's a small bar, but still. He will also be wearing a sun block so strong I think he'll actually be albino by the end of the day.

I get to the kick off point right at noon and there is good old Rob. In spandex. From head to toe. He looks like the Michelin man. Yet, somehow I don't think I've ever seen him happier. Hey, on Pride, spandex is an undeniable right to all Latinos. I, however, am wearing silk shorts, (they just happen to be cool, that's all) and a tank top. We hug and kiss and wish each other happy pride.

"I've always wanted to do Pride with you, Javi," Rob beams. "Now, what do you think about my outfit? Too much?"

"Oh no. The fanny pack saves it."

He punches me good-naturedly and we blend like tiny cinnamon colored specks in the giant crowd. We watch the parade kick off with the Dykes on Bikes.

"They always start us off, it's a tradition."

I feel like a virgin. I have no idea of the order, participants (gay and lesbian, got that) or nothing. This is my first time at this jamboree and I actually find myself tearing up. I remember the first time I held hands with Jason in a public place and feeling so brave, unaware that his money was better than a team of body guards to keep me safe, but today, today it's just your run of the mill queer walking down Fifth Avenue for all the world to see. We see Joel and wave like lunatics to him, calling out his name but he doesn't hear us. So many of us, and how different we all are. We hear the thumping of club music and a huge bar float comes by, boys shaking it for all they're worth.

"They should pace themselves," I tell Rob, sounding like somebody's maiden aunt.

"Honey, with what they're on they could dance for weeks!"

More topless men (and topless women!) follow. The women have put duct tape over their nipples, so legally they're covered. Float after float, display after display. It is overwhelming. I feel like I've swallowed a kaleidoscope. And then Victor's float shows up. He is in his (ahem) rightful place at the very center and wearing gold lame short shorts and channeling Iris Chacon in her hey day. The boy is fierce! And pale. He glows like he were made of ivory opal or something equally pale and shiny. And not an ounce of fat anywhere on his body. Rob jumps up and down until he catches Victor's attention and Victor smiles at us and waves. Now I'm glowing. Look, it's contagious.

The group right after Victor's is Latino Gay Men, they are carrying a banner and chanting "Somos Gay! Somos Gay!" My emotions are getting the better of me, I feel like my heart is about to burst. I'm not alone. I belong to a group of men (at least I guess I do, should I join? Is there a paying membership?) And then, sweet Jesus Cristo, Rob grabs my hand.

"Come on!"

He is joining the parade. With me! Me! Oh no no no no. Not happening. But Rob won't let me disappear back into the crowd. He adds us to the people carrying the banner and I go from observer to participant just like that. I walk like in a daze. I can't do this. It's too soon. Time out. I'm actually looking at my feet, not at the crowd. Rob is beside me, screaming until he's hoarse.

"Somos gay, somos gay!"

What if my parents see me? Sure, they know, but do they need to hear me screaming it?

"Come on, pendejo, this is your party, too!" Rob smiles.

And I look up and people are smiling and cheering and I start whispering, "somos gay, somos gay." My voice gets louder, it cracks, but I keep hollering. People wave from the crowd, blow kisses. This old Puerto Rican woman gives us the finger and mimics a gay man and I find myself laughing at her. This is what I was afraid of?

We get to St. Pat's and that's where I see the protesters holding up signs that wish us death, that wish us hell and eternal damnation and proclaim that AIDS is God's retribution for our sins. We keep chanting to drown out their chants of "Faggot! Faggot!" "Somos gay! Somos gay!" The Red Castle float with our Victor is stopped directly in front of them with a frenetic version of La Bamba playing over their loud speakers and Victor explodes. He is obviously now dancing for the protesters. Insanely dancing. Possessed dancing. The sweat pouring off him is making him glisten and then he does it. He moons them! It is a direct hit! They are outraged into a beat of silence and then they amp their hate, but we move on. Victor pulls up his pants and blows them a kiss as the Latino Gay Men fall in step behind the Red Castle float. I feel like I just went sky diving and Lived! Rob has to yell in my ear to be heard over the crowd.

"Let's amp this baby up!"

I'm not sure what he means.

"X!"

"I've never done it."

"Oh please." He dismisses.

"No really, Jason was totally against any drugs."

"Well, he's not here, is he?"

"I'm already having fun."

"Take half."

"What's it gonna do?"

Rob suddenly kisses me, and I realize, it's not a kiss, he has the ecstasy on his tongue. What the hell. I swallow. He gives me a swig of water and we continue marching. For a few blocks. Suddenly, it hits. IT HITS!!!!!! and I begin to walk faster. My heart begins to beat fast, like it's going a thousand miles an hour. Hello! Hello! Hello! Hello! Hello!

"Damn loca, that was quick. Slow down, enjoy it!"

Is he nuts? I am skewing the banner by walking so fast, but I can't help myself. I have to move and quickly. Rob finds two other guys to take our places and I'm tearing down Fifth Avenue at the fastest walking pace ever recorded with Rob right behind me.

"It's good right? It's real good!"

"I'm gonna kill you!"

And as we hit 14th street, it changes. The frenzy disappears and is replaced by bliss. Absolute, total bliss. Yes, I don't have a pot to piss in, yes I'm alone at 39, yes my prospects look grim and yet I'm absurdly happy and accepting of all this. And horny. Other worldly, alert the media horny. What's in that damn thing?

I lean against a wall with Rob, both of us totally at peace.

"I'm gonna be totally bald in a couple of years," he says.

"Yeah, you will, but you can still act," I dreamily reply.

"Thank you."

"I'm getting love handles," I say and smile.

"That's true," he agrees.

"I'm horny. My asshole is twitching," I just blurt out. Rob laughs so hard he slides down the wall, I laugh too and join him, then we get up and dance over, way down to the dance floor on the pier. Having never danced on X before I can tell you it's an out of body experience. Endless energy and endless joy. And Rob, who's always so self conscious about his body whipped off his spandex tee shirt and let his man boobs get some sun. I took off my shirt, too and pretty soon we are engulfed in a sea of men, all sweating and dancing. Oh God, I'm so happy. Right at this moment, I'm so happy. I hump everything that moves in front of me. I am dancing as if I were 19 again and telling myself, letting myself believe that I am at one with everybody. Every so often Rob will get us a bottled water, but I don't leave the dance floor. Today is my declaration of independence. Today belongs to me. Hey Diary, do you know what happens to silk shorts when they get wet from sweat? They stick to your skin! They kinda disappear so I might as well be dancing in my tighty whiteys. But damn, I feel good!

I look up, and there by the speaker, there he is. Jason. And I smile. The biggest smile of the day. Soaking wet, hair flying all over. Okay, so it's a hallucinogenic now? But, no, it's really him. What's he doing here? Who cares? I hold out my arms to him. Join me!! He smiles, shakes his head, no, and I continue dancing. I see "the boy," my replacement, from the back as he tugs on Jason's arm and they dive into the VIP crowd. Diana Ross is asking us "Who Was The Boss?" and I catch a glimpse of Jason just before he disappears and he turns around and looks at me and licks his lips. Did I just turn him on?! Victor joins us on the dance floor and by the time the fireworks happen, which end our festivities, Joel is with us. We all ooh and ahh to the jewelry in the night sky (that's how I think of fireworks, jewelry on a big scale). By the time we have our late meal, my pants have dried and I have mellowed. Joel is heading to one of the many after parties, Victor is going back to the Red Castle to hold court and Rob has hooked up with a real cutie. I cab it home. A ridiculous expense in my current situation but I'm at peace with it. Not quite as horny, but a hand job is definitely in order.

Okay, ecstasy is nice, very nice. But it's a one time a year event. If that. And will anything come close to this glorious first time?, I think as I study myself in the mirror. I will let today live in perfection. I will not regret or change anything about it. I see I have a message on my machine and hit play and a drunken Jason's voice fills the room. He says one word.

"Damn!" Which he manages to fill with both admiration and lust. A perfect day indeed I think as I masturbate to images of Jason until I am sore. Nothing. Fuck. I can't cum. Well, it was almost a perfect day.

Dear Diary:
"FUEGO!" closed!!!!! My life is over and shit...

I fell into the Grand Canyon of funks. I didn't know enough to know that the show stunk big time, all I knew was that it way my identity, my independence. When I filled out my first tax return and wrote "dancer" on profession I could back it up with a pay stub. And it also meant I wasn't just Jason's boy, I was a working man. I was. Then.

So I went back to classes and auditions. I took every class I could afford cause I wasn't about to let Jason pay for my dreams. But every audition I went to I was always among the first they cut. Jason, seeing his newly minted dream boy beginning to look like one of those sad eyed big headed kids painted on black velvet decided I needed a boost. And what could be a bigger boost to a showbiz manboy than Madonna. Not a concert, but a dinner. Jason made an obscene donation to the charity of her heart and lo and behold we were given seats next to her Madjesty at a formal dinner. I, of course, almost killed Jason. "What the hell am I supposed to say to her?!" I whined/screamed. Matters took a decidedly uncivil turn when Kearn, not one to be left out when it came to one up yours manship, donated one dollar more than Jason and completed the table.

On the night of the dinner, Kearn and his newest paramour, Kevin, who took an immediate dislike to me, and wasted no time in letting me know it, showed up at our place.

"So you're the chorus boy, huh?" he smiled. "God, I hope they don't play disco all night, though you'd probably love it. Jason darling (he barely knew Jason, what's with the darling?) back a revival of West Side Story and give this boy a job."

All that in one satanic breath. To be fair there was nothing I could slam him on. He was perfect. The kind of guy Jason should have been dating. Smart, elegant and model good looking as opposed to street cute.

The ride to the event was interminable with Kevin holding court and dropping enough obscure reference in his monologue that I was totally at sea. Kearn looked at him with adoring eyes while Jason kept massaging my neck, telling me how nice I looked. I'm doomed.

We get to the dinner and are already seated at our table when SHE (caps mine!) arrived. There is a flurry of photos as SHE is led to our table, you could just about catch a tan from the flashes, and SHE is immune to it all. Regal, graceful. There is one group photo of all of us and then we sit. Jason makes me take the seat to HER left while Kearn, monkey seeing monkey doing, positions Kevin on HER right. I didn't have a prayer. No, not "Like a Prayer," I didn't have a mother fucking prayer! Kevin launches into an exclusive discussion with HER about the Freudian aspects of HER music and videos while I am left to pretend that I am fascinated by the croutons in my salad. I try to join the conversation but there'll be no co pilot for Kevin on this voyage. Kearn, fuck I disliked that man, is Cheshire cat smiling as Jason motioned me with his head to dive into the deep end of the conversational waters. Kevin was sharing his thoughts on all things Germanic opera, you can't make this shit up, when La Bella Madonna turned to me. Either out of boredom or as an escape.

"You don't say much, do you?" SHE said in a totally unreadable voice.

"I'm..." oh look at that, I found part of my voice. Unfortunately it was the part that also cracks. "I'm kinda nervous around celebrities."

Celebrity was definitely the wrong choice of words. Kevin stopped trying to win HER back. He was just gonna sit back and watch me burst into flames.

SHE eyeballed me, but said nothing.

"I shouldn't be," I stammered, "cause I'm in the business, too. I was."

Please God, Helen Keller me or kill me. Your choice.

"I was in FUEGO! on Broadway. I got to meet Luba Potamkin. She came to see the show. She was really sweet."

At the mention of Ms. Potamkin's name Kevin's hand shot up to his mouth. To stifle a laugh or a scream, I'm still, to this day, not sure.

Madonna looked at me in a way that only years later I came to recognize as "are you putting on an act or is this you?."

"Yes, she seems very sweet." SHE half offered.

Either nerves or foolishness propelled me on, and SHE seemed to be waiting for more.

"Everybody got a picture with her, well 'cept me. I didn't have a camera and I went out and got a disposable one but she was gone already. She was…luminous."

And SHE, Madonna smiled.

There is a way that the very famous make their presence and their wishes known. I can't do it, and neither can you, but trust me, SHE can and did. SHE sat perfectly straight and flicked HER head just so and presto, the photographers were back. And then as the flashes popped, SHE kissed me on the cheek. Shit, even Jason was stunned.

"Tell me about that show you were in. I'm so sorry I missed it," SHE said.

For about fifteen minutes we talked dance and auditions as Kevin developed an excruciating headache/nervous tic and left. Madonna left early, too, after having barely eaten a thing. Before SHE left SHE took my hand and wished me good luck.

The limo ride back was a decidedly different trip. I was like one of those crazy bouncing balls in a very contained space. Even Kearn had to smile and Jason, my man was beaming. And even though it was a cold night Jason and me turned up HER music and danced on the roof garden. I danced until I couldn't dance anymore. With renewed commitment and energy I went back to my classes and back to auditioning, but I never got another dancing job again. And soon Jason and my life became so full and chaotic that I told myself it didn't matter. That it was all for the best. I would still go dancing with Jason, still have that release, but even that became less and less. And that, ladies and germs, because sometimes it does take a brick to hit me on my head, is when I began to disappear. When I didn't out grow my dream, I just let it go. Like a child who had outgrown a balloon but spends the rest of the summer looking for it in the sky, secretly whispering "come back to me."

Dear Diary:

I've now added dog walker to my many skills. People are hiring me cause it's too hot to walk their own damned dogs and so I'm left trying to herd their drooling, and in some cases, incontinent four legged family members. This is the summer of my fucking discontent...

The hotbox that is my dwelling is, of course not a/c'ed and I sweat even when I'm taking a shower. I see women in advanced stages of pregnancy and want to say, "Really, carrying around another 30 pounds during the bake and broil months seemed like a good idea to you?" I tell myself that spending every free moment in the cooled environs of the Red Castle is practically a medical necessity. Boy, do I miss the temperature controlled bubble that was my world. I must sleep with my windows closed because being a basement apartment apparently qualifies my place as a trash receptacle, that and every kid on summer vacation seems to stay out until midnight only to have forgotten their key and so have to caterwaul "Ma, throw me a key!" And you know, oddly enough if you politely ask them to shut their piehole they take offense. Go know.

It is a particularly hot Tuesday that I ran into an old school mate. Actually, 'mate' is a friendly way of saying an old school bully. He was that oddity. A ferociously femme big boy who zeroed in on me and made my life hell. The thing that got me, that pissed me off so much was that no matter how Ms. Thing he was, he would just joke with everybody and they would leave him alone; while I became the "Fua" king (or queen) thanks in large part to him. He was also the one who added the cherry to my humiliation sundae by calling me 'sister' in front of everyone. "Hola hermana!"

I would try to hide, oh look, I'm so engrossed in my math text book, how could I possibly see or hear him. Looking back on it, I still have a little intake of breath whenever I think of it. A desire to duck, to just vanish. Fag-B-Gone, coming soon to a theater near you.

But today, I'm at a store, a dollar store, natch, where I saw him again. I'm restocking my pantry - hey, first go to the Dollar Store, then hit the A&P, when I see him. As my Moms would say, "Como castiga la vida (how life can punish you)" Hermana boy, has seen better days. One hopes. He is missing teeth, hair and from the elbow down, his right arm. We are about the same age, how did this happen? I have to remind myself to breathe, and for Christ's sake, reach for something. Anything. As I reach for the bleach he says, "Excuse me, could you get me one, too?"

So polite. But the voice. It's him. It's fucking him. Except back then there was no humility to his voice. Ah, but then he wasn't asking a stranger for a favor, he was fucking up a confused kid's life. I put the bleach in his basket and he thanks me. It's then that he recognizes me. I can tell. I want to say, "Soy gay, hermana, so fuck you.," but I don't. I mean what's the point. Move on. And then he reaches out his nub, sorry I don't know the polite term for it, nub, stub, his elbow where his forearm used to live, and he tries to touch me with it. I'm like in shock. I try to back away, but have you seen the aisles in the Dollar Store? He sees the horror on my face and it gives him pleasure. He touches my chest. He gives me a practically toothless leer and hisses, "I hope you die, lucky boy."

I leave everything and run out of the store. I'll have to find myself another Dollar Store, luckily not too hard in my hood. Why did he unnerve me so much? That night, I tear my place inside out until I find my high school yearbook. I never technically graduated since I dropped out when I got the show, but I still got a yearbook. I look through the pictures, so many people that I was afraid of and I wonder, was I the luckiest person in the history of HS 45? I never even got a chance to rub it in their faces. God, how much more would they have hated me then? That night I write a letter I know I'll never send. To my now one armed bully. I tell him I'm sorry about his arm, his teeth, his life. It coulda been me. Maybe yes, maybe no, but when I signed the letter I didn't hate him anymore. I don't know what his story is, but sister has paid his dues.

Dear Diary:

To celebrate my fourth birthday with him Jason is going all out. He has given me an extravagantly expensive gift everyday of the month leading up to the day of my actually getting hatched and is planning a huge blowout for me, but I tell him I don't want a party, (certainly not with his friends) so Jason has planned a nice catered dinner for just the four of us. Yes, my beloved has invited my parents, who he has yet to win over. This will not end well...

Jason hired someone who claimed to be the number one Puerto Rican chef in the country and El Trio Los Panchos (my Pops is crazy mad for trio singers. He could listen to their harmonies for hours). While this started out as the day to celebrate me it is clear that Jason was trying to win over the inlaws who still looked at him as a temporary lapse in judgment on my part before I settled down and married some nice vecina next door.

Jason was a bundle of nerves and spent almost an hour debating with himself over which car to send for them. The stretch? No, didn't want them to think he's fronting (trust me, he's not). The town car? Too old. Hey, they are old. They're my parents. My mother is not much older than Jason, who finally decided on the Silver Cloud Rolls Royce (oh yeah, that's casual Friday).

Los Panchos had already arrived, eaten and had begun playing. I think they were expecting more of a crowd, but Jason was probably paying them Elton John rates so they crooned away in the room off to the side of the dining room. The place settings were set with gorgeous Haitian carved wooden plates. I smiled as I remembered the first time I ate on them. I thought they were place mats until a server plopped some mashed potatoes on them. I made a note to myself to warn my parents, not wanting them to be embarrassed. My parents were buzzed in. Jason was all in beige, no, beige would have been too out there, he was in ecru. Ecru, Brutus? He was never really close to his family so he was really making an effort for my folks.

Now when you're a Hispanic child, the first thing you do when you see either one of your parents is to ask for their blessing, "La Bendicion." My Moms never let me get it out, she spat out her response so she could get it out of the way and start talking. My Pops upon hearing the gentle singing and guitar strumming, broke out in a child like smile when he saw Los Panchos. Score one for Jason! Except that Pops dropped us to go talk to them. When I gently steered him back so we could eat I had to explain to him that "they're not gonna eat with us, they're gonna play while we eat." Pops looked at me like I was nuts and I told him, "They're working, Pops."

"For Jason?" my Pops asked.

"For you, really. Jason did it for you. And for Moms." Pops accepted the answer, but you could see it made no sense to him.

Moms had gone directly to the kitchen and it was looming to be a smackdown in the okei corral. She was tasting everything and while the chef looked on in horror, she was reseasoning the food. Oh, she was very nice about it and she laughed like it was the most normal thing in the world, but I was sensing only a major tip will make this right.

Jason was offering up some of his finest wine, but my Pops was on high blood pressure medicine so he shook his head "no" as he continued listening to the original boy band of his youth. Moms, of course, took some of the white and then warned, "I may not be able to estop talking if I drink." Really? The woman has been a silent film up until now? I was the bridge to small talk so as Jason would say something and I would translate or my parents would say something, you get the picture. My parents could understand English, but in entering this mini Puerto Rico that Jason had created for them in the heavens of Manhattan they felt like they were back on their island. We sat down to dinner, finally! and Moms turned to the chef with her first mouthful and said, "Esee, it tastes better now!" I thought the chef was one step away from sticking an apple in her mouth. I tried to talk to Jason, but Moms constantly interrupted and Pops was leaning as far back in his chair as he could so as not to miss any of his music.

I looked at Jason. He tried so hard to make this special for them and I felt sorry for him and mad at my parents, so the next time my Moms said "Translate for Jason" something she just said I told her, "You tell him. You speak English."

Big mistake. Huge.

"Do ju know that until Javi was three I juse to dress him like a little girl?"

Okay, Moms, put the wine down.

"Jes, he was eso pretty. Efrain hated it." She laughed and gestures to my Pops who is of no help to me now.

"And he was fat!" She squealed. Good lord, shut the woman up!

"Gordito," she continued. "Had a big belly, that's cause he was eso gassy!"

At this Jason began to roar and I evil eyed my Moms into the next century. She was oblivious.

"Moms, la comida esta bien buena, verdad?" I quickly said in Spanish, hoping to get her back on the Borinquen Express, but that train had left the station.

"We were once at Woolworths." She was laughing so hard at this upcoming memory she could barely get it out.

"Moms, eat!" I stammered, which of course made her laugh all the more.

"Ay, ay, ay." She was holding her sides. The hilarity of it all was killing her. And me.

"And Javi went, 'mami, caca' right in the middle of the store!"

Of course just as she delivered her line Los Panchos decided a cigarette break was in order so her rim shot landed in a room full of silence.

"I was fucking three years old!!!!" I spewed, and my anger just made her laugh all the more.

By the time we got to dessert I was ready to have myself declared an orphan. Jason was uncomfortable, I was mortified and my Moms blissfully continued her roast of me. Then Pops, who could probably have landed an airplane on the head of a pin, turned to Los Panchos and said, "Mi hijo bailo on Broadway." The last word is the only one Jason understood, but it is the money shot. The trio looked at me and nodded with respect and Moms, not missing a beat, added "I always knew Javi was talented."

As the evening ended my Pops got to sing along with his idols, and the day, for me became perfect. He can really sing, you know. My parents gave me my gift as they left, a crucifix on a gold chain. "What more gift than that song?" I told my Pops. I hugged them and told them I loved them, cause I really did, you know. And my Moms held on really tight to me and whispered, "Ju will always be my baby."

My Moms thanked Jason, and gave him the "look." It's her 'mono que se viste de seda mono se queda (dress a monkey in silk, it's still a monkey. Hey, I grew up hearing these things.) What that look really meant is, not yet Jason Wilcox. I still don't approve of you for my son. But then I saw Jason, just as courtly as can be, with a look in his eyes that tells me, "I got this, trust me." And I did.

My parents went home in the Rolls, this time with Los Panchos serenading them. I'm sure that Moms talked through most of it. We stood in the doorway, Jason and me, until he broke the spell by half whispering/half giggling, "Now I know what you're gonna be like in twenty years."

"You better hush," I laughed back, and we chased each other around the apartment.

My last diary entry for that day was: "Best. Birthday. Ever." And it was. It was perfect.

Dear Diary:

Well, today is my birthday. Forty. Officially. For some reason it didn't hit me like I thought it would. I just want to sleep through it. Pretend it was any other day. It's my 40th birthday and I have no idea who I am. I was an "us" for so long that the me part of me is MIA. I'm embarrassed to be this old and this inept...

My Pops cooks me breakfast while my Moms sits and smokes, her ever present ashtray in the palm of her hand.

"I haven't been to the beach in fifteen jears," she says, "that's what keeps me looking jung." "You mean it's not the Lucky Strikes?" I reply.

She hacks a laugh and we eat and I have to make up this

fun filled day I have planned just to get them off my back. Last year I spent my birthday in Barcelona, this year? Well, I'm staying closer to home.

Moms wants all the details so I make up an itinerary chock a block with so much fun that it would kill a celebutante. My Moms eyes glow the more I go on. All they want is for me to be happy.

"So good, you're busy," my Pops says, "so you'll need this."

Their gift for me is a cell phone. I am humiliated and grateful in the same breath.

"It's a good plan. We researched it." my Moms says. And as they go on I feel like I'm watching myself from far away. I have been without a cell phone for, what, six months? Ever since D day. But to get one from my parents, what am I a teenager? makes me feel even more like a loser, a grateful loser, but a loser nonetheless. "Gracias," I say and kiss both of them. I notice for the first time that my Moms holds the hug longer than I do.

As I'm about to leave I see Kearn's limo outside. My Moms is standing beside me as Kearn bounces out (at almost 70!), and leaves a small box outside the door. He leaves never even ringing the bell.

"Who?"

"Kearn."

"He rich?"

"Filthy."

"Ay!," she says, giving me a big wet kiss on the cheek. "Ju still got it!"

"I don't love him."

"He love ju?"

I shrug.

"No seas sangano. Reel him in. Ju had love. Ju need esecurity."

Pops brings in Kearn's gift to me. Sunglasses. My Moms

looks disappointed, but I assure her they're expensive. How expensive? Jewelry expensive. Easily major ca-ching ca-ching.

I wear the most over the top outfit I can throw together. Sometimes the outside can change how I feel on the inside. Plus I needed something to set off my new sunglasses. I go for a walk, all over the city. Today it's my city. Music seems to play from everywhere. My life is a damn musical! Cars, stores, some kids singing on the street with a hat to gather money. I give them a twenty. What can I say? I'm a birthday fool. They are so young and so full of hope. This is my first birthday without "J" in so long. I have to fight the impulse to still turn to him. Ask him something. Make some lame joke that he'll always laugh at. I call Rob and give him my number.

"Oooh, happy birthday sucia!"

And Victor.

"Cabrona, you don't look a day over forty!"

"I am forty," I deadpan.

"Oh. Your first drink is on me tonight!" he salvages himself.

I would call Joel but he never gives out his number. Then, THE call. To Jason. But I hang up before he can answer. And even if he *69'ed me (and who came up with that number? Now really.) It's Saturday, late summer and I have eighty dollars left of the hundred I saved for my birthday (damn those inspiring kids and their singing.) Eighty, just for me. Which before would have bought me, what, a pair of socks? is now my gift to me. And ay virgen, how long did it take to scrape that C note together. I have a couple of hot dogs and an unidentifiable beverage (is it juice, is it soda? no one knows) and still am flush. I could blow it all tonight but I know the guys want to treat me. So, what would make this rapidly aging boyman happy? I call Kearn and thank him for the sunglasses.

"Ah, you found them," he says, sounding like he's on his first drink, still happy, but cuidado. "Just say the word and I'll whisk you away to Timbuktu for a birthday you'll never forget."

I beg off, family you know. "Of course," he says understandingly.

Before he hangs up he blows me a kiss on the phone, then drops it. I hear him curse up a storm looking for the phone. I hang up so he won't hear me laughing.

What I wind up doing is going to a bar. The most exclusive bar in the city. No name outside, doesn't need it. Jason and me would meet there for drinks before dinner. With my bankroll of eighty I can afford one drink. I'm not kidding. Tipping is how you earn your stripes in here and I'll be damned if I don't out tip every cabron here.

At the bar are two trophy boys, exhausted after a hard day of shopping. They air kiss me, we sort of know each other and they congratulate me on Kearn's interest in me. So word is out, huh.

"Good for you, landing on your feet!"

"Or something," Trophy Two cackles.

I order my first drink and exhale. Every thing seems right. I'm here, where I should be, in the lap of luxury. They compliment me on my sunglasses. I find out that obscene doesn't even begin to cover their cost. They ask me where I've been keeping myself and I say Manhattan (hey, it's not a lie). "But we never see you."

"I'm always at the Red Castle," I say before I can pick a more appropriate place. But then I stop. I look at these young, perfect men I want so desperately to impress. Like me! Notice me! And, yes dear diary, fuck this shit.

"It's a dive," I add, looking at both of them squarely in the eyes, "but it's near the basement apartment my parents are kind enough to let me have since dog walking and apartment cleaning don't really pay all that much."

And scene.

I leave a two dollar tip for my drink. I hear an audible gasp from Trophy One. Trophy Two may have just fainted. I pull out my generic cell phone and the first message there is from my friends. They've sent me a picture of a birthday cake with the words "Happy Birthday Puta" on it. Ahh. I get up, leave, and this time I do get to be classy. No cursing or tripping or nothing. I head to the Red Castle and we order Chinese and eat it at the bar. Even Hector comes by. And I pay. I treat my friends. And look at that, I still got a couple of bucks leftover! I go home and begin looking for you. I have kept all my diaries since the very first one. Why? I don't know. Maybe I figured when I was famous someone would want them. I was ten when I got my first one, picked it out myself. Beige, with a little snap on it. I would hide it in my underwear drawer, then between the mattress and box spring, then deep in the closet (no cracks!). You were always in movement like if you held state secrets as opposed to "lunch sucked at school today," or "I really hate gym class." No, what was incriminating was that I would draw a little heart and put my initials and the initials of the boy in school I thought was cute. And I would enter those initials backwards (try to crack that code, Moms!). You became my secret best friend and like all secrets that made you all the more tantalizing, and like all friends, I eventually took you for granted.

I find the diary I am looking for with the entry that changed everything.

"Dear Diary: Today I met HIM! He is the person I'm supposed to spend the rest of my life with. I didn't jump up and down, we didn't even talk much, but I just looked at him and I knew. Peacefully knew. Just like, "oh, okay, this is him" knew...

I reread the entry, with a drink or two or four, pick up the phone (danger Will Robinson, danger, danger!) and call Jason's direct line. Did I mention it was 2am? He doesn't pick up, which means either his phone is off or he's screening his calls. I head out there.

The doorman takes one look at me and knows I'm a little wobbly. Do you know how hard it is to stand upright when all you want to do is lie down? "George, please call Jason for me."

"It's awfully late."

"It's only getting later."

"You should go home."

"This was my home. Tell him to come down. Now."

In all the years I dealt with George I never used the diva voice. He looks at me sadly and calls up. It takes forever but he whispers into the mouthpiece, listens and hands me the phone. George also tries to will himself to disappear as I take the phone.

"Javi-"

"No. Get down here."

"Happy birthday, Javi."

"That was yesterday."

"Yeah, cause it's almost 3am."

"...you didn't even send me a gift." Oh shit, this is not about that.

"I didn't think it was appropriate. But please, pick whatever you want and put it on my tab."

I don't want to cry in front of George.

"I met Philip."

And now it's Jason's turn to be quiet.

"I never knew about him. Jason?"

"I'm here."

"I said I never knew about him."

"What do you want me to tell you?"

"Why did you keep him a secret?"

"I didn't keep him-

"You told him you would cut him off if he ever made himself known to me."

Silence.

"Please come down here."

"I think you should go home."

Silence.

I hear in the background when he moves from one room to the next. Eric must be sleeping. Sleeping Beauty.

"I didn't ask you about your former lovers."

"That's cause I had none (I want to add "cabron" but I contain myself. Good boy). You were the first and you were supposed to be the last."

I hear him sigh. He's exasperated. The mother fucker is exasperated. His belated birthday present to me is his patience in not hanging up the phone and having me forcibly removed.

Then.

"I thought you were going to be the last one too. Javi, I still love you, but…"

And I hang up. I scrounge up what I have in my pocket, nine dollars and change and give it to George. He refuses to accept it at first, but then I think he gets it. One working class man to another.

"Thank you, Mr. Javi."

I have no memory of how I made it back to my apartment, but I did.

Dear Diary:

Jason now has my number and after my b'day meltdown left a couple of messages. That's it. A couple of polite messages. I heard them over and over again looking for some hidden meaning, but I don't think there is any. No shift in tone, clutch in the throat. He has moved on. Time I did too...

I am running. It is a brisk, beautiful day and I am in red and white broad striped running tights and a black "Flash Dance" (what a feeling, indeed!) inspired top. Hey, get off my case, back in the day this was styling. I'm running through the hood, shades and ipod zoning out people when the rains of Ranchipur erupt. I duck into the nearest bodega, where unfortunately a brigade of the saggy jeans boys have also taken refuge. I might as well have come in wearing a target. Quickly looking for something to focus on (gay boys are well trained in the art of survival) I spot the lottery counter and amid the hopeful and the hopeless I lose myself. I, having actually won the lottery of love and abundance, have never played this particular game of chance. I also remember clearly a saying my Pops has, "Quien juega por necesidad, pierde por obligacion." [Those who bet out of need are obligated to lose.] And Diary, how is it that you are not bilingual after all this? I have no intention of betting anything, hell, I got no money on me. Oh, and side bar, the designer who comes up with concealed pockets on spandex is destined for immortality. Mark my words. I'm standing there, faking that I'm looking at the lottery ticket, hoping the boys, I'm forty years old and still afraid of boys? shoot me, will either leave or get so boisterous they are asked to leave. I notice one of them look at me and nudge his friend. Puñeta. I'm dead.

"You need a pencil?" An old woman standing next to me asks.

"Huh?"

"A pencil." I can't quite place the accent. A little like a drunk Meryl Streep slurring her way through some award winning performance. Blasphemy! I will deal with me later.

She offers me a pencil and points to my lottery form. I take the pencil and fill in the little squares. She proudly shows me her filled out ticket and smiles.

"Not today, but someday," she says.

I nod and kinda smile back. What is the shelf life of dreams? When I'm done randomly picking out my numbers I notice she is gone. So are the boys. In fact, the only one under the watchful eye of the store clerk seems to be yours truly. I've got no money to play this thing, I'm sure he must know this. But when I pick up the ticket to throw it away I notice the mystery woman has left a folded up dollar bill right next to me. The guy at the counter grunts and I read it to mean, "just play the damn ticket." So I do.

And that, Dear Diary, is how I won the Mega Million Lottery. The press! The numbness of it all! I knew it was a dream, but a dream I didn't want to wake up from, you know. I never found out how much I won, only that now I was officially one dollar richer than Jason and it really burned him. Then it was all like little vignettes of me being super rich and it would go from color to black and white and Cher floated by, dream, remember? and it sort of nonended when I'm in this glam fab limo and I know Jason is in his and we get to this event but we play chicken. Neither one of us want to be the first one to get out of our royal carriages. I've got my own little twinkie kissing on me, but I just keep looking out my tricked out limo window waiting for Jason.

When I wake up it's dark. I look up and out my basement window and feel like maybe I should bay at the moon or something, but I don't. I go back to bed, hoping to rejoin my dream, currently in progress. Hoping still that Jason will get out of his limo and we can finally meet, equal to equal. But hey, if my love couldn't make us equal, money just ain't gonna do caca.

※ ◉ ◍

Dear Diary:
Caught up on everything! Walked my last dog, scooped my last poop, painted my last trim and ironed my last shirt. Oh yeah, I'm taking in ironing now. All to bankroll my mini vacay with the boys. Oh, and brace yourself, Diary, we be traveling coach...

Before I can make my escape I am drafted to work in my pop's vegetable garden. At first I have to admit, I hated it. I hate getting my hands dirty, okay. But my Pops is out there everyday with a straw hat and his trusty machete, so when my Moms said, "Ju not doing anything, go help him," I had no excuse. He starts at 6am, my Pops does, "before the sun gets to be burning." I find a pair of coveralls (when the fuck did I buy those?!) and join him. I tie a "let's get physical" bandanna around my head, put on some work gloves and meet Manuel Labor. The sun, the mosquitoes, ...the quiet. The city noise fades and it's quiet. I slowly begin to understand why my Pops loves this so much. "Watch the root. Give it a berm."

I tell you it's a new language. I come to treasure his little asides. My Moms rarely comes into the garden so it really is his domain. His world where his voice is the only voice you hear. Every so often we can hear Moms on her phone, not giving the other person a chance to get a word in edgewise and Pops smiles and rolls his eyes at me. Occasionally something will remind him of the Puerto Rico of his youth and he'll tell me a story. A short one. Getting this man to say more than three sentences in a row is close to impossible; but his memories, both good and bad, have made this man I call my Pops. He only got to third grade, he slept on a chair when he first got to New York and to see me happy he would eat rocks. Okay, that last one confuses me. He was the first man in my life, and look, he's still here. Just when I'm about to get totally Hallmark my posse arrives. Dressed for Fire Island. My Pops is always kind to my friends even when they are scantily clad, and gives them a grand tour. They ooh and ahh but their collective heart is not in it. "Aren't vegetables the things you find in a salad bar?"

"No, stupid, that's tofu."

My group is a witty group. Their indifference disappears when my father shows off his pride and joy, his zucchinis. They are humongous, insane. My friends are speechless until Rob blurts out, "Slap a car battery on that thing and it's my next husband!"

"We need to catch a ferry!" I quickly add. As my Pops sees us out he gives each of us a lime for our cocktails.

"I know you boys like your drinks," he says. "Hey," he adds, "how do you make a Cuba Libre?"

Victor immediately says "Rum and coke."

"No," my Pops cackles, "you kill Fidel."

And with that we leave. Me to first change into appropriate Fire Island attire, not to mention packing the necessary wardrobe changes, and then we're off via mass transit to paradise. It's a gayapalooza on the train, but I notice that me and my boys are actually kind of quiet. One by one, we pull out our limes and smile. Here is proof positive that a straight man loves us. And then Joel sighs and says what we're all thinking.

"Javi, your Pops is cool."

And they nod, and I nod. Yes, Don Efrain Rivera is cool.

I have never been to Cherry Grove. Jason for some reason hated it so the one time we went, to the Pines of course, was for some charity thing and we went by yacht, natch, and left the second it was over. Cherry Grove was not my choice, nor was it anyone else's but Victor being Victor, cadged us a weekend at some guys place by mooning him. Yes, Victor has a nice ass, but is it real estate worthy? I mean, now really. Victor is a little glum that it's not in the Pines where beauty like his can be lusted by one and all but the Pines' loss is Cherry Grove's gain. We've each packed more than we could ever wear, basically a different spandex outfit (okay, puta, we're dated, shoot me!) for every meal and cocktail. Even Joel has put aside the political tee shirts in exchange for something a little more, well skanky. His "Will Blow for X" may have been a little over the top, but hey, who am I to judge? The only one of our queer quartet who is making do with only one bag of clothes is Rob who has himself a "what's the point?" attitude in need of adjusting. The house itself is blah and true to his word, Victor's ass man is not there. It's just us, Rob, Joel, Victor and myself plus all the food and booze we could carry.

We all immediately change clothes, save for Rob and have our first cocktail, something very lethal, and head out to scope out the scene. Victor is dressed all in gold, the better to be set off by the sunset, and walks slightly ahead of us on the narrow boardwalk. What must it be like to be that fucking gorgeous?

As we enter the bar, Victor smiles and says, "Putas, it's on!" and we flirt and dance and drink and carry on. Victor is the belle of the ball. And then out of the corner of my eye I see him. A Greek god. Marble come to life. So perfect. Too perfect. And he's wearing Victor's exact outfit. And this kid is a kid, he's gotta be barely legal. I try to flag Victor, get him outta here! Now! But it's like watching a car accident in slow motion. Victor and Perfection catch sight of each other. And Victor blinks. Egowise, he loses his footing but it's just enough for Mr. No More Calls We Have A Winner to take the lead. A dancing Victor misses a couple of steps, bumps into someone, looks around and sees me. Sees that I've seen the whole thing. Victor hurries out. His gorgeous tail between his legs.

I find Rob, hugging a wall and nursing a drink.

"Victor needs us. His ego is hurting."

"Yeah, well," counters Rob, "welcome to my life."

Joel has disappeared, probably on his way to the USDA meat rack, so I take off after Victor. As someone who's had his ego erased and reerased I don't want him to be alone.

I am butt grabbed and turn around to see Kearn. Slightly drunk (heaven help me) and smiling, leering.

"If I had known you were coming I would have...." And the rest, mercifully, is drowned out by house music.

"Listen," I say, trying to smile, "I gotta run."

"Don't be like that."

"No seriously."

"Fine, bitch."

I let it go. My one weekend on the island and he decides to go for the Grove? What kind of a stereotype is he?

Victor's showering when I get back to the house. Joel shows up in somebody else's pants and surprise surprise Hector crashes the weekend.

"Yo, am I late for happy hour?" Hector grins.

"What the fuck did you tell Sonia?"

"Relax, she's off to see her family, so dig it, I'm here with mine." And he hugs/strangles me..

"We don't have enough beds."

"I'll bunk with cuz here."

Hector has also packed. A box of 24 condoms. "What, no Viagra?"

"Not yet, baby. Forget about getting it up, I can't get it down."

Victor avoids eye contact with me for the rest of the night. Our first Saturday night in Cherry Grove and Joel and Hector are planning to tag team the rack, Rob just wants to hang back and Victor has oddly disappeared. Nothing sadder than a King dethroned. And I'm the fucking witness. The lone witness, so I may be sent overboard on our return trip.

One friend sinks, another rises. To truly unexpected heights. The bar we hit for our after dinner drinks greets Rob like a long lost son. It's blazing hot and Rob and all his love handles, (I love him, but it's the truth Ruth) has removed his tee shirt. Once the doorman gets an orbful of Rob he ushers him in like the prodigal ham.

"Hey, new meat!"

New meat indeed. We have chosen the bar hosting the bear cub competition. What the fuck?! A path is made for Rob and his every step is greeted with applause and wolf whistles. And my friend, who disappears into himself just to survive the gayborhood, begins to come to life. Now listen to me, Eunice, I'm not drunk, cocktailed though I may be, Rob is the new kid in town, the belle of the plus size ball. His every shy smile and awkward step seem to enchant the crowd. Rob, let us not forget, is an actor and he plays to the crowd. I catch sight of Victor and he is crying, for Rob or for himself, I'm not sure. We look at Rob playing his "aw shucks" role to the hilt and with total sincerity. Hector and Joel are AWOL, well, they're missing history being made. Rob wins cub of the summer and is given a leather sash with his title that he wears proudly nestled between his man boobs. Sniff. They grow up so fast.

I congratulate Rob, who is being joyfully manhandled by his new tribe and go for a walk on the beach. Victor is off somewhere nursing his wounds and I'm alone for the first time this weekend. Alone. That's what I am. The stars, the ocean, the stuff of romance and I'm alone. Damn Jason for taking away his half of my heart. Fuck him and his new boy toy. I catch myself walking to the meat rack. Well, it's either that or go back to my room and jack off. I stop at the end of the boardwalk, one foot in mid air. I can't do this. I've had sex with three guys in my life, I can't just jump into the deep end of the pool.

"Hey, you blocking traffic."

Two guys, leading each other by their dicks, brush by me. I follow them into the abyss.

Okay, so I get it, it's like a giant gay bar, without alcohol, just sex. It's all about the lighting here. Let the moonlight hit you just so and viola, twenty years gone. Most guys are shirtless in just shorts, some are naked. Some industrious soul has set up a sling and smiles as I walk by. Fistfucking on the beach? With all this sand?! Are you nuts?! I catch sight of Hector, barely pulling up his pants, when a hand reaches out for him and he disappears into the bushes. Gay men likes their sex.

I hear a guy pissing, more like guys pissing and I follow the sound to a group of five guys, all surrounding this one guy on his knees, jerking off as the group pees on him. Kearn. His white hair is matted to his head. He sees me, blows me a kiss and cums.

What am I supposed to do? Feets don't fail me now! I half smile back, catch myself about to wave and head out. Kearn's into golden showers? Ye Gods, it is all about the liquids with him. I get lost and find myself groped and grope back a couple of times but there's no zing so I just continue on my maze-like way to the boardwalk. The guy with the sling is still there, peeling off a recently used latex glove and snapping on another. His head motions me to the sling. I shake my head "no."

"Never know until you try," he smiles, "Whassa matter, ain't you got any fantasies?"

And that stops me. Actually, I don't. Damn it. How the hell did this happen?

Dear Diary:
"What's your fantasy?" Do I know how to kick off a Sunday brunch or what?...

We are seated around the breakfast table knocking back Bloody Marys and bacon.

"Well, as cub of the year-"

"Yes, pendejo, we were there, remember?"

"Not all of you," he says as he arches an eyebrow at Hector and Joel. "but, in answer to your question, I vow to win an Oscar for bestest actor to add to my leather sash."

"Sexual fantasy," I clarify.

Okay the table is back in the game, even Victor, behind his dark glasses perks up.

"Somebody. Anybody." I add.

Hector starts. "I want to have sex with six different guys at once."

Joel deadeyes him, then says "You did. Last night. I was one of them."

Not skipping a beat, Hector says, "Seven, seven different guys at once."

I look at Joel who smiles and shrugs, "It's not like I didn't look for you."

Rob refills his glass, downs it. "I want to be, nobody look at me, treated like a dog."

Hector throws a bagel, "Fetch!"

"That's felch, and shut up. Not by any of you! Oh why did I say this? Because I'm cub of the year, that's why! I want to be treated like a dog, made to walk, sit and eat like one, by the man of my dreams."

"And that would be?" Victor ventures forth.

"...Dick Cheney.," Rob confesses.

Spit takes all around.

"There's something about his snarl that just conjures up rolled up newspaper to me. There. I said it and I'm not taking it back. Victor, what's yours?"

"To be worshipped."

"You are," I say, channeling Tony Robbins.

"I mean forever."

"You have been, ever since I've known you." Rob says as one desirable person to another.

"Yeah, well tick tock," Victor says glumly.

"Fantasy is something you haven't gotten around to yet, right?" Joel asks.

"No, it can be something you've done." Hector leers.

"In that case, I want to be gang raped by a motorcycle gang and then turn the tables and do all of them."

Forks drop.

"And, ahem, let me reiterate, ahem, you've done this?" I'm looking at Joel as if he were suddenly an alien life form.

"Hey, Javi, your turn," he offers as a smug non answer.

"Exactly how many members were in this gang?"

Joel starts a chant of "Javi! Javi! Javi!"

"I don't think I have any."

I'm pelted with bacon.

"Liar! She's a liar! Loca sucia!"

"No, seriously, that's why I asked."

"Cuz, don't hide it, share it with the rest of the class."

"I was with a gorgeous, super rich man and we had sex all the time. I'm good."

"Nothing you wanted to try? A threesome?"

"No."

"A little B/D, S/M, W/S?"

"Nope."

"Miss Priss."

Joel takes charge. "I know that to be a lie." I forklift my jaw up. They all lean in. Even I do. What the fuck is he gonna say?

"You want to be in control," Joel say, "You want it your way, when you want it and when you're done you want to leave. You want to be the one to leave. Oh, and you also have anger issues."

And there you have it, a perfectly good sex discussion is ruined.

After everybody leaves for the beach, Victor and I sort of stay behind, clearing the table, cleaning up, boring stuff, that is until Victor drops trou and stands before me naked as the day he was engineered, uh born. Oh my. He holds out his driver's license.

"Look," he says.

"Trust me, I'm looking. I'm also worshipping."

"No, look at my driver's license."

"This face could be on the cover of any bar rag. Flawless." I overdo.

And then Victor does the unthinkable. He removes his thumb from over the year of his birth. I try, badly, not to gasp.

"Am I really that old?" my friend asks me.

So I told him the truth, cause it was easy. "Victor, you are heart stoppingly beautiful."

He leads me outside to his nemesis, direct sunlight. "You've never seen me in the sun without concealer, bronzer, and sunglasses. I'm in the shade nine times out of ten. I work in a bar where I control the dimmer switch."

"You were so gorgeous on the float."

"Bare minerals." He points to his face. "This is the most naked I've ever been in, forever. Forget the body."

"As if anybody could." I say, but it receives just a wan smile from him. "Age is just a number."

He parts his hair and reveals the beginning of a bald spot. "I use something like dark brown talcum powder. It covers it."

Victor, the Victor I know is becoming smaller and smaller before my eyes.

"I will not become the bar doorman! It's not gonna happen! It's not gonna happen! It's not gonna happen!"

Just then, Hector comes back for a towel/lube and takes one look at Victor and says, "Hey, you should catch yourself a disco nap."

Victor is off like a shot to the dimmer indoors.

"Tact. Every hear of it, Hector?" I hiss at him.

"Tact is for losers, cuz. Go get laid."

At sunset I head to Sunset, a new bar/dance club overlooking the bay. Victor is wearing a caftan and sunglasses while Rob is wearing the smallest speedo known to man and the ever present leather sash. Joel is chatting up a barback and no matter how many innuendoes I hurl in his direction we don't seem to be headed towards sex. He looks at me with a very friendly "been there, done that" smile, so we all just take in the sunset, kinda at peace. That is before Hector barrels in, grabs me by the hair and thrusts his tongue deep down my throat.

"Sorry I'm late, baby!" he practically yells for one and all to hear. Before I can recover, what can only be described as the male version of Sonia (oh yes, complete with muffin top) storms in, clearly in hot pursuit of Hector. Miss One Size Does Not Fit All takes one look at me and does the whole finger in the face thing.

"Listen beyotch!" Hello, is he's talking to me?! "It's over and you have got to let him go!"

What the fuck?!

"He's my man now," Divalicious continues. He's itching for a fight, a hair weave tug fest as Hector tries to sheepishly calm him down.

"Yo yo, I told you it was just gonna be a fling."

And looking right at me, this puta boy, this cuera says, "You don't owe this senior citizen nuthin!"

Okay, throwdown!

"He's like yesterday, and I'm today, so," eyeing me and in full voice for the Jerry Springer crowd that is now taking this in, "pack up your polident and hit the road!"

Now, I should have told HoHo that Hector was not my man, not now or ever, but fuck it if the rage I've been feeling over Jason and his little junior miss didn't just kick in. This was pus that just had to come out. And it did. In spades.

"Who the fuck do you think you are?!" I scream at him.

HoHo (the name fits, trust me) loving the drama, goes for me, but pent up rage is an ugly and strong thing. I push him back and stand over him and unleash, and I swear to Nydia Caro that little mother fucker backed down. I let it all out. The betrayal. The anger. The fuck you, fuck you, fuck you of it. I honestly can't remember everything I said but I know when I finished the first thing I noticed was the silence. Utter, complete silence. In a gay bar. During happy hour.

HoHo got up and left and I fell back into the waiting arms of Victor and Rob. Of course that's when Joel licked his lips at me and said, "Let's do it!." I shot him a death stare and he backed off.

Hector looked at me, and being Hector, uttered the evening's most memorable line. "Man I knew you wanted me and shit, I just didn't know how much."

The bar returns to normal and I go off to get a drink. The bartender puts a ginger ale in front of me.

"From the gentleman in the corner."

Kearn salutes me with his drink and a smile.

"Ginger ale, get it?"

"Thanks."

"Or maybe I just pissed in the glass."

I turn away and order a drink.

"I guess you can't wait to get to New York and tell everyone, huh?"

"Kearn, I'm tired."

"You'll feast off spying on me for weeks. Well, if you tell anyone I'll just say you were right there next to me!"

"Hey, at least then I would have a fantasy."

This actually stops Kearn.

"Whatever gets you off, that's your business. Yours." I tell Kearn as I go to pay but he stops me, won't let me.

"You know, I've been banished from the Pines." He says.

"For a golden shower? Oh please."

"No, for being rather unpleasant."

"Hard to imagine."

"I'm like Glenn Close at the end of Dangerous Liaisons. Persona Non Grata. That's why I'm slumming it in the Grove. I....."

"You want to join us?"

He looks at me and almost like a little boy says, "What if I get drunk and nasty?"

"We'll throw you over the railing."

He laughs. I add, "I'm not kidding." So we sit for the last sunset of our weekend with Kearn, who keeps offering to buy us drinks. 'Next time', we tell him and he sorta smiles.

We take the ferry home that night. Kearn is staying on for the rest of the week. On the ferry there is a lesbian couple, about sixty, holding hands and sleeping on each other's shoulders. I think to myself, yes, sex would have been great this weekend, but my fantasy, what I really want is that eternal connection.

We're on the upper deck, just quiet, looking out at the

inky water. Victor and Rob both still taking in the weekend and the shift their lives have taken. Victor will bounce back, I hope, but will Rob? Now that he's tasted being wanted how can he go back to nothing? Hector is making out with yet another stranger/energizer bunny. When I asked him how he was gonna explain his tan to Sonia he just shrugged. He'll think of something. He always does. Joel is asleep. I swear that boy can sleep anywhere. Then I laugh to myself. Boy? None of us are boys. We're men. Men who are supposed to be, at this age, fortyish, solid men. Men not on the verge, but there. I was there. Once.

The waves caress the ferry full of fairies and not for the first time I think about jumping. During the day it's useless, they'll find you. But at night, ah, I would just disappear.

Yeah Diary, I've thought about suicide, but I'm afraid. Afraid it would make me a total loser. So for now I just look at the water. Seductive, mysterious, final. God, I wish I weren't a coward.

Dear Diary:

Tonight is Hades on the setting of broil. This heat wave has knocked me to the ground or I should say the roof. It is Victor's day or night off from the Castle and he doesn't want to spend it there, even though we'd be air conditioned, so here we are on my parent's roof. What little night breeze we have is being shared by me and my boys oh and Hector, who has made something he calls mojitos but I think is just lime flavored Janitor in a Drum. And Sonia's up here, looking like a stuffed canoli in a tube top her mother gave her...

"Can you believe it? She was just gonna throw it out!"

Considering it's the size of a napkin ring it wouldn't have been such a bad idea. She is also in shorts so short they redefine toes for camels everywhere. But see, here's the thing. Ms. Sonia thinks she's hot and somehow, wepa, she's hot. There is something about her that skinny girls should only be so lucky to have.

"Hey look, if it weren't for my Hector it would be girls night up here!" she brays. We collectively roll our eyes as Hector makes a big show of licking the spilled drink off her titanic tetas.

Victor is laying on his stomach, his full moon competing with the one in the night sky and Rob and me are sharing a headset as we listen to vintage Yolandita on his ipod knock off. Joel is drifting off to sleep. I am studiously avoiding the discovery channel mating of Hector and his Mrs, which is still, sadly in my peripheral vision. Suddenly, a shooting star flies by and we all start talking and pointing and wishing, cause that's what you're supposed to do when you see one. Wish.

"What you wish for, Mami?" Hector asks.

"I ain't a gonna tell you, it won't come true."

"Changa!"

"Fuck you!"

And they're off. Now his pinga hangs too much to the left and her pubes are too bristly. Did we just disappear? Can they not see us trying not to see them? Sonia finally throws her drink in his face. Pause. They dive into each other like they were the last piragua of the summer. Oh yes, they are humping each other with us right there.

"Hello!" I scream.

"What? You never seen foreplay?" Hector smirks.

"Ay papi, I like my sex deep fried!"

And that's it, they win. The roof is theirs tonight cause I don't think cold water, pry bars or pit bulls could come between them. We surrender the roof to them. Well, me, Rob and Victor do. Joel can sleep through anything.

Thing is I can guarantee you Hector is not doing this to play quien es mas macho with us. He is just really horny. The horniest person I have ever known. He has never known a dream that isn't wet, has probably never seen a porn film from beginning to end (but to be fair, who has?) and has probably used every kitchen appliance he owns as a sex toy.

"I don't let nothing come between me and what I wants. I go after it!" Hectors says as he rubs Sonia the right way. "I may not always be neat, but check it out, I am in motion!!!!"

As we exit and they dive at it, Joel softly snores and Hector looks up briefly enough from his meow mix meal to throw a kiss to Victor's ass. Coño nene, leave a little for the rest of us. And yeah, I was a little bit/a lot of jealous. He goes after what he wants, no apologies.

Dear Diary:
There's drama and then there's DRAMAH. I'll let you decide which is which...

I'm on my way to one of my jobs, dog walker to the stars, okay one star, Rosie Perez, I'm dogless however at the moment when I hear.

"Hey Javi!"

It's Jason, in the limo. He waves me over.

"Long time no see."

I look at him and my eyes can't keep still. Play it cool, play it cool, play it cool!

"Hey Jason."

He leans out and we lightly kiss. Initiated by him, trust me, I wouldn't have had the cojones.

"Hop in, we'll give you a ride."

We? Madre Santisima, he's with the harlot! Now, if you've been a good gay, eaten all your vegetables and minded your elders, when a moment like this happens, meeting your replacement, you're actually looking fab. Hair, clothes, weight all copacetic. I am pretty flawless as I get into the limo, and there in the corner, moving closer to Jason so he's practically sitting on his lap, is the boy. Eric. Twenty, doe eyed, fresh faced fresh everything, and an open yet shy smile.

"I've wanted to meet you for so long," he says.

He doesn't offer his hand. I just nod and smile. Jason, I swear to you, is petting him on the nape of the neck. Like a puppy.

"I don't mean to take you guys out of your way," I say.

"No, no problem." Says Jason.

"At all." Adds Eric. I feel like I'm being held underwater. "Where are you off to?" Jason asks.

"Work."

"Oh," Jason looks contrite. "Sorry."

"You shouldn't be." Eric chirps. Then looks at me with such sincerity that Marianne Williamson should sue for copyright infringement. "I think it's wonderful that you found this incredible strength in you to create a life on your own."

That's only cause you stole mine you bastard! Mother Fucker! I want to kill you! I want to..., but all that comes out from me is a very small "thank you."

Jason beams at me as if to say about Eric, "isn't he great?!"

I want out of this car so badly. And then Eric leans in to me, all dark curls, inches from my face and, oh no! he's tearing up! And he says, "I hope someday that we can be friends."

Oh no he didn't!

Jason totally forgets I'm there and holds Eric by the chin, and even though the car is not moving I'm about to experience car sickness, hopefully over both of them.

"Listen," I say, willing my voice not to betray me, "I've got to go to my first client, and they're right around the corner." I get out of the car.

Eric calls out, "Nice to meet you! Finally!"

I smile and wave. Jason leans out the window after I leave the car and takes my hand. He smiles. "Nice kid, huh? And he really respects you."

"I've got a client to get to."

"What are you doing now?"

"Hustling. What else?"

Hector would have been proud of me. Jason's smile turns into a frown as I turn and leave. I hope with everything that's in me that Eric breaks his heart.

Dear Diary:
Sonia knows! Sonia knows! Sonia knows! Sonia knows!...

The second contestant for the drama sweepstakes happened about 8pm. I'm conditioning my hair, hey it's beauty night, when all hell breaks lose. I think the building, fuck, the block is coming down. Screaming people running down the hallway above me, cursing and things being thrown. So I do what any grown up would do. I duck for cover, I'm not stupid. There is a mad banging on my door.

"Let me in! Fucking let me in!" It's Hector. But before I can get to the door, he's off. Sonia is in hot pursuit with her three kids, one of them in her arms. Junior, the little boy, is hanging desperately to Hector's leg (thank Judas for peepholes!) and the little girl, Cristina, a mini me of Sonia, is egging her mother on. Hoo boy, isn't some lucky guy in the future gonna hit the lottery when he marries her! My parents are at church so the only witness to this gang war is me. And I'm afraid. I admit it. Sonia looks like she is ready to kill and Hector is bleeding from the mouth and from the head. Miss Thing packs a wallop.

"Vente, hijo de puta, vente y niegamelo! Come on and deny it!"

She's translating. How kind. In case any of the neighbors missed that final class at Berlitz. Hector is allowed to say, "Pero mami," before she charges at him again. She throws roundhouse punches wildly, even as she holds a crying baby in her arm. She kicks at him, barely missing her eight year old son, who like his father is crying miserably. I actually feel sorry for Hector. Yeah, he's a dog, but Sonia, she's outta control.

I open the door.

"Hey!" I holler.

"Come on, you bastard, lie to me again!"

"Pero mami."

"Daddy's a bastard."

Ah, that little girl is a treasure.

"Sonia, come in here," I tell her. And yes, I'm crazy. "Come on."

And even with her rage at white hot, she allows herself to be dragged/coddled in.

"Hey Sonia," as soothingly as if I were talking to a pitbull, "come on, come on."

She looks at me, and I thank goodness, don't blink and she comes into my living room. The little girl and her attitude come in, too, while Junior stays with his father, both of them crying.

"You know Hector loves you." I say.

And she balls up her fist and slams my glass top coffee table, shattering it, but even it doesn't dare move. The pieces just hang there in place. We is all afraid of this woman.

"Okay, okay, I knows you have always wanted my man."

Hold the cell phone.

"So you think he's perfect," she continues.

"Uh no."

"But ese hijo de puta, ese…"

"Canalla," I offer. Hey it works on my Moms soap operas.

And suddenly, Sonia breaks. To see a monster break is a scary thing. You want to comfort it but you're afraid if you do it'll bite your head off. I keep my distance. I like my head.

"He…he…" she is crying so hard she can't talk. Did she somehow find out about Fire Island? Does she know I was there with him? Is she going to track us down, one by one, and deball us?

Junior runs in.

"Daddy's crying!" he wails.

"Que se joda!" Sonia bellows, her entire body shaking with the ferocity of her rage. The baby in her arms, Sully, actually laughs at this.

"Daddy's gonna kill hisself!"

"Himself," corrects mini Sonia. Oh yeah, she's a prize.

Junior runs back out to his father, Cristina makes a beeline for my TV, so much for her anguish, but I snap my fingers and point to a chair where she sits and pouts. Sonia is now sobbing and banging her chest.

"I will kill him. Esto no se queda asi. He must pay!"

Before I can blurt out that Fire Island was just probably an isolated incident, Sonia screams out "That mother fucker gave me the clap!"

I pour Sonia a drink, but down it myself. Oh Hector, you is dead.

"Are you sure?" I ask.

With her face only millimeters from mine she screams out for all our listeners to hear, "He's got a milky discharge on his pinga! I got clap! From him! He dies tonight!"

For a moment she is spent, her tears and his tears a duet of the inconsolable. Cristina, anxious to get the show on the road, looks at her mother and says, "So we gonna kill papi, right?"

"Go get your father and send Junior in here," I say.

"You ain't the boss of me." But one looks tells her that for right now I am. Junior comes in and hugs his mother and I can only hope that Cristina can be bribed into doing the same with Hector.

"I'ma leave him," Sonia says.

I take her hand. "If you think that's the right thing to do," I barely say, when she glares at me. "Oh you'd like that wouldn't you? Get your little faggot claws into him."

I yank my hand out of hers.

"Get out." I say as coldly as possible.

Sonia looks down. It takes her a moment but she finally says, "I'm sorry."

We are quiet. And, oh man, she begins to nurse Sully. She caresses Junior's head and tells him, "Tell your father to go back upstairs."

"He's gonna kill hisself," Junior sniffles.

"He ain't gonna do shit."

And like a tableau vivant out of Modern Parenting the little boy kisses his mother and exits.

Sonia looks at me. "Was that the only drink you had in this house?" I pour her one. "He gets one mistake." she says. "One. That's it. I'm not like you, Javi, no offense. I will not be a doormat." And it hurt worse than when she called me a faggot, cause it's true. I am a doormat.

"Stay here tonight," my mouth says before my brain can fully register the offer. But luckily she's up, up and still breast feeding Sully, away. We listen to Junior and Cristina lead their softly crying father back up stairs. Sonia gently burps Sully who rewards her with a little spittle.

"The sooner I get upstairs the sooner Hector starts to pay. Cause that maldito is gonna tell me who the whore was that gave him the clap!"

And my blood runs cold.

Diary:
My father died today. There are no words. There are. No words...

Dear Diary:
I am talking to you today because I have no one else. I'm forty years old and I have no one who will just listen. Who will not try to comfort me, who will not say at least he didn't suffer...

It was 9am in the morning. September 3rd. I was getting ready to go out for a run when I heard my Moms screaming hysterically.

"Efrain! Efrain!"

She never called my Pops by his full name. It's "Negrito" or "Rain" pronounced rah heen, so right away I know something's up. I run upstairs and my Moms is running downstairs. We collide into each other and it would have been comical except my Moms has a wild eyed look to her face. She pushes past me, slams me into the wall with a strength I never knew she possessed. I follow her to the backyard. And there, lying face down in his beloved vegetable garden is my Pops. The garden he tended to with such devotion and patience and yes, class. His trusty machete beside him. His skill with that thing would have made the Three Musketeers proud. He lies face down, humble even in death. My Moms throws herself on him and begins to weep, and I, tearless, hold on to his dead hand. Then his arm. He's gone. My Pops is gone. When the ambulance arrives, called by Sonia, I am cradling my dead Pops body whispering "perdoname." Forgive me. My Moms sits next to me, spent, and then wailing then spent again. They take him away. Who they? The boogeymen? The dead people taxi? I've never been in an ambulance before but Moms and me climb in. Me in running tights and a tee shirt that reads HARD and my Moms in a house dress and chancletas. A Moms and son hardly dressed for the death of the most important man of their lives.

The next few days are blank. I can recall snapshot moments of them, but an actual continuation of a moment is impossible to grasp and hold on to. My Moms and me have this trivial/monumental fight over whether he should be viewed in a suit or a guayabera, but at least the argument gives us something other than mourning to breathe in. My boys, Victor, Rob and Joel sticking out like gay sore thumbs, are at the viewing at the Rosado Funeral Home. They give me the space to be as lost as I am.

So many people, so much food. Floral tributes that each tried to outdo each other, but somehow perfect for a man who died in his garden. I want him to be cremated, to have his ashes spread over that small plot of land he called his Eden, but my Moms won't hear of it. He's going home to Puerto Rico. That was always his wish and that is what he must have. The numbness my Moms feels is palpable. Sometimes I look at her and we eye each other, both lost and empty even as we facilitate Efrain Rivera's wake.

Jason arrives the first day. Of course he should come by. He was, for all purposes, my Pops son in law for twenty years, but I am still touched by his presence. He nods to me and after offering his condolences to my Moms and me, takes a seat.

The first day of a wake is the hardest. People come and somehow feel they must emote. This is the day of the big emotions and my lack of any is scary to me. I cannot cry because I am too filled with guilt. Perdoname. For being his only son and being gay? Perdoname. For ignoring him at times, being impatient with him. Perdoname. For being, at the time of his death, a failure. Perdoname, Pops. Forgive me.

Condolences wash over me by each of the mourners. My posse takes their lead from me and keep their distance. Yet I never want for a glass of water or a seat. And if I had to cry I could cry with them, but see, I don't. At all.

The first day goes from 9am to 7pm. It ends with three rosaries said back to back and led by Sonia, who in a crisis rises to the level of goddess. She is dressed in full Sophia Loren mourning attire, outdoing even my Moms who sits like a zombie. Hector and the kids are perfectly behaved, yes even the devil child Cristina; either because she's afraid of the dead or her mother. Cristina takes a seat and remains there for the duration. At the end of the first day the mourners shake my hand and kiss my Moms. They all tell me, "You have to take care of your mother now. You are the man of the house."

The last mourner to leave is Jason.

"Can I do," and here Jason is at a loss, "anything? Anything at all?"

"No. And thank you for coming. My Pops...." And now

I'm at a loss. My Moms and me spend the last moments of the day alone with my Pops. My Moms doesn't cry, her tears have run dry for now. Mine have yet to be tapped. We go home to a sleepless night of if onlys. Did we ever say I love you enough to him? Did he know how much I respected him? Perdoname.

The second day of the wake is the hardest. It really just is the closest family members. People are either here for day one or three, but the middle day is just gray. The crying has been done (by most) the day before and the big emoters from day one are saving themselves for the big send off.

Jason arrives promptly at 9 am and sits in the back. In the same seat as yesterday. This is sweet, but unnecessary on his part. But I feel a little comfort every time I catch sight of him throughout the day. People drift in and out during their lunch breaks and it's the first time I actually see my Moms eat something. Ice Cream. Victor got it for her. The second day is the hardest because it's also the day people start reminiscing. And with the memories come laughter. I hear from all these virtual strangers that my Pops was a very funny man, and somehow I didn't know it. Perdoname.

The place fills up after work. More, "remember when compai…" and more laughter. The stories go from Spanish to English to sometimes both. And throughout it all Jason doesn't leave. Sits there in the back like a loyal soldier. Only he's not my soldier anymore, he's Eric's. But for the past two days he has been so present for me. This is why I fell in love with him.

Three more rosaries, more handshakes and kisses. I had hoped that today, feeling no opening night pressure, I would cry, but no. I am unworthy to cry at my Pops wake.

Jason is, again, the last to leave. My Moms and I hold hands over my Pops coffin and say our own prayer. That night we stay up the entire night eating ice cream, any flavor, it doesn't matter. And she tells me the story of how they met.

The third day of the wake is the hardest. I start to remember every kind thing he ever did for me. Things I never thanked him for, and I run to the bathroom, lock myself in and begin to weep. So hard I have to stuff a face towel in my mouth to muffle my sobs. Before I couldn't start, now I can't stop. I don't know how long I cry before Joel knocks on the door.

"You okay?"

"I'll be right out."

I wash my face and sit by my Moms. She looks at me. She knows that I've finally cried and simply says, "Okei then."

On this, the last day of public mourning, Jason has once again paid silent tribute to my father. Towards the end of the day Jason has a private moment with my Moms. I can't hear them but my Moms looks at him after he's had his say and kisses him on the cheek. Jason looks startled, as do I.

For the last three rosaries my Pops is SRO. Everyone is here. Where do they all come from? Why do I want them gone? Now! Please go.

The last of the mourners leave and as if on cue Jason comes to me. He doesn't say anything, just stands next to me. Then he whispers.

"He was proud of you. He told me so."

I look down at my Pops.

"Perdoname."

"He has nothing to forgive you for."

"Perdoname."

"He loved you."

"Perdoname."

"Kiss him goodbye."

And I do. And Jason is gone.

The next day my Moms and me took Efrain Rivera, Pops,

negrito, compai, to his beloved Puerto Rico, his final resting place. On Jason's private plane.

"He begged me," my Moms says. And I have no doubt that Jason, my Jason, would have done just that.

Dear Diary:

It is raining like crazy when we land in Aguadilla, but that doesn't stop my relatives from showing up, in droves. Smiling, sad faces that greet me as if I had just seen them last week as opposed to three years ago. I'm embarrassed cause I honestly can't remember all their names, and their husbands or wives names, and their kids names. How is it that they all remember me? Did they study? Seriously. I nod and smile and realize that my grief has won me a "get out of remembering anybody" pass...

My Moms, however is a different story. She remembers each and every one of them. Why shouldn't she? She's the Hallmark Queen. There is not a relative's birthday that goes by without a card from her and a little gift, be it homemade or from the dollar store. The odd thing is on her birthday, she gets a card from her sisters, but that's it. Everyone else is suddenly amnesiatic. It doesn't seem to bother my Moms. Me? I'd be bitter; but she just keeps on remembering, congratulating and blessing. Maybe that explains why her reception rivals that of any Caribbean Diva. It's sad to see her smiling and crying in the same breath. Happy to be surrounded by family, but missing her other half. The man who shared her everything with her.

From the airport we caravan directly to the cemetery

in Isabela. My pop's final resting place. There I see even more family members, everyone who couldn't make it to the airport. It's strange to see my pop's face on his sister, on his younger brother. Every family member of a certain age is dressed in black and the younger ones have something black on, even if it's just a handkerchief; something to show respect. We do a rosary at the gravesite and when the first shovel of dirt hits Efrain Rivera's coffin, Moms and me hold each other up. That's it. He's gone. Que descanse en paz. Then she reaches down and takes a handful of dirt and gently throws it in after my father. She is releasing him. Forever acknowledging his place in her heart, but ultimately, letting him go.

"Vamonos," she said.

And we left, followed by the motorcade of relatives, to a lechon diner with Puerto Rican rum. I introduced my cousins (the older ones) to my Hawaiian Punchtini and we stayed up until the roosters greeted the next day. Then we crashed, or at least I did. I finally slept so soundly that an orchestra of coquis couldn't have woken me up. I go running later in the day and get a chance to just be Puerto Rican. Not gay, not a failure, not anything but another Puerto Rican on an island full of them. When I come back from my run I sit on the deck until my Moms brings me a café con leche. We are both quiet. She smoothes my sweaty hair with her hand as we both drink our coffee thinking the same thing. I'm not ready to go back. Not yet. I call Jason who insists we keep the plane there until we're are ready to come back. He says goodbye, but not before saying "Take care of yourself, Javi." God, I miss him. My Moms goes to every spot she and my Pops shared. The schools, the beach, the flamboyan tree where she first kissed him. She's very proud of that. She was the one who initiated the kiss. "After that, he had to marry me!," she snorts. She was thirteen to his fifteen.

My Moms and her sisters spend hours dissecting the local novelas (you can NEVER have seen it and in one episode you are totally sucked in). I find myself cast as the older uncle type to my cousins. They were preteens when I last saw them; now they all have their boyfriends and their girlfriends. They are smart, funny and straight. Not a gay one in the bunch. What the hell ever happened to one out of ten? There is no gay scene, at least none that my trained and jaded eye can spot. José, can you see indeed. There is in San Juan and some of the other big cities, but here, alas no. As I look at my cousins I can't help but wonder if one of them were gay would they feel comfortable with me enough to tell me? Somos gay, somos gay. After the sturm und drang of the soap opera is over we all find ourselves watching a local comedy show. Skits, double and triple takes, the works. And I am reminded of why there was always a part of me that forever felt uncomfortable with Puerto Rico. In this macho culture the biggest laughs are reserved for las locas, las mariposas, those mincing, prancing comedians who play the maricones and are made the butt of all the jokes. Everyone in the room laughs, everyone but me. I love Puerto Rico, I really do, but I always get the impression that I am only nominally allowed in. That even though I was born in Puerto Rico, I really am only tolerated. We are staying in a small, rural area and since I don't drive, this is the area I remain in. On this particular afternoon, with all the cousins at school, my aunt sends me to the local store to buy some tocino (fatback, and yes! I love it) for her. The store is run out of somebody's house and the joy of it is that you can buy half a pack of cigarettes, fifty cents of butter and a limber (flavored ice). Wouldn't stores like this go over great in Manhattan!? The door to the house is open so I call for the old woman who runs the place, Doña

Toñia, but an even more effeminate voice answers me.

"¡Aguanta!"

Through the badly in need of a wash curtains, enters Salvin. Reptilian, plucked eyebrows, greased back hair and -shut up!- perfumed. He, we, stare at each other and I swear to you, no shit, his first words to me are, "Yo no le vendo a maricones." Hello? The man is wearing a hairnet! No brotherhood, though I'd settle for a sister-hood, here. He turns around to leave, and okay, he is definitely wearing woman's pants, and as acidly as I can I say, "¿Con permiso?." My Spanish is not perfect, but girl-friend gets it. Salvin stops, arches an eyebrow and slams me again. "No sell to maricones. You a maricon." And I go all grenade on him with, "Hey, you're a maricon, too!." I barely finish before, didn't see this one coming, he decks me, and like the movies all it takes is one punch and I'm out like a light. When I come to, I'm leaning against the wall and the mousiest looking woman on planet earth is pressing a cold towel against my jaw.

"I so sorry. My husband has temper," she says in broken English, but all I hear is the word husband. Husband?! He looks like a drag queen doing a mall run.

"Salvin, desperto," she calls out and Salvin enters. From the floor I see his faded pedicure and bright orange flip flops.

Husband? No, really. Husband?

Salvin glares at me and after some hesitant prompting from the Mrs., he sort of apologizes to me. "Sorry," Salvin hisses through clenched teeth and lips that have known their fair share of lipstick.

"What you want?" she asks and after a beat I remember, "Oh, yeah, …uh tocino." and Mrs. Cowering Inferno hurries off leaving me with the incredible Hulkette who even after my short nap looks gayer than an Easter basket. Somehow, my gayness has offended his macho sensibilities. The fatback is on the house, just "please no call police" his wife begs. I take my tocino and leave. Okay, if you rounded everybody in the gay pride parade, all of us together couldn't be as gay as this Salvin person is. Or as angry.

Dear Diary:

Today my Moms took me to where she grew up. The house was no longer there, and though she made a joke about it I could see it upset her. She talked as we walked and we retraced her route from her home to her school and she seemed surprised that it was so close...

"We juse to run this every day. Take our eshoes off and run like crazy people. Eramos niños. We were children."

Being on the island with my Moms has finally given me my A-ha! moment about her accent.

Here, in Isabela, surrounded by all things familiar and of her youth, her Spanish is beautiful and melodic. The lilt in her voice caresses the words more than pronounces them. I've never understood until now that her Sofia Vergara/ Googie Gomez accent was her way of always keeping her past with her. She is fearless in who she speaks English to, and it's really good, but her accent is her touchstone. I think to her it sounds like she's still speaking Spanish, and giving up her accent would be giving up her past, and that is something she will not do.

She touches everything she can, like she's trying to soak in memories from fences and trees. Moms is not wearing comfortable shoes but she is determined to go the distance from today to yesterday. My Moms was what was called "traviesa," devilish. Always getting into trouble and having to outrun the belt that was frequently used on her. She tells me about one of her pranks where she and her sisters were playing church (it's a religious island, what can I say?). Moms was playing the priest, all solemn and saintlike when her younger sister, caught up in the religious fervor of it all, knelt before her and closed her eyes to receive the holy communion.

"Open your mouth to receive the body of Christ," my Moms said, and the twit obediently did. So of course my Moms stood on a rock and stuck her dirt covered big toe in her baby sister's mouth. My Moms laughs so hard she can barely finish the story. Then she's suddenly quiet, not teary, just quiet which is worse. We get to her school and it is of course much bigger than she remembers it. Hell, it's a learning complex. She just stands and stares at it, hearing the children and the teachers inside. Should I say something? Should I share a memory? I just put my arm around her and take in the school. I get sentimental at commercials, what must she be thinking?

Moms returns with, "Let's get outta here before the little mother fuckers get out."

On the way back she goes from house to house, knocking on doors. "Do you remember me? I'm Don Ramon's and Doña Elena's daughter. The one in the middle." But the people who might have are gone. I hold her hand, partly to comfort her and also to stop her knocking on any more doors. We get back to her sister's place and for the first time I've known her my Moms seems old. Later she and her sisters will talk over "El Amor Lo Puede Todo" (Love Can Do Anything), the latest soap obsession that is paralyzing the island. The weird thing is they can be in the middle of sharing the most gut wrenching and personal memory from their past when suddenly something earth shattering happens with the televised lovers and they all shush each other as they ooh and aah over the scripted drama, momentarily forgetting their own heartaches.

I am sitting on the porch, nursing my umpteenth Medalla Light and swatting at the mosquitoes who have decided I am a delicacy. I have gone through Off, Cobra and Skin So Soft, but the mosquitoes are apparently quite willing to risk certain death for a drop of the orgasmic nectar that is my blood.

Three of my cousins arrive, Ñito, Pito and Tito (I swear). They've grown up with each other, have never lived anywhere else, have probably never been on a plane and they seem totally satisfied with that. They'll marry their local novia and raise their children here. They are each other's best friend, and as accepting as they are of their older gay cousin I wonder how they would feel about each other if one of them was gay? Would that make them a maricon as opposed to my visiting homosexual? How much of this is just in my head? I plunge in.

"So, are there any gay guys in your school?" I ask.

"Eww!!! You want us to hook you up?!"

"No! I just mean-"

They enjoy me sweating for a beat, then smile. "Oh yeah. A couple. And Sandy from la curva is a tortillera."

?

"Lesbian."

"Oh."

"There are gays all over, though a lot of people still feel they gotta hide it here," Tito adds.

"Like Salvin," I laugh.

And they grow very, very quiet. "You know he killed somebody, right?" Ñito whispers.

"Who? Salvin?!" I practically scream.

"For calling him gay," Pito says. "I wasn't even born when it happened, but he took this guy and whacked him to bits with a machete. In broad daylight in the square. Right outside the church. This guy had been teasing him for years, calling him a sister and Salvin snapped."

Ñito laughs, or maybe it was Tito and covers his mouth, almost like he's afraid that somehow Salvin will hear and reprise his ninja act. Later on I ask my aunts and uncles and find out that the guy Salvin killed was short and tall, fat and skinny, bald and uno de esos hippies. It's like no one can get a general consensus on the guy. Thalia, Salvin's wife is a pretty, if plain young woman who is afraid of her own shadow. Why she's still with Salvin is anybody's guess. They have no children (you're kidding!) and barely speak to each other. They eke by on whatever the store makes (Doña Toñia is Salvin's mother) and from some sort of pension he receives for being craqueo, crazy. I don't think he's crazy. There's a stillness to him that is so incredibly deliberate. I am sure he has not had a spontaneous moment in his entire life.

"What did he plead? Temporary insanity?"

"Oh no. He said, 'yeah I did it. And I'd do it again.' He served ten years and then they let him go. Now, anybody else would have left town, tried to start over somewhere else where nobody knows them, but not Salvin."

I think to myself, why should he leave. He sent out the message loud and clear. I will kill anyone who calls me a maricon.

I call my boys back home and they are true to form. Victor is sure he could seduce him, Joel decries a machista culture that has fomented this internalized homophobia (yo Joel, long distance charges. Ever hear of them?) and Rob wants me to secure the rights to Salvin's story so he can play him in "Maricon! The Musical."

My Moms has reached the saturation point with her sisters and we are leaving tomorrow. She never did find the tree where my father carved their initials, but she has taken a leaf from the tree that shades his grave and tied it in a handkerchief. That's it. She's done. I try to take a nap later in the afternoon, but the mosquito netting that hangs over my bed seems to be suffocating me and the sound of the coquis, which I usually love seem so angry. Like Salvin. I keep seeing his face, this dead soulless face of anger. Here, in this small town in Puerto Rico, lives a man just a bikini wax away (and I'm guessing here) from being a full on drag queen and the people are petrified of him. They know to call him a pato would be an open invitation for him to reprise his chef at Benihaha bit with their bowels. He has cowed teenage boys, for Christ sake, into leaving him alone and those can be the cruelest creatures on the face of the earth. I remember all the boys from my torturous school years, the "fua fua" boys. It never would have occurred to me to kill one of them. Even if it would have ended my torment. But, I stop myself, Javi, you cried yourself to sleep how many times because of them? You skipped school and faked colds how often? I even made a pact with God that if the boys would stop bullying me I would say a rosary every day. On my knees. But nothing changed. I wonder, Diary, if I could have sent a clear message to those boys would that have stopped them? I remember a particularly bad day, I had just gotten my hair cut and the way it fell just added fuel to their fire. Pato! Maricon! I began to cry on the subway platform and as I heard the train approaching, it hit me that all I had to do was head butt the ring leader and he would fall into the subway tracks and be crushed by the oncoming train. Manny. His name was Manny. I looked at him through my tears and I think for just an instant he saw what I was thinking. But he wasn't afraid. He looked me right in the eye and spit in my face. He knew I didn't have the balls to do it. Had I? Had I done it? One hell would have ended and another one would have begun. Salvin can never leave this town, cause here he is feared, anywhere else he would be mocked and he would have to kill all over again just to make it clear that he is not to be messed with. So he stays here, the town's fear a constant reminder to them and him of what he did. And I think that's why he gives me nightmares, cause I know that for a moment of relief, I could have been him.

Since I can't sleep I go for a sunset run, a sort of goodbye to Isabela. To avoid going in front of Salvin's house I take a short cut through a cow field. I'd rather step in shit than see Salvin again. I am going past the backyards of houses and the smell of Puerto Rican cooking is making me so hungry. I will not allow myself to get on a scale for at least a week after I get back to New York, but boy have I eaten well here. I turn by a well and he sees me before I see him. Salvin. There he is. Slicing green coconuts. With a machete. Cue the knees buckling. If there was ever a feet don't fail me now moment this would be it, but of course they do. I can't move. At all. He slices open a coconut. Just whacks at it. Damn, he's good with that machete.

"You thirsty, pato?"

Okay, see, that's just rude. What I want to say is, "Listen here Lane Bryant, drop the machete and ask me man to man," but what comes out is a squeak that would shame any mouse.

"Well, I'm thirsty, pato."

He starts to drink from the coconut, the watery milk spilling form his mouth to his blouse, excuse me, shirt. Good God, is he wearing nail polish?

"You scared, pato?"

Maybe I'm a three pato kind of guy, but I finally snap.

"Yeah, I'm a pato, but you're a wanna be pato!"

Boy, did the clouds darken suddenly. His eyes become the stuff horror movies are made of. But, hey, I'm in running shoes, he's in two inch wedgies. He suddenly leans back and throws the machete at me. Aims the mother right at me. This is no slo mo special effect shit a la Crouching Tigress Hidden Drag Queen, he has hurled it at me and I throw myself to the side on the ground and watch as the blade takes root in the exact spot where I was. We both think the same thing, but I'm closer and grab the machete (I've never held one of these things, hello!) and then he and me, we just lock eyes.

"So," he finally says, "you gonna kill me, pato?"

And his smirk, his smirk is gone. In its place is an exhaustion in his eyes that can only come from fighting yourself year after year. I take the machete and throw it into the field behind him. He scowls at me and spits at my feet. I walk, not run, away.

The next day Jason's plane takes me and my Moms home. I think about all the Salvins in the world. All these gay men and women who because of where they live have trained themselves to hate who they are. My Moms says, "Lissen, that man is loca, loca, loca."

"I hate that word, Moms."

"Well, excuse me, he's not gay. He's too esad to be gay."

Ay, Moms, you know, when you're right, you're right.

Dear Diary:
My Moms called on the night we got back from the island.
"Mijo, can I come downstairs and esleep with ju?"...

So I made some apple martinis and we sat up on my futon bed ("This is a bed? Ay, no wonder ju always look eso tired.) and talked. And were silent. And just breathed. And outta nowhere she says, "Jou're the only one who underestands."

I pour myself a refill. She apparently should be cut off.

"No listen, mijo, my esisters, the other widows, they

embraced me and esay "Ay, ju are one of us now. I buried two, Cuca esaid like eshe was bragging instead of crying and Petra held up three fingers. Three husbands! No, mijo, I lost the love of my life. And so did ju."

I am now crying into my apple martini. I can't believe that after all these years she has put my relationship with Jason on the same lofty plateau she reserved for her and my Pops. I kiss her and clink glasses.

"Ju underestand."

"Yes, Moms, I do."

I refill her drink.

"You know, Moms, after Jason left, I was even thinking of suicide-"

And that's as far as I got, when deftly switching her drink form one hand to the other she slapped me full force. She didn't spill a drop. I, on the other hand, was not so lucky.

"Coño Moms!"

"Don't ju ever talk about killing jourself. As long as there is life, there's hope."

"Okay, okay."

"Esuicide is a mortal esin!"

"Yeah, got it. Mortal sin."

"And he estill love ju."

"Moms, he lent us the plane out of respect."

"Esend him a thank ju card."

"Dear Jason, thanks for the use of the Gulf Stream. Here are some pasteles."

"No, he loves ju cause he came all three days."

Yes he did.

"Y se porto como todo un general."

He behaved like a general. Okay, doesn't translate.

"He esat there all those three days. No ecell phones, no text messages. Nada. Esilent and estrong. Jour cousin Leyda was downloading during the esecond rosary."

"She was not!" Am I surprised at Leyda or that my Moms knows what downloading is? "Jes eshe was! We're about to download jour father and eshe's downloading Daddy Yankee!"

My Moms is so vehement when she says this that we both begin to laugh. Healing, loud, life affirming laughter.

"Ju know he loved ju?"

"Pops?"

"Jes. And Yason loves you estill."

"He has somebody else, Moms."

"Oh jeah, where was he? Quien tiene tienda, que la atienda. He eshould have been tending the estore. I put my neck on the chopping block-"

Again, doesn't translate, bear with me.

"I betchoo that there was a fight from hell over Yason coming to the viewing and his little boy toy lost. Apuntalo!'"

My mind immediately jumps to when I met Eric, practically curled up on Jason's lap and purring like a pussy. Cat.

"No, Moms, he doesn't love me anymore."

And as my Moms attempts to mix her first apple martini she winks at me. "Ju never know. Where there's life, there's hope."

"And when do you give up the ghost?"

"Ay nene," she answers as she crosses herself. "Don't esay ghost! Ju know, esomething been bothering me esince the funeral. Why ju keep saying perdoname? Why jour Pops got to forgive ju for?"

"You know."

I point to myself. She looks at me, not getting it. I do a little feminine hand gesture, still blank. So I break out the full Walter Mercado.

"I knew it! Ju think jour Pops was ashamed of ju!"

"I was 18, and I come home with a man. I'm guessing it wasn't a dream come true."

"Ju guessing wrong. Okay, we was eshocked at first, but then eso happy ju weren't out there dating with all that AIDS estuff around. And jour Pops liked Yason, me not eso much. Till recently."

"But every time I talked to Pops I could always tell he was disappointed in me."

"No, papito, he was just esad that ju estopped dancing. He thought ju could really dance."

"He didn't think dancing was a little...." And again I do the full Walter Mercado.

And another whack.

"Coño Moms!"

"Jour father loved ju. No forgiveness necessary."

Dear Diary:

I'm gonna tell you something I've never told anyone before. Ever. So if it gets out I know where you live. ...Sometimes when I'm about to cum, be it alone or with someone, I, just for a moment, hear the taunts from the fua brigade. The maricon, the pato and then I shudder and ejaculate. Is it because, oh hell, you know why it is. It's cause deep down that's exactly what I think I am? So do I think my friends are, too? Do I think Jason is? All this pride pride pride, but is there a part of me that thinks I got what I deserved?...

I take my question to the man on the street. Hector, who has stopped by to 'borrow' a tube of KY. No, I'm not kidding.

"The past is the past, cuz, you gotta let it go."

"Just like that?"

"Think of those kids who called you names. They're all minimum wage losers, I guarantee you."

"Hey, watch it, I'm minimum wage."

"Yeah, but you got out. Even for a bit. I'll tell you something. Remember that nice restaurant we all splurged on at Fire Island?"

"You mean the trip where you came back and gave your wife the clap?"

"See, I'm reminiscing here and you gotta go there. We're all seated at the table and I was watching how you moved during the dinner, like you were used to be waited on. Not in a bitchy way, just like really natural. You were....stylish."

"Thanks, and that has what to do with-"

"It has to do with, I don't know, class. That's why those kids probably dumped on you. Cause you were different and they probably knew you were special."

I am speechless.

"Hey mariconcito, why do you think Jason picked you?"

Welcome back, Hector.

"People call me names all the time, well they don't, but if they did it would just roll off my back. Tell you what, tomorrow's Saturday, right, let's go to the old neighborhood. I'll go with you, bodyguard you. You can see you're not that wimpy kid anymore."

I barely got out a sincere, "Thanks," when Hector added, "You is waaaaaaaaaaay older."

So like that day years ago, I get on the subway, but not the Manhattan bound side, but the Bronx, so named because oh who am I kidding, I have no idea. We are just gonna walk around and I'll maybe forgive the Bronx and myself. I'm not sure what I'm expecting, that someone will call me out and I'll unleash Hector on them? Yes, I'm a pato, but I brought back up. We walk for a few blocks before Hector says, "Why you looking down?"

And like that sissy from the sixth grade that I still am deep inside, I begin to cry. This is my memory of the Bronx.

Sidewalks. Cause I was so afraid of people, of them seeing that I was a fucking easy mark that I would never make eye contact. "Hey, wait until someone says something before you start bawling like a girl."

I continue crying and shrug helplessly. I am so overwhelmed by memories, none of them good.

"See, that's why people made fun of you. Always looking down and shit. They knew you weren't stupid, so if you didn't meet them in the eye you either thought you were better than them or you were a coward."

"I was a coward."

"A what?"

"A coward," I say a little louder.

"And all cause people made fun of you? Fuck 'em. Maricon!" Hector yells it out at me in the middle of a busy Bronx street.

I look at him like Bambi meeting an uzi in a dark alley.

"Jodio maricon!"

I am going to kill Hector once we have safely returned to Manhattan.

And then he hisses, "Hit me."

I look at him like he's 64 flavors of crazy.

"Pato!" and he leans into me and says, "Open up a can of whoop ass, cuz."

So I hit him. And he overacts like he was doing the lead in some Greek tragedy. Oh wait, that would be me. His hand flies to his face and he cowers. Cowers!

"Yeah I'm a pato," I snarl like Nancy Grace, "so fucking what?!" I scream this out so loudly I'm sure I'm now a basso profundo. A Latina lesbian walks up to me and says, "Nene, dial it back a notch, it's not life and death." And that's it. No one else said anything. I realized this Bronx was not the Bronx of my tormented youth. Now I wish I could say I gave Hector a black eye (it would have been my first!) but he tells me I hit like a girl, even though he's still rubbing his cheek from time to time. My cousin, who has Britney Spears' 'Womanizer' as his ring tone takes me home where I forgive myself, and more importantly I forgive the boy I was.

Dear Diary:

I'm going back to dance! Yes, yes and yes! Give me one good reason why I can't?! I am going to reach back into my past and reclaim myself, the me I never should have let go of...

I announced it to everyone at the Red Castle. News I'm sure that couldn't be trumped. I was so wrong.

"I've been collared!" beams Rob.

"Come again."

"I've met him. The one. I'm his pup."

"What happened to cub?"

"And I love him and better than that, he loves me!"

"Lurid details, please." Okay, I can't help myself.

"I was actually seeing him for a couple of weeks, he gave me a collar a few days before your father's wake. I didn't think it was appropriate to wear it to that."

"Why not, it was black?" says Victor, to whom I shot the "you will pay" look.

"I've never been happier. I've never been more me. He's an avant-garde director and I'm his muse. He wants me in everything he directs." Rob is practically dripping with happiness. "Oh, but I'm sorry, you were saying you were going back to the dance?"

Victor can barely hide his mocking smile, "Aren't you a little old?"

"Forty is not old. I'll pick it right up again," I say, "A few classes is all I need. Haven't you guys ever heard of muscle memory?"

"Don't you have to have muscles to have the memory?" says Victor.

"Victor, oh look, thin ice, you're on it. I was born to dance."

"And I was born for spandex. What's your point?" Victor reasons.

"The point is I'm gonna pick up my dream where I left off."

"Yeah, twenty years and twenty pounds later."

"Victor I have ammo." I say, then mouth the words "Cherry Grove."

Rob's phone rings, he checks the caller id and "arf arf arf's" to the caller.

Victor and I eyeball each other and down our drinks. I wanted to mock Rob, but he was becoming exactly the man he wanted to be. At 40. He wanted to be collared, he's collared. He wanted to be a pup, he's a pup. Would I ever become the man of my dreams? Victor must have read my mind, but being Victor he couldn't just let it go.

"He better not think I'm gonna pour his drink into a bowl and put it on the floor."

A glowing Rob returns.

"Lassie is one crazy bitch. In heat." Victor sneers.

Okay, is Victor's good-natured ribbing taking a turn towards the darkside?

"He wants me in all of his plays!"

"Off off off off off-" Victor digs.

"Yes, way off Broadway, puta," Rob is still smiling, "but all I ever wanted was to be a working actor."

"And collared."

"And now I have both."

For some reason, Victor's jealousy was a vibrant shade of green that he could not seem to hide. He was not about to let Rob be happy."

"Boy I would love to be a fly on the wall when you take him home to the folks."

"Victor," I sigh, "give it a rest."

And Rob, steady Rob, centered Rob, turns to Victor and says, "Joe Bear sees me first thing in the morning, scratches me behind my ear and calls me beautiful. I know I'm not, but he thinks I am."

Victor drops the attitude and becomes quiet.

"It's not like I was born beautiful, I'm just a dog with a master who loves me." And here Rob, with a steel in his spine I never knew he had, decimates Victor, the show stopping bartender. "I'm nobody's idea of beautiful, except the man I love, and that's enough for me."

Victor turns and begins dusting top shelf liquor not knowing that I can see him crying in the mirrored back splash. Rob leaves, but I can't. I stare at Victor's gorgeous back as he cries.

"Is he gone?" he barely gets out.

"Yeah."

He doesn't turn around. He just keeps dusting dust free bottles.

"I…." And Victor can't speak.

"Hey, it's okay."

Victor, perfect Victor, finally gets it.

"He's gonna become more beautiful the older he gets, you know."

"I think so too," I tell him.

Barely audibly, he whispers, "I wish I were Rob."

Dear Diary!

I'm so excited! I'm taking my first dance class in decades, wow, that didn't sound good, uh, in a few years, yes, that's better. I'll tell you all about it tomorrow. Wish me luck!!!!...

Dear Diary
Breathing hurts. Kill me now...

Dear Diary:

I'm a few weeks into my dance classes with students who would not fit in my dance bag. I am still sore. And sore. How does any male have a 28 inch waist? No seriously now. I'm a 32 waist. Normal and healthy. FAT by comparison to these boys who don't sleep, eat whatever they want and drink whenever they want. Okay, we have that last one in common. The thing is if I lose weight I look like the fucking letter I. No vee shape, no tapered waist. I never noticed it so much until I was in a room with these slivers in tights. I hate them...

One of them actually ran into the wall. I kid you not. We're going corner to corner and this boy, this ego laden, could I be more perfect boy, can't take his eyes off his own visage in the mirror and slams into the corner. Why am I the only person laughing? All the other boys crowd around him with "Ooh, you poor thing," and "I hate when that happens." Hell peel your eyeballs off yourself and it won't! Mirror boy gives me the evil eye for laughing at him. In the dressing room later I hear a bitchy "I didn't know leotards could stretch that much" aimed in my direction. I pretend I'm deaf and head out. To rain. Deluge. I'm wrestling with my collapsible umbrella when mirror boy suddenly appears holding open a huge umbrella. He stops and looks at me, smiles and says, "Hey, you heading to the subway?"

I am fucking his brains out fifteen minutes later. His apartment is as spare as mine only his clothes aren't couture and therefore are scattered all over the floor. I am pile driving my dick into him when he starts screaming.

"Fuck me daddy! Fuck your boy!"

Ground control to Major Tom we're losing altitude.

Daddy? Boy?

Hey, I was the boy. When the carajo, pardon my Spanish, did I become Methuselah? I keep fucking, partly because it would be rude to stop and partly because I wanna try this new role on. Like a hat. Daddy.

"Take me daddy!"

So I took him. The kid practically tattoos his number on me. We both know I won't call. Daddy. I'm not a daddy and today, okay I'm slow, is the first time it hit me full force, I'm not a boy either. So what am I? A doy? A boddy? No, just, …okay I don't have an answer for that yet. Gimme time. It's only been less than a year since I stopped being Jason's old boy. I look at myself in the broken vestibule mirror where my wanna be boy lives. Is it just me or is this really REALLY bad bad lighting? I should stop drinking.

At the bar Victor is on tap. Flirtatious, sexy, coy. Only one of his nearest and dearest, yep moi, notice that he is extra bitchy to the younger bar back. I wonder what would happen if one of them had the temerity to call him daddy. I'm guessing public beheading. At least. Joel shows up, that little political rabble rouser, and having just heard Amy Goodman he is hot to trot. But I'll have none of it. This is the guy who wore the same Eagle's Nest tee shirt and tacky jacket to my Pops funeral three days running. Hey, if you don't respect my Pops, you don't respect me. I zone Joel out. As the night progresses it becomes one of those down the rabbit hole nights. I'm on my fifth or something cocktail and Joel is cruising with politics. How does that man ever get laid? Victor is getting angrier/ older as the night progresses, all we need is Rob having a Alpo martini to make us complete. I turn to Joel, cause I'm hammered enough not to care and because I've been wanting to get this off my chest, and say, "Yo, the next time my Pops dies you better show some respect and wear a fucking tie."

Joel looks at me a beat, I can tell he's made a decision, and he says, "I don't own one."

"A different shirt then."

"That's all I had."

"Another jacket for pity's sake."

"Ditto."

"Oh, what's up? You donate all your clothes to MoveOn. org?"

And maybe cause he's drunk or cause he knows I'm drunk, he blurts out.

"I wore what I had dot dot dot, I'm homeless."

And suddenly I'm sober. And small. So small. "Homeless? Since when?"

"We met in March? Since April or so."

"That's fucking seven months!"

"Yeah well," and he dot dot dots me as he trails off.

I thought I had downsized going from a triplex to a basement apartment, but Joel, he's got no roof at all over his head. Fuck, he's got no walls, no floor.

"Where do you, you know, go to the bathroom?"

"There are public restrooms everywhere. I could do a walking tour of the finest toilets in the city, and the ones to avoid. Showering is tricky. Literally. You score a trick and shower at their place. I travel light and I keep some clothes here and there. I get money whenever I can land a temp job. Eating is sometimes an issue."

He's saying all this like he's ordering a fucking Cobb salad. I begin to cry.

"Sssh," he says. His mask falling. "Please, throw your head back and pretend you're laughing. Please."

I do as I'm told.

"The only reason I told you is cause I didn't want you to think I was disrespecting the memory of your father. I wore what I had. Period. Not out of lack of respect. It's what I had."

I nod and order us drinks.

"I have some money," he says.

"Joel, please!" I stress. Like I would let him use his money to pay for my drinks.

But he counters with, "We can't be friends anymore if you're gonna treat me like a deadbeat."

"Baby, you're not."

"Hush. I'm a forty two year old man who has yet to find his way. And things ain't looking great for self discovery in the near future."

"Come live with me."

"Javi."

"How can I sleep at night knowing you're just out there."

"No."

"I'll start crying again. And child, you've seen me bawl."

Joel smiles, "And we've balled. We're fuck buddies, okay. I can't live with you."

"Fine. I'll give up my apartment, you move in and I'll move in with my Moms upstairs."

"The woman who drives you crazy?"

"That would be the one."

Joel leans into me and softly kisses me, not romantic or anything. A very soft kiss.

"You would do that for me?"

"In a word, fuck yeah."

"That's two words."

"Split hairs why don't you."

"Man, what happened to my selfish little bitch?"

I hold out my keys, but Joel shakes his head, no.

"If you tell anybody, you'll never see me again, if you treat me differently, same thing. This is part of my journey, and I gotta believe it's happening for a reason."

We sit and drink in silence, he smiles and says, "Hey, maybe I'm supposed to be an advocate for the homeless. How can I do that if I haven't walked a mile in their pumps."

"Shoes."

"Open toe sandals, and that's my final answer."

We drink and make chit chat, I finally get him to at least take the keys in case of some dire emergency, but we both know he'll never use them. When I go to bed tonight, for the first time in a very long time, I won't ask God how he can be so unfair to me, but rather how he can let some of his children just slip through his fingers. Indeed, God, Universe, Angels, how do you sleep with yourselves?

Dear Diary:

I can barely afford them but the dancing classes give me, finally! a sense of peace I haven't had in eons. Now we both know I'm not gonna be a professional dancer again, hell I was barely one the first time around, so I'm taking the classes for the sheer joy of it. I'm not as good as even the weakest dancer, splits? forget about it, stamina? one production number and I would be in the ICU, but this fucking class makes me happy. My Moms always says, "if ju are born to be a hammer, nails will rain down on ju." This is what I was born to do, even kinda badly, and so I take my classes. I won't audition again, that's just like too ridiculous, but I watch Dancing With The Stars and pretend I'm on it, and of course I win. And Jason sees it and realizes what he gave up, and what I gave up for him. Wait, did I give it up for him or did I just give up?...

Dear Diary:

Hell froze over, pigs flew and I was carded at a Gay bar in Chelsea, okay, now I'm depressed, but all of those things were more probable in my lifetime than what started the day. I was just rolling out of bed at around 11am, rough night, when I hear Sonia yelling outside my door...

"Hey, this door is locked!"

Which, I think to myself, should insure me a lifetime without you.

"Open up!"

What fresh infierno is this? I soon find out. There, outside my door is Sonia, an almost demure looking Sonia, and by that I mean she has dialed back the red on her lipstick and has topped her tube top with a fetching (or retching) bolero jacket. She foists the baby at me.

"Here!"

What the deuce? I can't even think of the little pernil's name. "I forgot I have to go to court for my sister. I'm her character witness." She says all of this while still smacking her gum. "I can't take care of him," I barely get out.

"You can, and you will. You familia. And your Moms at the Beauty. Ah yes, Moms weekly visit to the beauty salon is a full day of gossip that she has never missed, and while that's lovely I am currently holding a baby that I'm sure

Sonia's programmed to piss and poop the second she leaves.

"Here's his doody bag," - Oh God - "and you gotta pick up Christina and Junior for lunch and then take them back to school and pick them up at the end of the day."

"No no no no no," I interrupt like a frustrated rapper. Oh like she's even listening.

"I don't know when I'll be back. If she gets sentenced for beating up her baby daddy it could be a while."

I smile nervously at that and decide not to argue. After all, she did think of me to take care of her litter. Looking me up and down while I hold her offspring she says, "Man I hate being this desperate."

She really should be giving etiquette classes.

She kisses pernil's head (I still can't remember his name) and leaves but not before getting in another slam.

"And Junior better not have himself no lisp when I get him back. Oistes?!"

Ah, the great ones make it look so easy.

After the exit of the Tasmanian She Devil, pernil and I just sort of eyeball each other.

"I could use a drink, how about you?"

For all the scatter shot insanity that is Sonia, Pernil's (at least I capped it this time) diaper bag would make Martha Stewart proud. No seriously. Everything is in its place and there is a detailed list of what to feed him and when and even instructions on how to clean him after he's nastified himself. I pour myself the tiniest little double rum and guava juice, all one handed mind you, as I'm petrified to put the little fellow down. What if he makes a break for it? Well, this is ridiculous, I've got to. I've got to pick up his sibs in, oh fuck! ten minutes. I put the wee one down in the kitchen sink, it keeps him from rolling around, and I did cushion it with some towels. He gurgles, probably telling me I'm a saint in baby talk. How have I not been canonized? After putting together an outfit that I hope screams "Fun Uncle!" I see that Sonia has left a carrier for little Pernil. It looks like a sling shot in chartreuse green. In other words I'll be carrying a child strapped to my chest in what looks to be Borat's swimsuit. How is this thing not a gay sex toy? For real. The teeny ham hock slides right in and is the proverbial bug snug in a thong, and we're off. The mission is to blend in, hence the whole wearing a child as a broach thing.

As I walk to the school I soon notice the little one gives me a protective shield I've never had before. Oh sure, money buys you safety, let no one tell you different, but a baby - whoa. I am, to the outside world, a father taking his child out for a stroll and in deference to the baby, I know it taint me, we are left alone. People will smile at Pernil and their smile carries on over to me. "Such a cute lil fella." "He looks just like you!" And seeing as he's drooling, how flattered am I by that little comment.

"God bless him and you."

Okay, that last one got to me. I'm not a religious person simply cause I never thought there was a place for me in the church, but hearing those words from strangers, "Dios los bendiga," I feel so stupidly touched. Ah Pernil, you are a child of magical powers. You have somehow made me worthy to my peeps by your very presence.

At the school, I join a small group of parents. I'm guessing most of the kids just eat in the cafeteria. Why Sonia would trot on down here in her cork wedges to pick up Junior and Christina for lunch, only to bring them right back in 45 minutes is anybody's guess.

Christina comes out of the school first. At ten years old she is already rocking her mother's too tight, too flashy, too trashy look. Her nails are polished blue and, I swear, she has glitter in her hair. Majoring in Disco I assume. She rolls her eyes and makes a sound of distaste, that I don't even have to hear to recognize, when she sees me. I, like the moron I am, wave and smile. She holds up her pudgy little hand in a "later for you" gesture and air kisses her girlfriends goodbye. For fuck's sake, she going to lunch not the French Onion Soup Foreign legion. And, oh shit! what am I gonna feed them?

Junior comes out of the school next. He is wearing reading glasses and I'm kinda ashamed to admit I didn't even know about that. As much as I think he's headed for gaydom when he grows up I also know he's a lonely child. Unlike his Miss Congeniality sister who is surrounded by her friends he is almost willing himself to be gray. Okay, this is the time for me to step up to the plate and be the kind of semi fabulous uncle I can be. I do a giant wave and smile and call out "Junior!" and he looks up and - dies. He looks down so fast I'm sure he'll try to sue me for whiplash. Hey Pernil, I think we just got dissed. Big time. Christina immediately leaves her little group and goes to Junior, giving me a stank eye that makes little Pernil start to cry. What'd I do? Then I see it and I smash cut back to a kaleidoscope view of my past. Some of the other little boys must have gotten the notice in the mail about the future gay boy in their midst. I see the little shoves, the snarky looks and even though I'm an adult I slip back into my past as easily as a noose around my neck. Javi, do something, I actually say to myself out loud. But I don't have to. You see, while I weathered this storm alone, Junior has a shaped like a fire hydrant sister who is willing and able to take on all comers. She joins Junior and the taunting marauders disperse a lo pronto. This is what awes me, she has somehow come to her brother's defense without drawing attention to herself or to him. It's like a sign has gone up above them that reads "STAY AWAY, OR ELSE!" and that's just what the other kids do. I finally remember I can walk and hurry up to them, only to have Junior give me a look that half begs, half demands to steer clear of him. So I do. Christina snarls at me as she hisses under her breath, "Purple? Really?" I go into panic mode. What? Then I remember, on my head is a purple baseball cap. In silk. And it hits me like a truck, Junior is ashamed to be seen with me. I stay five steps behind them on the walk back. Christina always talking to Junior, cracking jokes (some of which were at my expense, I'm sure). When I call out that their Moms asked me to pick them up on account of her going to court, I am cut short by Christina. "We know! Mami texted us." Okay, now I'm beginning to get a little p.o'd. Am I such a fucking embarrassment? There were only a handful of kids there anyway. It's not like I showed up in full Carmen Miranda drag at three p.m. in front of the entire student body. What do you think, Pernil? Could you see yourself as a headdress? Well, apparently I wasn't the only one offended, Pernil took that moment to let 'er rip. And yes, those disposable diapers do retain moisture, but fuck it's a clammy, sloshy feeling against my chest. Then little Pernil looked me right in the eye, laughed delightedly and promptly dropped a load. Phew! What's your mother feeding you, cement with rotten eggs? Okay, a lot less blessing from the common man on this return trip, more like holding up crucifixes and garlic. And I can't get away from the stench. I'm wearing it! Oh fuck shit, I'm gonna have to clean him. I tell you there isn't enough vodka in the world. We get back to my place where Christina commands, "Gimme him!" and I swear to you I cannot get that baby off fast enough. As I'm spreading any newspapers I can find on my futon, she's laid the baby on the floor and like a magic act - Poof! - doo doo be gone, baby be cleaned and rediapered. She hands me a ziplock with the soiled diaper and sarcastically adds, "You're welcome, loca." I give her a fish eye but mine is a minnow compared to her whale. My gay powers are futile against her superior diva attitude. With Pernil resting comfortably in a make shift playpen, she turned the coffee table upside down and surrounded it with throw pillow, who knew she was the MacGuyver of the toddler set? I steal a moment to try to bond with Junior.

"Hey, those are nice glasses."

"Lunch!" Christina bellows, alerting foghorns everywhere that it is her feeding time.

"Whaddya got?"

"Okay, your Moms didn't give me much time to prepare."

She smacks her tongue disdainfully and just looks in my fridge. She grabs a few things, including a jar of cocktail olives.

"Uh, excuse me," I barely get out.

"Mami says we always has to have something green with our meals."

While she whips together God knows what from crackers, Vienna sausages and pimento olives I again try to reach out to Junior who is lost in his school books.

"I like your glasses."

"I'm doing homework."

"Oh."

"He said he's doing homework!," Christina yells in case I missed it the first time. We eat in silence, hey she even made enough for me, and we have apples for dessert. Wait, I had apples? We start out for school again and without having to be told I lose the offending purple hat. Hey, better hat hair than hatred, you know what I'm saying. I drop them off and wave to them. Junior enters with his bodyguard sister right behind him. The message is clear. She has his back. She will annihilate all haters. It's one p.m., do you know where your unlikely heroines are? I look at Pernil and say, "Okay, bro, we got two hours to up our game."

So far not the best of times. A boy who may or may not be gay is ashamed to be seen with me, his sister who treats me with a degree of contempt that would make her employee of the month at Bloomingdale's and a baby who dumped a load on me that I'm sure dropped the air quality reading for the entire city.

Returning home I go through practically my entire wardrobe, trying to find the outfit that will not shame Hector and Sonia's progeny. Pernil is of no use as a stylist/fashionista, barely a gurgle as I hold shirts over pants over sweaters. The trick is to achieve the look favored by the thug elite, I must find a pair of pants that land as far away from my waist as humanely possible. I don't own pants like that. I mean, who came up with this look? It totally de-emphasizes the butt while at the same time providing easy access to it. Thus asking the musical question, so is you is or is you ain't my baby? I bite the bullet and wipe away a tear as I rip the waist band off the baggiest jeans I own and I pray that if Dolce doesn't forgive me, Gabanna will. I put on the biggest sweater I have over the largest tee shirt and I put on a black roo hat. I practice saying "S'up" in the mirror. Pernil laughs. "Yo," I tell him, "there's a toxic waste dump with your name all over it." I lose the green baby sling shot (NOTHING could make that work) and slide Pernil into the stroller that Sonia illegally keeps in the hallway. I tie a black bandanna around Pernil's head and the two butchest bitches are ready to rumble.

3pm

We are standing outside the school. There are a lot more parents now, mostly mothers. They all seem to know each other. Pernil and me are the men of mystery, but they are much more into their bochinche than either of us. The doors open and the kids flood out and - damn, some of those sixth grade boys are huge! They could kick my ass, let alone Junior's. Once again Christina is out first, surrounded by her clique. Miss Thing is popular. She sees me, and be still my heart I coulda sworn I saw the faintest trace of a smile on her pouty lips.

"Hey, Pernil," I whisper, "looking good."

Junior comes out, (well not COMES out), uh exits the school next. He sees me and is about to react but before he can - SLAM! he is body slammed by a boy maybe twice his size. My fucking blood boils but before I can charge over and possibly get whipped by a bunch of sixth graders, Christina knocks the boy to the ground with one very solid round-house punch. Dang! Gurl didn't chip a nail neither. The boy, easily bigger than Christina, gets up and quickly disappears into the crowd and for a moment, a beat, I saw why. Christina had a look on her face that scared him. It clearly screamed "I will kill. Not maybe, not try me, I WILL KILL." A second later it's over and she downplays it, kissing her brother on the cheek and laughing. Junior looks at me again and waves, and I kinda die inside and wave back. Why do I want to cry? Cause I know what he's going through and this gentle little boy in glasses with his tank of a sister just breaks my heart.

I'm allowed to actually walk closer to them on their way home. Eureka! My ensemble must have passed muster. Joining us on our walk back are a bunch of kids from the school. Little boys and girls who for whatever reason fall into the category of outsider. And Christina mother hens them all, bossing them, cajoling them but with a, there's simply no other way to put this, a maternal touch that probably makes them feel very safe. I use the money I had been saving for an Itunes card and buy them all ice cream. When we get back, after one by one Christina has kissed them goodbye and her flock has dispersed, we find Sonia sitting on our stoop and smoking.

"How was court?" I ask as Junior and Christina run to her for hugs.

"Ay, please, it was a breeze. The judge wanted me, the lawyer wanted me, the what you call it, bailiff wanted me." She scans her body with her hand and adds, "all this is a curse."

And I could think of several, but choose just to smile.

"Everything okay?," she doesn't ask me, she asks the kids.

"Yeah, except his lunch sucked.," Christina smirks.

"But he bought us ice cream," Junior quickly says, coming to my defense.

They all head upstairs. I offer to help Sonia with the stroller but with one hand she picks up both the stroller and Pernil.

"I got it," she says.

Before she goes upstairs, Christina turns around and says, "Hey, thanks.," and doesn't add the word "loca." Junior surprises me by hugging my legs before following his two strong women upstairs. I stand there for a moment, then hurry downstairs when I feel myself tearing up. Uncles can be such pussies.

Dear Diary:
Rob has invited us all to dinner to meet Joe Bear...

I didn't mishear it the first time, Joe Bear. Joel, Victor and me meet at the bar beforehand to steady our nerves. Joel talks about moving back with his parents, just for the winter, and I keep reminding him that mi casa es su casa, but Joel is proud. Too proud. We have to talk in code in front of Victor, who still doesn't know that Joel is without an address for the moment. "What if he makes us eat off the floor? If I walk in and there are like dog bowls on the floor I am outta there!" Drama, meet Victor, Victor meet Drama.

We laugh and nod, but yeah, all of us are curious. An S/M dinner party? What the hell is a good hostess gift? "Crisco," I say in my outside voice, inside thinking, Rob I'm glad you're happy, but you should have left us out of this.

Just as we're leaving, Hector arrives, all gold chains and cologne and insists on joining us.

"Spend the night with your wife for a change." I say.

"Nah, whenever I do that she get 'picious."

"How did you get out of death row after giving her the clap?" inquiring minds and Joel wants to know.

"Shit, I have a doctor friend who told her I got it from swimming in the pool at the gym."

"You swore you practiced safe sex."

"Cuz, I do. And practice makes perfect now. Condom broke. Oh, like it's my fault I'm hung like a real man."

"Someone hail a cab so it can run over him. Please." I say, and we're off.

We get to the lower east side. Way lower. Outside the building is a wreck, but inside, let's just say if this is Rob's dog cage he's done well for himself. Rob scampers up, I gotta stop that, walks up to greet us with a big smile on his face, and there beside him is Joe Bear. Very nice looking. With a warm, secure handshake. He is, quote me, dreamy! Joe Bear zeroes in on Hector.

"And you are?"

"Aw, my bad, I sorta invited myself along. I'm Hector."

"No cologne."

"Scuse me?"

There is a dead silence as we watch this unfold.

"No cologne in my house. I told the other guys, since you weren't invited you didn't know. You're more than welcome to stay, but no cologne."

Even in the mandatory gay dim lighting I can see Hector burning red.

"I'll make us all drinks. You join us after you've scrubbed down. Bathroom's over there."

Rob looks at his man with unabashed love and we retire

to the stage set that is their living room. Joe Bear is quite successful, not just as a theater and opera director, but set and lighting designer as well. "He also makes costumes," says Rob, who promptly sits at Joe Bear's feet. Should we all be on the floor? What are the rules here? Hector, having decided to tough it out, joins us. Joe Bear serves us the manly drink of a single malt scotch, lights up a cigar, not before offering each of us one, we all pass, except for Hector, who I get the uncomfortable feeling is trying to play quien es mas macho with our host. Joe Bear is incredibly charming, asking us about ourselves and when Hector puffs up like a peacock and says, "I got myself a wife and kids," Joe Bear grins and counters with, "And a healthy love of cock." We all laugh. Rob is blissed out. Joe Bear suggest he check on dinner and smartly smacks Rob's fleshy bottom as he heads to the kitchen. And Rob? He looks, there is just no denying this, Rob looks beautiful. His face is lit from the inside with that joy of having arrived at the destination that is yourself.

I sense Victor and Joel, and let's not kid ourselves, me too, lean in to every word that comes out of Joe Bear's lips. He is like a magnet. I swear if George Clooney and Mario Lopez both walked in stark naked Joe Bear still would have held the floor. Easily. Effortlessly.

"See, I can't get into that whole S/M shit." Note to universe, why hasn't my cousin been struck dumb. Or dumber as the case may be. "I mean, what is it, sewing and mending?" And Hector laughs at his own joke. Well, that makes one of us.

"Actually," Joe Bear offers, and we focus on him as if he were the only source of oxygen on the planet, "you seem like a boi that could really benefit from a good hard spanking."

"Okay, hold the phone. I'm a man, not a boy!" Hector mans up.

"A good. Hard. Spanking."

"Well, J.B, that'll be a fantasy you'll never get to live out."

"Right back at you Hector. Dinner?" And Joe Bear rises and we would have followed him anywhere, but alas it was just to dinner, which was cooked by, you guessed it Joe Bear.

"Okay," says Joel, "is there anything you can't do?"

"Yeah, let me up for air," Rob giggles. And at that moment, the way Joe Bear looked at Rob, I recognized that look. He really loves him. Joe Bear loves Rob. The rest of the meal is a happy blur. Victor pulls me over after our first round of after dinner drinks and points to Hector. "Check him out." My jaw falls as I see my downlow, Mr. Man cousin find every opportunity under a gay moon to bend over and stick his ass out in Joe Bear's direction.

"Oooh, look at these books on the bottom shelf!"

"What kind of rug is this?"

"Gee, I almost tripped on this electrical cord."

Skankanella, fueled by scotch, wine and cognac is channeling La Chacon in a desperate attempt to get spanked. I swear! I saw it and I still don't believe it. Joe Bear ignores him and we just enjoy the last drop of our drinks. I help Rob clean up, take him aside and hug him as tight as I can.

"He loves you."

"Yeah, he does." And his smile says everything for him.

We are loading up the dishes, Victor and Joel are not moving from the living room. They can't miss a moment of the telenovela that is "Hector Becomes a Bottom."

"So you like him?" Rob asks.

"Pendeja, that man has man written all over him." Rob beams. "And he's nice, you know."

"Honey, who cares? I'm talking Sean Penn kind of man. Woof."

Rob stops loading the dishwasher and looks at me kinda funny.

"Oh don't worry," I immediately pledge. "He's totally off limits. He's yours, period."

"I'm not worried," Rob says as he begins the Bustelo.

"Loca you should be. The drunker Hector becomes the more brazen a bottom he becomes. He's one drink away from lowering his own pants and laying across Joe Bear's lap and screaming, "don't you dare SPANK ME SPANK ME SPANK ME!"

We both laugh so hard he has to put the coffee down.

"Seriously, baby," I tell Rob as gently as I can. "Hector's not gonna be the only one. Men are gonna throw themselves at your man. Take it from someone who's been there. Hold on tight."

Rob shrugs, "If he wants to go, he'll go; but I don't think he will." He picks up the tray and we head out the swinging door and then Rob stops and says, "It's strange, you know, everybody always talks about how rough and tough and manly he is. And what I love about him is his vulnerability."

We enter the living room to the sexcapades that is Hector. We have our coffee and on our way out, Hector accidentally on purpose falls over an ottoman, ass up, as a gift to the icon that is Joe Bear. I blame that extra cognac. Joe Bear doesn't let on, and just helps him up. "Steady there, boi." I could have sworn I heard my tres bolas cousin whimper.

"We should hang out sometime…." Hector blurts out. Joe Bear smiles patiently and sees us out. Hector barely makes it to the curb before he vomits. The next day he'll claim not to remember anything, but the rest of us do. We were there to watch and testify that Rob Tamayo had landed the gold cock ring.

Dear Diary:

I have been haunted by that look Joe Bear gave Rob and so of course all I can do is think about Jason...

Since my Pops funeral we have spoken once by phone. How does that make any sense? I can't call him. What if I get el petite puta? How could I stop myself from blurting out, "Does he scream out my name during sex?" and the brat would probably have the phone on speaker and, well, it would not be pretty. So instead I jog and fume. I'm angry. So fucking angry. So FUCKING angry! I'm running past people blasting "fuck you" music through my ipod which if it breaks I am fucking screwed cause I can't fucking afford a new one cause fucking Jason decided he wanted an upgrade.

I fucking run into, calm down, I run into Joel, who has been off the map for a bit. He jokes that's the plus of being homeless, nobody can leave you any messages. But today Joel is excited. "I scored a job! Okay, a one time thing, but the pay is insane!"

"Baby, that's great! Best fucking news I've heard all day!"

"Yeah, and this is where you come in, loca sucia, I need a favor."

"But first insult me why don't you."

"They need one other guy, so if you do it with me, it's a go. Otherwise they just gonna go with some other tag team. See, they need two guys-"

"Got it. What is it? Does it involve heavy lifting, cause you know-"

"Sangano, no, cater waiter."

And scene. The one golden rule I've had since Jason and me broke up is I won't do cater waiter. The embarrassment of having to serve somebody who once dined at my table would be too much.

"I'll get you somebody else." I say.

"Rob's already working and Victor can't."

"I know other people."

"Who?" Joel rightfully asks.

Okay, he's got me there.

"It's tonight. Look, I'll make sure you never have to leave the kitchen. You can be the guy who makes up the trays. How's that? Please."

The thing about Joel is that he's too proud to beg for money, but a favor? That's different. So that night I'm at the maisonette of Lord and Lady Smell Me on the upper east side. The place is gorgeous. It's weird to recognize their taste, know their crystal and linens, their place settings, know exactly where they shop. This was my world. Now I'm relegated to the kitchen where a chef has the cojones to look right at me and ask Joel, "Does he speak English?"

"Yes," I answer for myself. Pendejo. I arrange the trays, load up the hors d'oeuvres, keep it moving; basically just keep reloading. Joel comes in every so often and gives me a tray with one still left on it which I pop into my mouth. Hey, this is my dinner. I have not seen any of the guests and the knot that was my stomach has begun to release itself. Joel and me have done our trade off, when suddenly the bartender comes in, grabs me, and puts a tray of champagne flutes in my hands.

"I need him outside!" He calls out to the chef who curses him in French. I try to say "no" but a mouth full of salmon puff pastry leaves me speechless. I am thrust into the room. This is my worst nightmare. I am beyond ashamed. Tierra tragame. Joel sees me but can't do anything to help me as he has a society belle who is trying to decide between four identical white chocolate swans. They're all the same bitch! Pick one!! Okay, I gotta move. I just can't hug the wall. Joel needs this money, and fuck, I could use my chunk of change too. I look around, nope, no one I know. I slowly start to make my way around the salon. Hands grab flutes, put empty flutes on tray. I concentrate very hard so as to keep everything balanced. One of these glasses is worth more than I make in a week. "Circulate" the bartender hisses at me. I head to the foyer, the library, still nobody I know. I thought I knew everybody in the upper echelon. What? Did they grow a whole new batch since my downfall? I have one full flute left and am heading back for the bar to drop off the tray and head back to the sanctuary that is the prep kitchen when I hear Jason's voice.

"I'll take one."

I turn around to face him. He stares at me. And I kid you not, the mother fucker begins to blush. He's embarrassed for me. "Take the drink."

"Javi.."

"Take the fucking drink." I say as levelly as possible. Which, trust me, wasn't too levelly. The bartender senses the discomfort and being the brown noser he is, winks at Jason and says, "Don't be too embarrassed, I slept with the help a few times myself."

I swallow and Jason takes his drink. The bartender gives me another tray and I put on my big boy pants and start fucking circulating. Jason falls in step alongside me.

"You can't do this. People are coming, they know you." Jason whispers. "I just left them. Lorraine, Kearn, the crowd. I know you could use some money, listen, just call the office, I'll get you a check."

"You'll get me a check?!" I say a little louder than I should. Cocktail music can only cover so much sound. Jason grabs me by the elbow and steers me into the closet. Okay, that's Freudian. It's a walk in closet, but still.

"I'm helping a friend," I hiss, the tray of mostly full champagne flutes between us.

"Just take money from me. We were together for twenty

years, think of it as fucking alimony! I'm not going to have you serving our friends. No. That is non negotiable."

"Okay, first, you ain't the boss of me." I say, and push the tray into him. "And who are you more embarrassed for, me or you? Afraid your friends will see your ex serving them drinks?"

"They're your friends too."

"No, when you dumped me, FUCKING dumped me, I found out just who's friends they were." Yeah, I was loud and I didn't care. Jason gives me one of his, "you are beneath even arguing with" looks and turns to leave, but me and my tray maneuver ourselves to block the door.

"When did you start cheating?"

Jason blushes. Even in the dimness of the closet I can see it. "Javi, get out of the way."

"When?! Cause it didn't just happen overnight. When did you hook up with him? Then you would come home, get in bed with me and pick a fight so we wouldn't have to have sex? Let me know when I'm wrong here." Jason is totally silent. "See, this is the thing with you Jason, this is how you argue. You are a terrible liar so you don't say much. You fucking realize that I know only so much so if you don't say anything, you don't run the fucking risk of giving me some info I don't already have. So you lie by not saying anything. You let me believe that you and me were still together when you had already left us. The us I still thought existed. You disrespect me, you humiliate me and you're worried that your friends will laugh at me? You don't think they were laughing at me the entire time you were cheating on me!!!" I jam the tray into his chest and the glasses and the champagne all hit the floor. There is absolute silence on the other side of the door which is flung open by the butler. I fall backwards, I fall out of Jason's eyes, and onto the marble floor. The mess, the total fucking mess of it all is final. Jason takes a step to help me but I jump up and run out. Run out of the house like if somebody had started yelling "Fire!" Joel runs after me. Jason, does not.

Joel holds me as we sit on a park bench. I am still shaking with rage.

"Let it out papito, let it out."

I have never been this angry. I have never been this hurt. And the numbness, that awful feeling I've had in my heart over Jason, is finally gone.

"You did good, for somebody who doesn't get angry much."

"You needed the money, Joel. I'm so sorry."

"You needed this more than I needed the money. Trust me."

Joel walks me home, but won't spend the night. He's too proud. And I'm proud too, that Joel calls me his friend.

I later find out that Jason paid for all the damages, and there was plenty. The glasses, the clothing in the closet. He also makes sure Joel got paid. And me. Only he added a few extra zeros to the end of my check. I set the damn thing on fire. My heart has been broken. He shouldn't have to pay top dollar for it even if he's the one who broke it.

Dear Diary:
Woke up feeling very mediocre, but not in a bad way. Like all the supporting players in the story that is my life have somehow slowly taken center stage and that I'm no longer the center of the universe. Almost like I'm nothing and everything, all at the same time...

When I was a kid, my Pops used to take me to his job at the hospital where he worked. It was in the Bermuda

Triangle as far as I could tell, but once every summer he would wake me at 5am and while I bitched and moaned (under my breath, I was no fool. Pops was a gentle man but the man had aim) he would half drag half carry me outside and we'd take two subways and get to a train station and travel forever to get to where he worked. As long as that trip seemed in the summer, it was only years later that I would even realize that Pops did that same commute year round, even in the dead of winter. Starting his day in the dark and coming back in the dark. Pops would get me a window seat and while I was still fighting the last vestiges of grogginess the train would leave the city, I would see trees and private homes and immediately sit up.

"Someday, mi hijo. Someday." I would imagine the people who lived in these house and that they never fought, never thought about bills and had cars. Like the people on television. The mothers wore ironed dresses when they cleaned and the fathers wore suits to work and his idea of being casual would be to take off his jacket and tie and don (I love that word) a sweater vest. They had no accents when they spoke and their only son was cute and popular and looked a little like me, only better.

"Someday, mi hijo. Someday."

My Pops would tap me on the shoulder when it was time to go and I would let go of perfection and follow him out to a mini bus that would finally deposit us at the hospital where he worked as a maintenance worker.

Everybody who worked in maintenance and everybody who worked in housekeeping (and they were two very different departments my Pops would stress) would make a fuss over me. One of the ladies from housekeeping would make me a tuna fish sandwich while all I did all day was watch my Pops mop floors.

All I did indeed.

He was sharing how he made his living, how his co

workers laughed at his jokes and the little songs he would make up while he worked. But all I saw was a man, my Pops, mopping the floor.

"Someday mi hijo. Someday."

And where I wanted to be was in that better world we had ridden past.

Now I think of Pops and all the years he worked and I am humbled, but in a good way, you know. Hey Pops, I finally get it. Perfection was sitting next to me on the train, not outside the window.

So sometimes, when I really miss him, I make enough tuna fish sandwiches for two and "we" take the train. And he finally, finally hears me say gracias.

Dear Diary:

Out of the blue my Moms decides to host Thanksgiving at her place. She never did much with Turkey Day before but since my Pops passing she says she wants to look around the table and see family there. So that means Sonia, Hector and the kids. Oh and me. "If ju can tear yourself away from the gay bar for one night." I ask her what can I bring and she first says "nothing" than adds, "maybe some of jour apple martinis."...

She has been cooking and cleaning for a week, complaining about it every day and hopefully enjoying every minute of it. Sonia has been helping her, so they talk all day long. I think this is just what my Moms needed.

All my boys have plans for that day except for Joel, who I'm allowed to bring as a date "but no funny business." Like what, we're going to do each other between courses? I had already promised to help Joel serve food at the homeless shelter, but I convince him we can do both. At least that way I know he'll have a good meal, and lots of it.

Joel being homeless is something we never discuss. It's like I don't want to make him feel bad so I never bring it up and he seems more than happy to ride that lie of denial into the twilight zone. We meet at the shelter at 10am to set up. I am assigned to the mashed potatoes and Joel's the bread and butter boy. We are told to expect quite the crowd. Now, here's the thing about New Yorkers, their volunteers come from all over. There's a woman who reeks of old money, a guy who looks like Hector and he just reeks, period, and others, thin, fat, young - you get the picture. For a second I can't help it and I think to myself, "aren't we good people," and I catch myself. One afternoon ladling out potatoes does not a saint make. I wonder how many of our crew are volunteer vets and who are, like me, newbies.

"They're all new," Joel explains. "Nobody likes to do it two years in a row, it's kinda depressing." And with that we are told to man our stations and the doors are opened.

I had no idea people had been waiting in line, cause, they just pour in. I wanted to say the poor pour in, but the glibness leaves a weird taste in my mouth. These are people, either by themselves or in families that have come to get what they don't have. Food. Over the top? I don't think so. You weren't there, dear Diary. Man, do I feel small. We are told, "no seconds, because we are trying to feed everyone." Some people smile, some avoid your eyes. Joel tells me to follow their lead. If they say "thank you" acknowledge it, if they cry - wait, someone's gonna cry?

Some of the first timers do. So I serve and become totally subservient. If they would have asked me to yodel I would have faked it.

I am so tense that Joel tells me I'm about to sweat in my potatoes, which have been restocked three times, and these trays are huge! and it's only two pm. Most people don't ask for seconds but a couple do and it's the supervisor who has to tell them "no." I don't think I could. No, I know I couldn't.

At 2:45, just as I'm beginning to unclench my jaw muscles, a woman, mid thirties I guess, Sarah Jessica Parker New York beautiful, is on her way to the food, tray in her hands, when she stops. Looking down at the floor, she hollers, "I don't need this! I don't need this food!" Her embarrassment is so total that I half expect for everyone eating to make a mad exit for the doors. But people, they just continue eating. This is not the sound of silverware on china, but of plastic on paper. The muted sound of lives lived in sighs. After her outburst the woman awkwardly makes her way to us. And then stares at each of us, not defiantly, just, I don't know, burning holes into you stares, as she gets her meal. I have suddenly never felt so tired in my life.

We were supposed to go until 4, but we ran out of food at 3, and after improvising Spam as turkey, yes I said Spam, we call it quits by 3:30. I offer to help clean up but Joel wants out. Pronto.

We don't take the subway to my Moms, we walk. A mother fucking long walk. I joke that we are burning off everything we are going to eat, but Joel says nothing. Block after block. Silencio. Then.

"Libraries. That's where you go when you get tired of walking. You can sit and they can't throw you out. Look around next time. Just a bunch of people grateful to have a free place to go and read, and look at pictures. I never used to go to them. Now I'm there all the time."

There is so much I want to ask him, and in this moment, right now, I think he would tell me everything. But I don't. What am I afraid of, that I'll remind him he's homeless?

"Shelters were never for me. I tried one early on."

We are three block from 'home' and I can't even think

the word without feeling odd, when Joel sits on the curb. I, couture be damned, follow suit.

And it comes out. "It's not that I didn't work, but I just never really worked at anything that really paid me well. I never thought of my future, cause see, I was always gonna be twenty five. Then 30, then.... I guess I got lost. Man my head hurts, does yours? Sabes, that woman today, I was her, cause at first you deny it. You are so embarrassed. I still am."

"You're not like that woman at all. You have a better butt.," I offer.

"Yeah, well."

Then I ask Joel the question. "How come you ain't angry?"

"At who?"

"I would start with God , you know, but that's just me."

He shrugs. "I was raised a catholic."

"So was I, but I gotta tell you that would be a real deal breaker."

Joel sends me further into my pagan love song abyss when he tells me he still goes to church. And to confession. Every Saturday and Sunday. Just to give thanks. I say nothing cause quite honestly I can't think of anything to say that wouldn't be, God hasn't earned your thanks. And it isn't like the Catholic Church has rolled out the E red carpet for us of the pink persuasion. How can he not be pissed, shaking his fist at God?

"Look, here's the thing, you either believe or you don't. There's nothing I can tell you that's gonna change your mind. I don't believe in preaching but I tell you what I do know is true (and here he points to my heart with his finger) I know God believes in you even if you don't believe in him."

"So how do you think God feels about us being gay?"

"He judges us for hating, not loving."

"What bible did you read?"

"The bible was written by man. It's not like God dropped

the book from the sky and said the original "Whoop, there it is!"

"Oh look, they just opened up six hundred acres of hell for you."

But I look at him, and okay, here's what I think. I think Joel has to believe because to be a decent person, to be basically a decent, caring person and wind up on the street you can either go full tilt hate or you can go to sleep every night, no matter where you may wind up sleeping, telling yourself that something good is just around the corner. Do I think it's a lie, yeah, but I so wish I had a little of that in me.

We get to the stairs of my parents' building and Joel stops, and I'm so afraid he's gonna bail on me, but he doesn't. He kisses me softly and smiles.

"You're lucky," he says, "you'll always have a place. Right here. No matter what."

And that dear Diary, was the last day I made fun of my basement apartment.

We went upstairs and ate and drank, both of us with just a little more determination than anyone at the table. Joel cracked jokes and charmed everyone, he even danced with my Moms. And then he snuck out before I could ask him to stay. I hope he scores a date tonight, I pray he scores a bed.

Dear Diary:

As Lucy would tell Ethel, "I got an idea!" and you, dearest diary, are my Ethel. I can't stop thinking of my Joel walking the streets, and not in a good way, so I've come up with something that will get him off his feet and on his back where he belongs. I have ordered/invited Joel for happy hour at the Red and unbeknownst I have invited Kearn as well. Why shouldn't they be a couple? Kearn is always looking and Joel is always horny. It could work. Oh, like right away I can't pimp out a friend?...

Kearn got a gander at Joel in Fire Island and I could tell he was impressed and while Joel wasn't, maybe I can sell him on Kearn's finer points. I figure I would have thought of them by the time I got to the bar. No such luck.

"So let me get this straight." Rob says.

"Good luck with that," I say back to Rob, who has the good breeding to ignore me, "Jason was more embarrassed that his friends would see you working than you were yourself?"

"Yeah how about that?"

"Well, to be fair, work is an alien concept to him. He would be devastated to be a drink jockey at a party and he thought you would be too. El ladron juzga por sus condiciones."

"Okay, Rob, now you're channeling my mother. So switch the channel."

Joel enters. Looking, okay not his best. "Joel, cupcake, loca, just a little freshen up in the bathroom."

"I barely slept a wink last night."

"Oh honey, were you just-"

"No, I had a bed. And a nice trick in it. Unfortunately he was twenty two and had the energy of a twenty two year old. Cabron! I couldn't find the little mother fucker's off button."

"Well, throw some water on your face and come back and be perky and sexy and all those wonderful things."

Joel leaves, giving me a "you is a crazy pato" look. But I want him to be at his best for Kearn. Sweet Kearn who had sent a huge HUGE floral arrangement for my Pop's service. Kearn arrives, I greet him warmly and, oh, who's this?

"Javi, you must meet Santos."

Santos is gorgeous, if monosyllabic, and Kearn can't keep

his hands off him all while Santos stands perfectly still, his hands clasped in front of him. I tell you the guy is a Beefeater.

"Santos is studying to be a dental hygienist." Kearn says this as he almost licks Santos' face, a face that clearly reads "this too shall pass." "I just had to show him off, give everybody at this dive a gander at what a real man looks like." I roll my eyes at this last comment and Santos catches it, and finally there is the faintest trace of a smile.

"Did I mention that Santos is an insatiable lover?"

"Not yet." Okay, just how looped is Kearn? Joel joins us, but both he and Kearn totally ignore each other. Every attempt of mine to circle the wagons together, bring Kearn and Joel into each other's orbit, crashes and burns. They couldn't be less interested. Joel just wants to sleep, practically yawns in Kearn's face, while Kearn is riding the ride that is Santos, and jumping in his seat. I am about to hurl, I am slightly disgusted at how Santos barely tolerates Kearn pawing him, but the guy is wearing some major bling so I guess Kearn thinks he's worth it. This was, it turns out, not one of my better ideas. Joel is face down on some cocktail napkins on the bar, drooling in his sleep. Hector pops in, "Hey, I just told Sonia I was with a client at Hooters, and then hung up and turned off my cell phone. That'll drive her nuts, huh?" He smiles, proud of himself. Oh sure, Joe Bear and Rob are the ones into S/M.

Victor is pouring with a light hand, especially Kearn's drinks. I should mention that ever since his unfortunate ego incident at the Grove, Victor has been dressing like a Buddhist monk. He's told everyone there will be a grand unveiling of his new and improved body for Christmas.

"You know, do not open until Xmas. I am chiseling my body into perfection."

"It is perfect," I tell him.

"No, I want an eight pack."

"Baby, you've got a six pack."

"Zac Efron has an eight pack."

"Zac Efron is twenty years old. You are dot dot dot, slightly older."

And that's how I lost my free drink privileges. But Kearn is buying. Drinks all around!

"Now you won't mind if I partake too, will you, Javi?" Kearn asks.

I shrug. Kearn is not my problem. Santos is sitting nursing a diet coke. He looks like a miserable little kid sitting outside the principal's office. Hector is giving Santos the eye, he's back to his topdog ways. Kearn knocks back his Long Island Iced Tea and announces, "I'm getting him a condo." Shit, that could have been for sleeping beauty Joel. I drink my drink and am silent. Curses, foiled again.

"And a car," Kearn adds.

"Goody," I vaguely muster.

Kearn orders two drinks at a clip. "Charge cards, ecstasy, anything his little heart desires." The two drinks disappear, two more take their place.

"Lots of things, lots of good things. That's why Jason lost you, he stopped-"

And that's as far as he got cause I turned to him and hissed, "Jason never bought me. He loved me and I loved him which is more than I can say for you and Santos." And Kearn blows my mind by saying, "I know."

What the fuck?! How much did I have to drink?

Kearn continues. "You remember, I never liked you. I thought you were in it for the money."

"You hated me."

He shakes his head and signals for two more drinks. "I called you, knowing Jason was out, and told you the world had turned upside down. Jason had lost everything. All his money. And you said..."

"I said we'd deal with it. I didn't even remember that."

"You were with Jason cause you loved him."

"Duh."

"You still do, don't you?"

Okay, no sarcastic answer for that one. No answer at all, except a guilty silence.

"You think Santos could learn to love me? Or is he the poster child for 'gay for pay'?"

Kearn doesn't want an answer, he wants another couple of drinks. "Two by two. I'm the Noah's Ark of the bar world." He laughs bitterly, then really looks at me and says, "You're not that young anymore."

"Neither are you," I counter.

"Or," he goes right on over me, "that cute or that thin. So why do you still haunt me?"

"Kearn, that was probably one drink too many."

And with that, Kearn slams his unfinished drink on the bar, grabs Santos and beats a hasty retreat with his feelings, after having stirred and shaken up mine. One and three quarter glasses of Long Island Ice Tea later I call Jason.

"Hey."

He's on the treadmill. Or having sex. Jesus Maria y Jose, let it be the treadmill.

"I'm taking dance classes again."

"Good for you."

"I really stink."

He laughs. He's slowing down to a brisk walk.

"I'm sorry we fought."

"Me too," he says.

There is a silence I foolishly feel I must fill.

"I always loved your vulnerability," I blurt out.

"Huh?" He stops.

"I mean you didn't have to be superman for me."

"I know that."

"Did you know it then?"

"Are you drinking?"

I shake my head no, as if he could see me.

"No."

"Javi, sleep it off. You were always a lightweight."

"Do you call out my name when you're having sex with him?"

"What?!"

We hang up, me first, him first, I don't know. Drunk dialing is nobody's friend.

Dear Diary:

For every high there is a low, for every low a lower low and for every lowest low, my current job in retail. After having been fired for being too old for Old Navy, not gapped tooth enough for the Gap and you don't even wanna know what they said at Abercrombie and Bitch, I have found my niche at the sex emporium, "Spanks For the Memory." Joe Bear's former slave owns this high end chain (wait, slaves can own stuff? What the fuck?!) and here I sit, among glass, chrome and more celebrity dicks than anyone could have imagined. Who is Rod Deep and why does he have his penis in this store?...

It was very sweet of Joe Bear to hook me up. I was sitting at my stool at Red Castle, where Victor has now taken to wearing Bill Cosby sweaters (hey, it's cold and shit) as he knocks back his protein shakes. I was bummed about once again being jobless. How can they expect you to have experience if they won't give you a job in the first place?

"Oh, honey you get the jobs, you just get fired cause you stink." Victor offers.

To quote the great Julia Roberts in her Academy Award winning role I counter with "Bite my ass, Krispy Kreme."

Victor looks like a deer caught in the headlights, his shake falls from his hands.

"Hey, I've had funnier lines, but that wasn't that bad."

Hector enters as Victor disappears behind the bar to clean up his muscle building mess.

"Well, I hope Sonia and myself didn't keep you up all night. Man, our sex was mad crazy."

"Hector, you live on the third floor, I live in the basement, how would I have heard you?"

"I'm just saying my girl got it every which way." Hector chews on a toothpick and grins, "I've been digging out pubes all day."

Now there's an unnecessary screen saver.

"I just pounded her all over the place. The kitchen, the bathroom, the closet."

I bite my tongue.

"Your Moms had the kids for the night so it was full steam ahead."

"Wait a second, you thought I could hear you in the basement, don't you think your kids could have heard you in my Mom's apartment?"

"It's good they should know their parents have a healthy sex life."

Hector leans over the bar to get Victor's attention , who's still dealing with the clean up on bar floor six, and he sees Victor bent over.

"Ooooh baby, check out the tail on *that* whale!" Hector gushes.

Victor immediately snaps to. Hector ogles him. "Hey Vic, ass is looking mighty fine."

Victor slams a beer down on the counter for Hector and shoots death rays at him.

"Hey codpiece, Victor is getting ready to be Mr. Olympus, so shut the fuck up." I snap at Hector.

"It was a compliment. I like me some junk in the trunk."

"Okay, you're in here doing a blow by blow about last night's sex olympics-"

"Oh, and early this morning."

"with your wife, and you come into a gay bar and cruise men?"

And with a shit eating grin Hector replies, "You know, I'm like that commercial for the candy bar. Sometimes you feel like a nut, sometimes you don't."

"You're bisexual?"

"I've never had to pay for it."

"Not buy sexual!" He's laughing at me. "Oh fuck you!" I snap.

"You wish."

And that's when my savior enters. Joe Bear with robpup (yep that's what he wants us to call him). You can practically hear the bar stool disappear up Hector's butt as they take their seats next to me. robpup asks about my job search and Joe Bear takes control.

"You need a job? In retail?" he asks.

"Well I don't have many skills." I demure.

"Unlike me," pants Hector. robpup rolls his eyes.

Joe Bear pulls out his cell phone, yes encased in black leather, holds up his finger for silence and makes the call.

"Pussyboi, I've found your worker. He'll be there tomorrow at 10am." Joe Bear says this looking directly at me, I of course nod. "He's a cutie, so take care of him." He winks at me and hangs up.

I push robpup off his bar stool and throw my arms around Joe Bear! Reality check. I blush and just nod my thanks to him.

"You'll be working at his sex shoppe. It's strictly high end. I get all our toys there."

robpup nods in agreement, "Even lesbians shop there."

"Pussyboi offers a full health plan and dental and he pays very well for this kind of work. Don't," and at this Joe Bear leans into my face, just a bit, but wow, "let me down. Order us a drink, pup." And he heads off to the men's room as we all sigh. We sigh, Hector swoons.

"You'll like Pussyboi, he's a nice slave," robpup smiles.

"What am I supposed to call him? I can't call him Pussyboi."

"P.B. is fine."

"Like peanut butter?" Victor says, his eyes lighting up.

"As a matter of fact," robpup smiles, "he does this really neat trick with peanut butter."

We all groan, save for Hector who pulls out a pen and a bar napkin and says, "Don't leave out any of the details!"

Dear Diary,

PB has turned out to be a really cool guy, sweet, but nobody's pendejo. The store, sorry, emporium, takes up the entire basement of a town house in Hell's Kitchen. (What is it about me and basements?) It's basically toy central for adults. There's even a motorized fucking machine, in and out in and out, that's all it does, fuck you, that I've taken to calling Junior after my first crush. I talk to it when I'm alone, he's a good listener, not like you of course. Don't get jealous...

It's a floor model so it's not going anywhere. When I open up the shop at 10am it's slow, but come lunch time the customers file in. PB has an upscale clientele and they have to be buzzed in, that's part of what I do. At forty I've become the Studio 54 doorman of marital aids. People come in and out all day and between waiting on them, restocking and dusting the paraphernalia the day flies by. Junior and I share inside jokes and I think I may ask for a discount and take him home to meet Moms.

And speaking of discounts, Hector spends every lunch hour at the store, trying to get me to give him my employee discount.

"C'mon cuz, hook me up!"

"If it were by your nipples and the ceiling I just might." I retort.

"Tease," he winks.

"And stop trying to make the DVD section into a back room. We don't have one."

"Not yet."

robpup comes by with Joe Bear. They very casually restock their toy room with robpup announcing, "We're moving on to fisting!" with such glee you would have thought he was accepted as a new breed in the American Kennel Club. At least robpup is working on his craft in a play directed by his beloved. Which is more than I can claim for myself, being totally craftless.

I meet PB's new owner, Mistress Daisy. Wait, he went from a master to a mistress? Are slaves allowed to do that? Mistress Daisy looks like Patti Lupone and is regally charming. PB never raises his eyes from the floor when she's there. She's totally nonchalant with me. The very first time we met, she shook my hand, very strongly, and looked deep in my eyes and announced, "We must do a three way." I merely nod and smile. I could never get the whole three way thing. Knowing me, I would call out "shotgun," which would be gauche. Or worse the entire thing would be like the Disney chipmunks, Chip and Dale. "After you." "No I insist, you first." "I simply won't hear of it, you must go first."

I've been there for a little over two weeks, thinking of what I'm gonna get everybody for Christmas, when my cell rings. Dionne Warwick's "You'll Never Get to Heaven if You Break My Heart." It's Jason, and yes, it's his personal ring tone. "Yo," I say, sounding as butch and as happy as I can. I put my hand over the mouthpiece and mouth, *It's Jason* to Junior.

"How are you doing?" he asks.

"Great!"

"Good to hear it."

"Yeah!" It's like I'm trying to sound like Eric, a preschooler missing his ritalin.

"Listen, um Eric and me–"

I lean on the countertop, fingerprints be damned.

"–are having a little Christmas party–" That was our thing. "–and we'd really love it if you could make it."

Oh shit, I stopped talking. I'm supposed to say something.

"I can't."

"We'd really love to have you."

"I'm working now. I'm a working girl, boy, man, whatever."

"What's up?" whispers robpup.

"Jason, Eric, Christmas party."

"Gotcha." robpup nods.

"Please," says Jason.

"You're going," says Joe Bear, all authority.

"Excuse me, Dr. Phil," I answer.

Joe Bear raises one eyebrow and I immediately add "Sir" to my sarcastic retort.

"This would be good for all of us," says Jason.

"Let me talk to him," I hear Eric say to Jason and suddenly my phone becomes radioactive.

"Don't hang up," says/orders Joe Bear.

"Hey!" Eric's voice is absolute honey.

"Hi," I answer, hearing my own heartbeat like a drum machine.

"We would really love, I would really love for you to be

here. You'll always be an important part of Jason's life and-"

He's still talking, the mother fucker is still talking.

"It won't really be Christmas without you! And please bring your friends!"

Again, a silence I am supposed to fill.

"Um." I can't bring myself to say his name. "I don't think that's a good idea."

"Promise me you'll come. I've already bought your gift! Jason let me pick it out! I hope you like it!"

Jason takes the phone from him, "So?"

Joe Bear nods.

"The twenty second, right?" I say so softly I'm surprised he can hear me.

"No," says Jason. "That was our date. We're doing the twenty third. See you then."

I nod, then add, "yeah," and hang up. I turn to Joe Bear and say, "I can't do it."

"You have to."

"I'll kill Eric."

Joe Bear laughs. "No. You'll finally put a period to the end of this sentence."

robpup smiles at Joe Bear and they kiss. He is right of course. "He wants me to bring my friends."

Joe Bear looks at me as I scan their purchases. robpup breaks the tension by reminiscing, "Your xmas parties were insane. It was the only time I saw you sangana (meaning me), once a year at your party, where you were too busy playing hostess to ever hang with me. But look, this year you get to be a guest, like us."

I wave them off. "Enjoy your fisting supplies," I call out. In this store no one blinks.

"Oh we will!" they answer in unison.

A guest. In my own home.

"How about that, Junior?"

Junior smiles, wraps me in his arms and- oh snap out

of it. My cell rings again. Probably Eric asking me to go caroling with him.

"Hi, it's me."

"Hi Victor."

"...Do you want my gym membership?"

"What?!"

"Come over to my place after work. You can walk me to the bar."

Victor is the only one of us who lives in a doorman building. He has to, he tells us, because some guys get so enamored of him that only a doorman can keep them out. *True lust* is what he calls what they feel and he's not bragging. So after kissing Junior goodnight and locking up the joint I head to Victor's, who by the by went away for two weeks to get in shape. One of those boot camp places that will either kill you or get you in the best shape of your life. And with Victor they had perfection to start from. I'm happy for him. Cherry Grove be damned!

Victor's apartment is just like him. Not a thing out of place. Pillows on the sofa in the right order, move one and he'll know. On the elevator ride up I think of him. Even though I've only met him this year, he calls me his closet friend. He never speaks of a boyfriend or a date for that matter. For a while, after his ego deflating he was so dark and gloomy but ever since he started his body building regimen he's been happier than ever.

I knock on his door and I hear his voice say, "It's open." I'm barely in the foyer, my hand is still on the door knob and Victor is standing there, fully naked. There are certain sights that elicit certain sounds, the Grand Canyon, the Eiffel Tower, the VIP shopping room at Tiffany's, seeing a naked Victor, I choked, and not in a good way. He had packed on at least 25, 30 pounds. And not of muscle.

"Close the door."

I am speechless. Victor swallows. As I approach him he slowly turns around, giving me a full 360 of the new and, well the new Victor.

"Twenty eight pounds," he volunteers. "Not of muscle, but of fat."

The sweaters, the caftans, all the hiding.

"Say something." He says.

Go with the truth, lie? What? I got nothing.

"You're my friend, tell me what you see."

I'm in a mine field. Danger all around me.

"You've put on-"

"Twenty eight pounds, I said that. I'm fat, Javi. I'm fat."

Yes, Victor Lugo is fat.

As I watch him dress, he tells me the entire story. How easy it was to go from no fat to full fat, how he hasn't been to a gym in weeks, how he's involved in a menage a trois with Ben and Jerry's. "And I don't care. I really just don't care anymore. Let them make me a bouncer, let them fucking fire me. I just don't care. I want to eat carbs, I want salad with dressing right on it, not on the side and not just balsamic vinegar either. Life is full of desserts and I want them."

"But you were perfect."

"No honey, I was just renting perfection. This," and he squeezes his love handles, "is the real me."

We walk to the bar. "The only exercise I do now!" Victor squeals, I mean exclaims. He keeps up a constant chatter about finally giving up the ghost of that Greek god that he was. "You know the older I got, the sadder I got, the angrier. Come on, how long could I fight time?" And on and on. I realize it's not just for me, it's for him. The closer we get to the bar the more Victor starts blinking nervously and the more "up with fat people" he sounds.

"We're here," I say, stating the obvious. We both know

it'll be packed, uh filled with regulars.

"No sweater tonight," Victor says to me, but more to himself. "Tonight I'm coming out as a, say it." Victor grabs my hand and squeezes it. "Say it, please."

"Victor," I helplessly shrug, "you're fat."

I wish I could read the expression on his face, but I can't. He's like Garbo at the end of Queen Christina. Before I let go of his hand I ask him, "Are you happy?"

And his face relaxes and he smiles and says, "Yes I am."

"Just remember that, my friend."

In the bar I join my crowd, I want to pull them aside, warn them so that-

"Holy shit!" Hector as always keeping it on the downlow.

There is Victor in his gold spandex shorts. And his gut, front and center. The shorts, pulled to their max, just make him look fatter. There is a death silence in the bar. This, I realize, is not gonna be pretty. "Okay guys," Victor says too loudly and too cheerfully, "I've put on a little weight."

"A little weight would be an Olsen twin," someone calls out. Note to self, hunt down and kill.

Victor's smile falters, but he's a game lad and on he goes, but he's toast. Hot buttered and jammed toast, but toast. "Coño man," some other guy sneers, "you pregnant?" When beauty falls the jackals come out in full force, almost as if they were waiting for the demise of his beauty. Okay, Victor did lord it over most of them, but still, these sucias are going for blood. Lorena, the drag queen from Hades, hisses "Nothing taste as good as being thin." That's when Victor stops dead in his tracks and eyeballs the haters. "Bullshit!" he brays, "Pernil taste as good as being thin! Flan tastes as good as being thin! Tembleque, amarillos, maduros!!!" He's preaching to a room full of latino gay men, so they are beginning to feel him. What he needs now is something to push the scale, if you'll pardon the expression, don't be hating, squarely towards his round self. And the calvary arrives in, who else but Hector? "Are you guys fucking crazy?! Look at that junk in the trunk!" He immediately holds out a ten to tip Victor, stuffing it in Victor's overstuffed shorts. "That," announces Hector, "is what a hot man should look like. I want me some cushion for the pushin!" And just like that the tide turns and we're in the "Them There Eyes" segment from Lady Sings the Blues. Victor is running all over the bar collecting tips and people are squeezing his ass, his tits. When Hector stands next to Joe Bear you just about hear the two sides of Hector's brain fight for control. He wants to top Victor but he wants to bottom for Joe Bear. Ah, what's a versatile to do? By the end of the evening Victor has scored more tips and numbers than ever before. His job is safe and so, thankfully is his ego.

"I still got it!" Victor beams.

"And in the large economy size!" I can't help adding.

"You feel like sharing," leers Hector. Victor sits on his lap, grinding his phat ass (oh look at me, so hip all of a sudden) into Hector's crotch.

"Go home to the Mrs." Victor purrs.

"See, now you got me primed." Hector leaves, walking stiffly home. Joe Bear and robpup leave too, but only after "atta boying" Victor to death. They are the tag team of positive thinking.

"You ever gonna diet again?" I ask Victor when we're finally alone.

"Never again. Ever. I mean, I don't want to take up two airplane seats, but I want to eat what I want to eat when I want to eat it. Life is too short. It's just too damn short."

I think back on how Jason and I would panic if either of us would gain a pound. As Victor ends his shift I stare at him behind the bar, reaching up, bending over, his body in constant movement, and it hits me. Victor's not fat, he's voluptuous!

Dear Diary:

My Moms has decided to spend las navidades in Puerto Rico. She never liked the cold much anyway and she really wants to be with her sisters. She wants me to come with her but as she put it, "I realize jour career in porno retail comes first." We exchange early gifts and while I'm gifting everyone else a little something from PB's emporium I just can't bring myself to go there with my Moms. I get her a Tabu gift set, her favorite, and she gives me pajamas and an invitation to stay upstairs while she's gone. I pass on the invite to Joel, let him stay upstairs. I'm getting used to my Laverne and Shirley existence...

Back at PB's, Junior and I agree (isn't it funny, we agree on everything!) that the saddest toy in the shop is the Kisser. Let me explain just what the Kisser is. It is a battery operated, molded rubber lower half of a face that you can kiss and will kiss back. That's it. I thought at first it might double as a rimmer, but no, it's strictly French mouth kissing. "It's kind of sad not to have someone just to kiss." I tell Junior, forgetting PB is right there.

"Some guys don't even like to kiss," PB shrugs.

I leave early, today's his turn to close up the shop. In my pocket is the Jason/Eric Xmas card I received this morning. Jason dressed as a sexy Santa spanking a naughty elf, Eric. I've memorized the card, the embossed lettering. "Don't be bad, have a good Xmas! Love Jason and Eric." Jason has added a "may next year give you ALL you deserve" under his preprinted name and signed it, while Eric has added a "see you on the 23rd!" in his adorable scrawl under his. And yes, he dotted the "I" in Eric with a heart. How is he not diabetic?

Joe Bear, robpup, Hector, Joel and Victor are all sharing coquitos with me before we head to the party. Without saying it I know all my friends want to go to the party to size up Eric and shower me with his imaginary faults. These are after all good people. Hector has convinced Sonia that he has to go cause it'll be good business. What business? The man drives for Fed Ex! But they've been getting along lately and as much as I criticize Hector, he is a good father. He is going to hurry home to read Xmas stories to his kids and put them to bed, then he and muffin top will try to build Barbie's Dream Dubai Palace.

"C'mon cuz, let's get going before the cater waiters get too busy for a quick BJ." Yep, the guy's Father Knows Best.

In the car, Joe Bear suggested/ordered we get for the party, the game plan is hatched. Everybody split up, do an informal poll on how people really feel about Eric. Find out who his friends are, if any. Then we all leave once the gifts are given. I wanted to leave before but was quickly pimp slapped out of that notion.

Going to the place I shared with Jason as a guest was surprisingly numbing at first. I felt I was revisiting the lack of feelings I felt when my Pops passed. I hope I can hold off losing it until I am safely and solely back at home. Please Universe, Angels, God, Brad and Angelina, let me just be the Mona Lisa.

The house staff remained the same as far as I could see. They greeted me as someone they used to work for, a boss they once liked, but not their boss now. I am history. In what had been my home I am history. Joe Bear, robpup and Hector go into circulation mode, all the better to get the inside dope on Eric. Victor heads gaily forward to the buffet. It doesn't seem to bother him that he's not the best bod at the party. He has accepted his new self with a gusto I truly envy. Ten months after being dumped I'm still in mourning for my previous life, but not the plus sized Victor, he's in food heaven.

The Christmas decorations are all out. Beautiful, fragile ones that Jason and I collected over the years. Mistletoes which I studiously avoid while Hector keeps parking himself under them. And a Christmas tree that would make FAO Schwartz cum. On a dimmer. Now really. I'm looking at things, at decorations, so I don't have to make eye contact. The place is full of people who knew me as part of Jasonand-Javier. Now I'm just Javi, the ex, who didn't even rate a phone call from them, but now they're face to face with me, so cue the "where have you been?, you look great, long time no see!" And I cue my fake smile until my fucking cheeks hurt. Lorraine is there with her latest in a long line of paramours and hers is the one look that brings me the closet to tears. Her smile is actually genuine as she says hello. I see Jason across the room and he smiles and makes a beeline for me, but he loses the race to Eric who effusively throws his arms around me, squealing, "You made it!"

Did I once call this boy a kitten? No, he's a puppy. A yapping little dog you want to throw out into rush hour traffic. Oops. Mask back on Javi.

"Hi Eric." I can't bring myself to hug him but I am saved by Jason who arrives to give me a safe kiss on the cheek."

"Thank you, thank you, thank you for coming!" Eric is practically jumping up and down. "Where are your friends? I want to meet them so much!"

"Eric's made Christmas cookies for them," Jason offers as Eric hides his head in mock embarrassment in Jason's chest. "He was baking all week!" Jason adds, apparently catching the exclamation virus.

"Wow!" I answer. Hey, when in Rome.

I corral my guys and introduce them. Jason has eyes only for his little Betty Crocker Eric who is soooo charming to everyone. Gets their names right, laughs at their little jokes and insist 'my home is your home.'

My home. My home.

As Jason and Eric disappear into their other guests I hear robpup whisper, "Steady Javi." I nod and join the masses. Making my way through, holding a flute of champagne in one hand, I hear, as the perverse DJ that is God, hits play on "Always Something There to Remind Me." I walk and smile, even though I can't feel my legs or my heart.

"Where have you been keeping yourself?"

"Oh you know."

"We must have you over to dinner sometime."

"Yeah well."

"Someone told me you're a working girl, that's not true, is it?"

"Excuse me, I need a little refill."

I am drunk, but not sloppy. Still able to walk straight lines and not slur, but for how long I do not know. Off the little alcove, by the library I hear the witches from McGaybeth as I am served up as the sacrificial lamb to their bitchiness.

"I heard Jason had offered Javi ten million to vacate the premises but he was holding out for more."

"Talk about delusional."

Evil chortle, followed by a comment I can't hear.

"Someone told me he went back to hustling."

"No!"

"Very hush hush."

"I wouldn't have had the bad taste to come. It's Eric's house now."

"Is he just divine or what?"

I want to say "or what" but my throat has become a desert.

"Listen, the only reason Javi is here is to try to score another rich husband."

"He's a one trick pony."

"Oh, he's had more than one trick."

Laughter.

And then I hear Kearn, drunk as a skunk and just as loyal (are skunks loyal?)

"Javi was the best thing that ever happened to Jason!"

Awkward silence. Kearn always did have a problem with volume control.

"Kearn, dear, Javi was just-"

"Was what?!" and there's a belligerence in Kearn's voice that makes the girl gang disband and go in search of safer quarters. I want to thank Kearn, but more than anything I want to get my coat. I run upstairs, mercifully the coats and I are alone. Until He arrives.

"You're not leaving, are you?" asks Jason.

"Yeah, ...nother party."

"But we haven't even-"

"What?," I cut him off, "Haven't even what?" On what planet does he think this is easy for me? This moron, this selfish bastard that I still love more than life itself.

"Why did you fall out of love with me?" I whisper. He visibly flinches. A low blow, but hey, I'm in pain here. "What did I do wrong?" There is no answer, just a face that looks away from mine. So I repeat. "What did I do wrong? What did I do wrong?" and I grab onto his lapels, "What did I do wrong? What did I do wrong?" And I throw my arms around him and kiss him, kiss the only man I have ever loved. And he kisses me back! His arms go around me, but wait, he's pulling me off him. Gently, but firmly.

"Javi.."

And Eric enters, absolutely angelic, he notices nothing, just says, "Javi, you're not leaving are you? Jason make him stay!" And turning to me with a smile as pure as I was once, adds "You have to help me give out the gifts. I don't know half the people here and they all like you so much. Please!"

"Eric…" Jason starts.

"Of course," I answer, smiling at Eric who takes my hand and squeezes it and leads me out. I look back at Jason who has a kind of haunted look, and I finally get it. Eric is the one thing I can never be anymore. New. The rest of the party is a razor blade. It cuts deeply and neatly. On the ride back I am silent. All the guys have scored great gifts, gadgets, clothes. I got a lovely, expensive, impersonal scarf. I finger the gift I had brought for Jason. It's still in my pocket. The framed ticket stub for "FUEGO!" on the night we met. I have always kept it and tonight I was going to give it to him, but…

Hector breaks the silence by volunteering to sleep with Eric. "That'll break them up!" No one laughs. They all think Jason is really in love with Eric. Only I know, for the briefest of moments, Jason kissed me back.

"I didn't meet any of Eric's people," offers robpup.

"Me either," adds Victor.

"Everybody was like from Jason's world. What's up with that?" Joel says. And the gift giving. Child, my nerves. There I was, still stunned from what will hereafter be referred to as "the kiss" being dragged from gift recipient to gift recipient as Eric would call out a name and drag me along. Almost as if the gift came from both of us. Almost. If he weren't the apparent reincarnation of baby Jesus I would have thought it incredibly cruel, but his smile, his glow, his total delight in giving and in sharing this with me made me border line nauseous. Never a question or a comment about Jason and me being alone in the coat room. A part of me almost, underline almost, wants to warn him. I too felt indestructible as a couple, and well, look at me now.

Everyone wants to go out for drinks, but I beg off. I go home, pour myself some Hawaiian Punch and domestic vodka and look at the framed ticket stub that was going to be Jason's gift. How inappropriate, Javi! I keep the lights off so no one will see I'm home and get rip roaring solo drunk. Gee Tiny Tim, this is the best Christmas ever!

Dear Diary:
Christmas is kinda a non event, with both my Moms and my Pops gone. My Moms calls from PR and I talk to all the relatives, and I hang out at Red Castle where we all order Chinese Cuban which we eat right at the bar...

There are a lot more take out menus there since Victor went AWOL from his waistline. Joel is staying upstairs at my Moms and has promised only to trick out, not in. I explain to him that my Moms bed is sacred.

"And I'm a pagan?" he asks.

"Okay, we agree on that."

At the request of my boss, PB (I still can't call him pussyboi even when he wears a collar that proudly proclaims it) I stop by before he closes up. He and Mistress Daisy are there.

"Here," she says, handing me an envelope. "It's your Christmas bonus. It's not much, you haven't been working here that long, but you're a real good worker. The floors positively sparkle. I can only get this kind of shine upstairs when pussyboi is scrubbing on his hands and knees."

"Thanks," I answer, "My Pops taught me how. He could clean anything."

What is the protocol with a bonus? I whistle appreciatively. Okay, they seem pleased with my reaction.

"And I'd like you to pick something, you know, for you." she says. I hem and haw and she looks directly at Junior. "So, you want the floor model?"

"Well, we've sort of bonded." PB helps me dismantle it, which thankfully is not too hard, and I box Junior up. Mistress Daisy throws in a couple of "accessories," oh Javi grow up. Dildos! Okay? Dildos! And I cab it home.

I feel like a kid who just brought home his first gay porno. Like everybody can tell what I have in the box. I get home just as Hector and his happy little family are exiting the building.

"Ooooh, what's in the box?" Cristina asks.

Thinking faster than I had any right to I spit out, "An old computer. Victor switched to a laptop."

"I'm surprised he can find his lap," Sonia sneers "from what I hear."

"Yeah, well you have selective hearing." I shoot back. At which Hector quickly hustles them out, while giving me a look that can only mean "we'll deal with this later."

"Adios pinga jockey." Sonia waves. "I'll come by later and help you set it up," Hector offers.

"No, I got it," and I hurry inside with my date as I hear Sonia snort, "He's just gonna download hisself some porn."

In the apartment I double lock my door as if I were carrying contraband and head to the bedroom. I'm actually kinda nervous. Hey, it's been a while. I fix myself a drink, shower, make sure I'm extra clean, blow dry my hair. I catch myself putting on concealer. Do I, in some Whatever Happened to Baby Jane twisted way, think this is a date? I put on some music to get plowed by. Laugh. Good. Laughter is good. I set up Junior. Gosh, you and me have been cruising each other for so long. Lubricant! Okay, got it. I decide to start with the smaller dildo first. No need to be greedy, work up to it. Oh what the hell, let's not wuss out. Medium it is.

Okay, Diary, have you ever used one of these butt fucking machines? I'm guessing no. It's all in the set up. You want it to be in a position for easy access, so some pillows under the hips are not a bad idea. You also want some firm footing for Junior. Nothing kills the mood like your date taking a header in the middle of a well you know, a "date." A fuck! A fuck a fuck a fuck! I get on my back, legs up, but the position seems hard to hold, so on my stomach it is. There's a part of me that can't help but feel pathetic. This is not a real man, but at least I'm not paying for it, I tell myself. As if there were some imaginary line of good taste that I refuse to cross. I grease up Junior's "dick" and my hole and slowly back into him. Should I have some poppers? How retro! I get up, find some and try again. Wow, Junior is packing. I ease him in, about two inches, and find the remote. I hit the slow option and Junior, like a sailor on shore leave, comes to life. He is a gentle and slooow lover. The moan I hear I assume is from me since Junior is also the strong and silent type. I take a hit of poppers and rev him up a bit. Hello nurse! He is moving in and about halfway out at a smooth and delicious pace. My breathing is jagged. Junior's aim is exact and true. There's an almost zenlike feeling to this ride. I look at the clock and realize I've been blissing out for about fifteen minutes. Another hit of poppers and I dial it up to about eight, which is almost about as many inches as are making their way in and out of me at a luxurious pace. Okay, who needs a lover? Andrea True's More More More comes on and I'm about to blow my wad, (oh that's so cute, I said wad) without even touching myself, when my phone rings.

"I can't come to the phone right now..." I answer along with my voice message, adding "I'm being fucked into next week!" Then I hear Jason's voice.

"Hey Javi are you there? It's important."

I lurch over for the phone, stretching my arm and getting Junior's remote jammed somewhere under my hip pillows. Junior has also moved on to the Faster Pussycat Kill Kill setting and has tipped over pinning me to the bed. Junior is now fucking me as if he wanted to get through me to the floor. "Hey Jason," I gasp into the phone while trying to disentangle myself from Junior. To no avail.

"Are you okay? You sound out of breath."

"Yeah…. I was working out. Charley horse." Oh great, I find the remote, but it's for the music. Suddenly the room is silent except for the sound of Junior gearing in and out of my ass.

"Is there someone there with you?"

"No, no. It's an exercise machine." I grit my teeth. "I'm still breaking it in." Or vice versa. I put the music back on low to disguise the unmistakable sound of an assault.

Jason begins, "Listen, I've had a couple of drinks, but-"

To get the old courage up!, I tell myself. He wants me back! Junior, we're over. Ouch! Junior does not take the news well.

"You know I will always care for you," Jason adds.

Care? Wait. No. The right word is love. I take a hit of poppers. I suddenly think I may need a little bit of help here.

"So I wanted to be the one to tell you."

I go to the poppers place. Calgon, take me away!

"Eric and I are going to get married."

And I push back into Junior. Fuck me harder! I can't breathe. Is it the poppers or the news?

"Javi, are you there?"

Ask Junior if I'm here. As I'm pounded into hamburger meat I hear a voice that I assume is mine say, "Can I call you back tomorrow?"

"I know it's hard to take."

"You have no idea," I say after a particularly virile thrust.

"Can I come over?"

"No!," then softer, "no. Tomorrow."

"Okay, but we will talk tomorrow."

"I'll meet you at noon at whatever, just send the car." I hang up, before I start crying. I could end my date gone bad, but I don't. I up the volume and cry as Junior fucks me into oblivion.

Dear Diary:
The phone rings off the hook all morning. I listen to the messages in a hot bath while I nurse my achy breaky asshole.
"Don't pick up the newspaper!" this is from robpup.
"Where are you, have you heard, are you okay?" Victor.
"Shit, he's marrying Eric! You lose!" my dear cousin Hector.
All morning long I have been playing on a loop Barbra and Donna as they preach/sing "No More Tears!" This is it. Enough is enough. I must name it and claim it. I will not cry one more tear for Jason...

In the car Jason is beside himself.

"I don't know how the papers found out. One of Eric's friends must have leaked the news."

"When did you ask him to marry you?"

"...Christmas. He said it was the only gift he wanted." I am silent. "He wants a birthday wedding."

"Yours or his?"

"... mine."

My silence makes him uncomfortable. Good. "In Claryville." he adds. That comes as a surprise. The house, estate, whatever, is not exactly Gay central, but it was always my favorite of all the houses. Maybe cause I was there from the purchase to the decorating to the landscaping. For all it's size, I still considered it our home away from home. Jason keeps talking, but I zone him out. His lips are moving, but I - his lips-

"Did you," I interrupt him, "or did you not kiss me back

at your Christmas party?"

"Javi-"

"Answer the question!"

Jason looks down, says nothing, thereby answering my question. "Stop the car," I tell the driver.

"Javi."

"Do me a favor. Have a beautiful wedding, have a beautiful life. Just don't fucking invite me." And I get out of the car. I enter the bar singing "No More Tears" at the top of my voice. To which robpup winces, "Honey, you're a dancer, not a singer."

"No, see, the thing is, the pity party is over. I am officially over Jason." I stand triumphant.

"Uh huh," says Victor, eyeballing me. "Nene, sit down, you make me nervous standing there."

"I'd rather stand." After last night, I may stand for a week! "We're done. We're done done. For the first time I got it."

After giving Victor *the look*, robpup turns to me and says, "Okay, Jason calls, says, I've made a terrible mistake! I want you back!! - you would…"

"Turn off the alarm and realize it was a dream. Or a nightmare. He's with Eric. He wants Eric."

"Of course he does. George C. Scott wanted Trish Van Devere." robpup says. The entire bar looks at him. "You people are so theatrically uneducated. George C. Scott was married to Colleen Dewhurst, major brilliant actress. They were young, tempestuous, and in love, capital L. Only she makes the mistake of aging, not him, her. So he meets and marries Trish Van Devere, who looked exactly like Colleen Dewhurst did when she was young, i.e. when he was young."

We're all still staring at him until Victor finally says what we're all thinking, "I never heard i.e. used in a sentence before."

"Jason is with Eric cause he makes him feel young again.

He dumped Philip for you cause you made him feel young and oingo boingo he's doing the same thing again, leaving you for Eric. Jason is searching for the fountain of youth and he thinks it comes in a men's size small jockey shorts." I forget about my sore butt and sit myself down, just astaring at robpup. "Man, when did you get so smart?" To which robpup barks happily. I gotta tell you, I have a brand new healthy respect for human pets.

Dear Diary:

My Moms has returned from the island, which means Joel is once again homeless. He won't let me help him, says, "Don't worry," but of course I worry. My Moms and me are upstairs in her kitchen. She is making pasteles and I finally realize I better learn how she does it. Diary, I would share the recipe with you, but I am sworn to secrecy. Suffice to say, that the next time someone gives you one of these root vegetable meat pies you better be very grateful. The work involved in making them is cabron. My Moms makes them the old school way, too. Plantain leaves and everything...

It takes all day, and I get to spend it with her. Every so often, she'll look out the window at the garden in the backyard, now covered in snow. The place where Pops was happiest. "Ju got to hear this." And she puts on a collection of old boleros. I used to make fun of these songs when I was growing up, stupid me, now I hear them and am overwhelmed by their beauty. "Esperame en el cielo, corazon, si te vas primero," she sings in a lovely mezzo. "Jour Pops courted me with boleros. He knew what he was doing." I smile at her memory as she checks the spices I've added. "A little more adobo, nene. I like it to have a kick."

"It was nice being in Puerto Rico, eseeing all the family, ju eshould have gone. They all asked for ju. I esaw jour Pops family. They had eso many pictures of him. Jour Pops was tremendo galan."

"I miss him so much. I can't even begin to imagine how you feel."

"Dios sabe lo que hace."

God knows what he does.

"It was estrange being in a Puerto Rico without him. I esat outside what had been his mother's house for hours. I thought of his wrinkled face and callused hands that did not match the jung man I fell in love with. His disappearing hair and eyes aged by what they had eseen and endured and I found I don't miss the young man, oh esure I miss the esweet first kiss of jouth under the flamboyan tree, did I ever tell you I was the first girl jour Pops ever danced with? But no, I don't miss the boy, I miss the man he became. That's who I miss most of all."

I can't help it, I hug and kiss my mother.

"You know it's strange, I always remember you two arguing."

"Oh we fought like crazy. That was our way. Didn't ju and Yason fight?"

I shake my head, no.

"Maybe that was the problem."

I ask Moms if she would ever move back to PR to live.

"No, this is my home, with ju and Sonia and Hector and the children." Hey, at least I got top billing. "Ju know eshe called me everyday I was gone and eshe would put Cristina and Junior and even the baby on the phone. Eshe makes me feel like I matter."

"Moms! Of course you matter."

"I know I won't have any grandchildren with ju muchacho, so those kids upstairs are my treasure."

Before I leave she loads me down with pasteles for the guys, an extra couple of them for Victor, and a copy of the boleros collection that my cousin Pito burned, just for me. "Ju need to visit the island more, they're jour family too, and they miss ju."

"When I go I'm gonna come back with my very own jibarito!"

At this my Moms throws her head back and laughs really loud. "Ju know, jour not the only gay in the family. Oh no. I counted five cousins of yours that are especial like ju."

"Bendicion, Moms."

"Que Dios me lo acompañe y bendiga."

I head downstairs. Wow! Five? I couldn't crack their code with a decoder ring. In the vestibule is, oh fuck, Sonia. Well, I won't let her ruin what is a lovely night. She is alone, smoking, staring at the front door. I try to sneak past her, but of course that's impossible. I await her snarky greeting but instead get, "Sit with me. Please." So we sit on the step, facing the door. The door that Hector will have to come through. Eventually. We don't say anything to each other. At one point, she leans her head on my shoulder and cries softly. Her fleshy breasts rising and falling in anguish over a man she can't ever fully understand. I am tempted to tell her everything. What loyalty do I owe Hector? But I know the wreckage would be immense. Forget them, the children, who they both adore, would suffer. What if Sonia moved away with the children? My Moms would be broken hearted. So I sit there and let her cry, cause that's all I can do. When she finally stops and dries her eyes, I get up to go. "Adios loca."

Okay, moment of sympathy shot to hell.

"Man, why you gotta say that? Lemme ask you something, Sonia, what would you do if your son was gay?"

I, being no fool, hold on to the banister awaiting the incoming explosion that is Sonia Suarez. This gal is not known for her subtly in dress, make up or hair, so this is gonna be epic. But she is silent for a moment, like she's really thinking about it.

"If my son was a maricon, big if, but if he was, I would march in every maricon parade, go to his first maricon bar with him and kill the first maricon who ever broke his heart." All this to the faint strains of my Moms boleros upstairs. Damn, how can someone change right before your eyes?

"I hate it when you call me loca."

"But you are. And a big one."

"And you're a muffin top."

"And proud of it. I ain't no skinny mini. Hector likes him some meat."

She has no idea how right she is. "Who's taking care of the kids?"

"They're at my mother's."

After dropping off my bounty from Moms, I grab Sonia's hand and hustle her out to a cab.

"Where we going, loca?"

"You'll see."

I take Sonia to La Escuelita, drag, dance Latino heaven, with some of the fiercest music anywhere. Hector hates it, I don't know why, so I know we won't run into him. We are frisked as we enter which apparently tickles Sonia no end. She may be going in and out all evening for a little touchy feely. Sonia looks like she's tripping. Has she really never been to a gay dance club? Scandalous! The music is pumping thumping and I get us a couple of shooters but fuck she don't want to drink, girlfriend wants to dance, and I so get to it. The ultimate tension release is to explode yourself in dance. I pull her out on to the dance floor and Miss Thang is craaazy! When did she become Ann Margret? God, I didn't even know how much I myself needed this. Sonia's about to pop out of her top, but she is not gonna stop. This is oxygen.

This is survival. Me, the overage boy toy, her the muffin topped cheated on wife. Oh no, baby, tonight belongs to us.

A drag queen waves a dollar bill in the air and dances up to us. She slips the bill in Sonia's ample cleavage and squeals, "Omigod, they're so real!!!" and Sonia smiles so broadly her gums take over her face and fuck she's never looked more beautiful, at least to me.

By the time we leave, 3am, Ms. Sonia, as she is now known at La Escuelita has cleared forty four bucks. We get back home, but she hesitates before going upstairs.

"What will I tell Hector?"

"Just let him lick the sweat off you, then tell him you went dancing with me."

"You and me, we both know what it's like to be with a man that other people want," Sonia says to herself and to me.

"That's not my problem anymore." I say.

"I wish Hector would leave me. I can't leave him. I can't."

"He's not gonna leave you." I say to her as we share a look.

"Adios, loca."

"Adios muffin top."

And she disappears upstairs to the man she can't help loving and I go downstairs and play my boleros until dawn.

Dear Diary:

It is an unseasonably warm Saint Valentine's Day. Not currently my favorite holiday, for obvious reasons, and not my Moms either. We are standing on the back door of their building looking out at the vegetable garden that used to be my Pop's pride and joy...

"Ju gonna take care of it?" she asks.

"Uh, no. You?"

She gives me a look that basically covers everything from ignoramus to "have we just met?"

"So, what do we do? When it's Spring, I mean."

My Moms and I share a cigarette. I don't smoke but we are both so lost in the moment that when she absentmindedly passes her cigarette to me I absentmindedly take it. My cough/hack drops us back to the here and sadly now.

"I don't want it to look bad." She says.

"Me neither."

And again with the silence. The silence that speaks volumes. "Get rid of it." she finally says.

"All of it?"

She takes back her cigarette. "Esurprise me," she says and goes back inside. I walk out and circle the spot where my Pops forever left me. A few days later I'm with my boys having piraguas de guava with some vodka, which is what they must serve in the VIP section of Heaven.

"I want to put a rock garden in," I say.

"And paths," robpup adds.

"And a water feature." We all look at Hector, who kinda shrugs and looks down. "You know, like a tribute to your Pops."

"He gave us limes, remember? From that little tree over there. For our cuba libres when we went to Fire Island." Yeah, we all remember. And even though it's not cold we huddle together, just wanting to feel each other's warmth and maybe the warmth of my Pops acceptance of each and every one of us. All my brothers from other mothers, each one of them hoping to make peace with their own padres. So we get to work. From that day on, any time any of us had free that's where you would find us. A tribute to my Pops? Yeah, and maybe a tribute to their fathers too. Some of whom weren't so accepting about their gay hijos. We're not loud, we don't even play music, it's like we just want to be in our own worlds. When the cold returned we just bundled up and kept working. We dig, we wheelbarrow, we break nails, and we keep going. Jason leaves a couple of messages, but I don't get back to him. No time. I'm sure he thinks I'm sulking because of him and Eric but I don't care. Joel earns his "boy is he gay" card, by going through a pile of stones to find the absolute perfect one for each spot. Joe Bear comes over and without asking just joins in. Every so often I catch Sonia looking out her window at us and she makes the shape of a heart with her hands. I don't get it at first but then I realize the water fountain, excuse me, - water feature-, is surrounded by small stones that form a heart. The cynical, jaded, Thelma Ritter part of me wanted to just make a circle, but hey, who am I to break my Pops heart? We are done two weeks to the day that we started. Sonia and the kids come down and so does my Moms, who just sort of nods her head and looks around. And cause I'm still at heart a son, I can't help but ask her "Do you think Pops would have liked it?" And when she answers with "Sangano" she invests it with such sweetness, such love that I kinda, no not kinda, I blush. My little motley crew of workers have calluses on top of their calluses, we have, for the love of all that is holy, missed happy hours. You're never really a man until your father tells you you are, and tonight as I fall into bed beyond exhaustion I know, I just know, I am a man in my Pops' eyes.

Dear Diary:
Joel is on cloud 9! He has himself a job, at the Center no less! Oh yes! Apparently the man is a whiz with a ball cock -

I'll wait - it's a plumbing term! Sure it is. So is plumber's crack, which begat I'm sure plumber's helper, but in any case Joel has scored the job of Super with, get this, residential privileges. Yes, the pay sucks, but it's indoors, indoors, indoors! As we toast him at the Castle he and I lock eyes and volumes are said. I could never, even on my best day, be as strong as he is...

There is one teeny glitch in paradise. The Center's heating system is positively prehistoric and as such may not provide anything resembling warmth when this mild winter actually decides to bring us to our knees. So the Center has decided to hold a yard sale, an event from which they hope to raise at least 5 g's, which would just about be the down payment on the state of the art boiler they are dreaming about. The guys and I have all volunteered to bring stuff and help. robpup is donating a custom designed dog collar (don't go there), Victor is donating a slew of art deco mirrors, and I'm sitting here deciding which Prada shoes to wear with the ensemble I've put together. Next to me is the sex toy from work that I'm donating, and that was donated to me. That's what I'm bringing. Sand to the desert. I'm watching New York 1 News out of the corner of my eye and the temperature is about to take a nose dive by the end of the week. I check me out in the mirror and ask myself, my friend can either spend a winter in warmth or I can be a fashionista. I call Hector. Yes, he can borrow a truck from work. "What the hell for?" he asks.

I hang up, take a deep breath and wipe away a tear as I look around me. "Daddy loves you," I whisper.

The sale at the Center is a decidedly blah event. Sometimes I think as gay men we all have the same movie posters, bric brac and music, so how can we sell to each other? Ah, but that is about to change. A bombastic Hector is playing the truck horn as if he were the original Mambo King. He nabs us a spot in front and with his help I unload the first rack of my clothes. The couture that defined me. Outfits filled with memories and heartache, but such a part of me that until a couple of hours ago the thought of living without them would make me even less than I thought I was. The audible gasp when I bring in the first one tells me I at least had good taste in clothing. I tell Victor, Joe Bear and robpup to run out and help with the other racks. Nine. Nine clothes racks in total. I kept one for myself, that's it. Joel looks at me with a look I can't remember seeing on somebody's face before, at least not directed at me. And through the modern miracle of tweeters the Center is besieged. Clothes, my clothes, nix that shit Javi, clothes are flying off the racks. Music starts blaring, guys start stripping in full view to try on clothes and we're suddenly morphed into the fashion montage from Shirley Maclaine's "What a Way To Go!" As my clothes/past disappear before my eyes I take it all in. What the hell am I feeling? I can't pinpoint it until Joel stands in front of me, and my fuck buddy smiles and says, "I'm proud of you, Javi." Oh shit, that's it. I guess I'm proud of me, too.

Dear Diary:
The invitations to Jason and Eric's commitment ceremony (and yes, I want them committed) were hand delivered by someone who looked like a Disney footman. Even Hector got one...

"Do you think I can go stag?" He asks.

Victor hits him over the head and Hector blows him a kiss. "Enough with the flirting!" I scream at them, then looking at the toxic invitation in my hand, add, "And I'm telling you I'm not going."

"Me neither." Says robpup.

"Hell no!" Says Victor.

"Que se vaya al carajo!" Says Joel.

"You think they'll send a car for us?" Yep, that was my cousin.

"It's agreed then. None," and I deadeye Hector, "of us are going."

When I see Hector about to make a move on a new piece of man meat at the bar, I intercept him. "Hey puta."

"Con orgullo," he smugly replies.

"Why don't you call it an early night, go spend some time with your wife."

Hector totally blows me off, "Man, you don't even like Sonia."

He's right. I mean, one night of dance bonding does not a sister from another mister make, but I hate cheaters. "How would you feel if she had somebody else, huh?"

"Baby, the rain must fall." He answers, before disappearing into a mustache.

Back at the Dusty Springfield record that is my life, once their engagement is made public it is impossible to avoid Jason and Eric. It's like their publicist is on steroids. A constant barrage of coverage that is, except for the blissfully dead, unavoidable. There is no mention of me anywhere. Not that I expected it, but come on! I was part of Jason's life for twenty years. Kearn sends me a card that reads, "now do you believe it's over?." I throw the framed ticket stub I was going to give Jason on Christmas into the river. Finito.

I actually enjoy going to work and disappearing among the other fake apparatuses. Most people are so intent on making their purchases and not making eye contact that I am anonymous. At night I go home to Junior, we have a cocktail and I pop in a DVD I've borrowed from PB's and go to town. Not every night, you understand, just those nights when I'm a little extra lonely.

There is a banging on the door and Hector hollers, "Hey, Javi!"

I don't know what perverse sense of "oh fuck it!" propels me but I leave Junior bobbing for apples and throw on a robe and answer the door.

"Hey, can I use your computer? I was in the middle of a chat when Sonia and the kids got home."

"I don't have a computer."

"Yes you do. Don't be that way."

And once again, "fuck it" takes over. I lead Hector into the bedroom and introduce him to Junior. "This is what I brought home, not a computer. This gadget is the guy I'm seeing now, who won't leave me. This is my fucking husband now!" I, having gotten all this out of my system, suddenly feel more embarrassed than ever before. I clutch my robe to me like a shimmering virgin.

"Yo, cuz, I'd fuck that sweet ass of yours. You don't have to get a machine." I hit him on the shoulder, even as I mouth "thank you." I feel his hand on my ass and snap, "Knock it off!"

"How does it work?" I show him the remote.

"Wow, if you got two you could get it from both ends."

"Man, you're never satis-"

"I'm just saying. ...Can I?"

"No. You know, maybe you should get one for Sonia, for when you're not there."

"Now why would she want a dune when she's been on Mount Kilamanjaro?"

My eyes roll so far back they may never see daylight again.

Hector nods and says, " I'll let you get back to it."

"That's it. No nasty comments?"

"Hey, I never criticize somebody's sexual needs. Won't go there. You two have fun," he adds, without a trace of irony and leaves. Ah, Junior, why can't you be rich instead of just good looking? I stop Junior, he seems a little tired, maybe he could use a night off.

Dear Diary:
There is a total blackout in all five boroughs in the city we call Nueva York. An invitation to Jason & Eric's wedding = a total blackout. Yes, God's an old time Catskills comic...

PB and me are closing up shop when - zip! we are plunged into darkness. He is counting the day's take and I'm in the stockroom surrounded by dildoes in every size, shape and texture. If they were actually attached to men it would be like the back room of Hector's dreams. I keep saying, like an idiot, "excuse me" every time I bump into one.

"Hey, P.B., what's with the lights?"

P.B. immediately tells me that it must be some new punishment his mistress is dishing out for some dire sin on his part. The man literally lowers his head and stands in a corner awaiting her arrival. I, meanwhile, look out the door to a blackness only alleviated by the passing headlights of cars.

"Uh, P.B., I think it's a blackout."

"Damn! I was so looking forward to a good session."

His cell phone rings with a command from Mistress Daisy that he is to stay where he is. From the smile on that slave's face I can tell she'll be coming downstairs to administer some tough love. Welts, when you care enough to give the very best.

I wish him a painful night and head home.

Blackouts, for some reason, bring out the best in New Yorkers. People direct traffic, help people up and down stairs. Flashlights appear and disappear like shooting stars, as some savvy folk, after having lived through a blackout or two in the Big Manzana now carry them on their person like bottled water. The last couple of blackouts happened in the worst of summer as air conditioners set the city over the top into Disco Inferno. Everybody hot, sweaty and muggy. Well, not everybody, Jason and his crowd, which once included me, lived in glass palaces that provided us with all the power our greedy little hearts and needs could desire. Yes, cause I needed to see me some Entertainment Tonight. Now, it's Eric's turn to be cocooned from reality as I make my way through the snow and slush clutching the invitation that makes it official. He's won.

After having tiptoed home, my shoes were made for appearance's sake not actual walking, I see Sonia on the front stoop holding court with some neighbors.

"Your Moms upstairs with my kids," she calls out. I can't tell if she's in the block party feel of it all or standing guard like a lioness outside the Public Library. As if anyone would take her on.

"Hector's out helping his fellow man." Sonia, Irony, Irony, Sonia. Helping himself to his fellow man is more like it.

I should go in but I can't. I don't want to be alone with that invitation that finishes me and my past once and for all.

I go to the Castle and it's of course closed. What did I expect? They sure as hell weren't gonna top shelf everybody for free. I stay at the door for a second, my hand on the handle. Now what?

"Cabrona, don't Bogart the bottle!" I hear. Victor's in there! Salvation, here I come.

"Victor, it's me," I half yell half whisper. Don't want

everyone crashing the joint.

After a protracted silence and a request for a non existent password I scream out, "Open the fucking door, puta sucia!." I'm allowed in. Hector, ropbup and I sit by candlelight at the bar. It would be romantic if I were not wishing death on all things romantic.

"Pour" is the only word I say and Victor, even more impossibly beautiful by candlelight, does just that.

"I think this lighting is just perfect," Victor purrs.

"I can still see your crows feet, muñeco," Hector says and is thus relegated to rot gut.

Look at us. It could be the end of the world and we're together. Joe Bear is texting robpup every fifteen minutes from Jersey where he is putting a group of senior citizens through, I kid you not, "Footloose." Joe Bear's grandmother is the lead. A former showgirl with gams! gams! gams! who promises to knock them dead. And with this crowd she just might. I take the well worn invitation from my pocket and put it on the bar.

"Please, join us to celebrate our love..." robpup starts, then stops. Even in this dim lighting I can see him and Victor exchanging the pity look. Hector being the cousin who's remains will be found in the East River, grabs the invite and covers his mouth to stifle his laugh. What's not to love?

Victor puts a water tumbler in front of me and top shelfs me. "No," I hear myself say. "I can't drink this away."

"You can try cuz."

robpup tap dances a text to Joe B.

"He thinks you should go," robpup says solemnly.

I think he should mind his own business. It was his pendejo idea I go to their Christmas party and that just fucking blew up in my face. Everybody has advice. Everybody would live my life better than I have. I'm the reality show you see just to criticize every decision I make, okay getting dramatica, maybe I should drink up.

The candlelight sparkles against the glasses and bottles. It's kinda borderline beautiful. My head is feeling a little lighter now, my thoughts a little prettier as I hold the invitation over the flame. Ashes to ashes, dust to dust. After a beat Victor asks me to go with him to the back to get some more vodka. Now, there's a trip I will go on.

"Oooh, going to the back room?" Hector growls and pants at the same time.

Victor ignores him and I follow his voluminous derriere to the back. Okay, before it was a bubble, now it's a zeppelin, yet it's still perfectly proportioned.

Once we're alone Victor says, "We'll go with you," knocking me out of my trance like state. I say nothing, which means no.

"What do you want me to carry?" I ask. I. Will. Not. Go.

Victor bends over to get me a box for booze and -

"Child, I'm gonna get you a license plate for that bumper," I say, unable to help myself. He laughs. Just call me Javi, the topic killer. He puts the box in my hands and begins to fill it methodically with joy juice. Victor holds a flashlight with one hand as he scans the labels. As whenever he wants to share something with me, he is facing away from me.

"My cat died last week."

"I'm sorry," I say. Victor never struck me as the pet kind, but hey you never know.

"His brother had died a couple of weeks ago."

Two cats. Wow.

"I took Bamboo, that was the first cat who died, and got him cremated. I never let Max see his dead brother. I thought it would be easier. But what happens? Max spends all his time looking for Bamboo and crying. Cats can cry you know. I think I should have let him say goodbye. You know what I'm saying?"

"Uncap that thing and get me a straw," I answer, gesturing with my mouth to a bottle.

"Max needed to know that Bamboo was really gone. It was the not knowing that killed him. Go to their ceremony, see it through and then let go."

".....i'm gonna embarrass myself," I whisper so inaudibly even I can barely make it out.

"Yeah. But Gurl, you know when I make a swan dive into that chocolate fountain fondue, and they better have one, no one will be talking about anything else."

"Love you, Victor."

"Everybody does, 'ceptin me exes."

Dear Diary:

Thank God for Joe Bear and robpup. In the hoopla that is "the wedding" and trust me if I could use smaller lettering I would, Joe Bear and robpup are opening a show! A deconstructed or reimagined or better like this, better like that version of The Petrified Forrest. With robpup in the Humphrey Bogart role. Hold for laughter. It's a labor of love as Joe Bear makes his big money staging operas, but this is his gift to rob pup. Me personally, I would have gone with a subscription to Dog Weekly...

We are going to meet at the bar and go to the storefront theater together. We may be the only people there, but we're a loyal bunch.

"Shouldn't they be doing a revival of Benji or something?"

Please let's get this out of our system before we get there.

"No it should be Annie with robpup as Sandy!"

"Or how about A Tree Grows in Brooklyn!"

"I don't get it." Says Hector.

I sip my drink and study Hector. My boy is frazzled. He's off his game. He also doesn't want to go to a show unless there's nudity. How this man makes it through a music video I'll never know.

"Hey Hector, what's the matter?"

"Nothing."

I shrug, make as if to move, when he adds, "When you went dancing with Sonia did any guy come on to her?"

"Honey, please the girl made money."

"No, a real man, not a, you know."

"Sonia was the belle of the blue balls."

"Okay, she is not allowed back there. She's the mother of my kids."

"Hector, what the fuck is in your drink?"

He motions me in closer, "Not a word to anyone."

"Yeah fine."

"Some guy's in love with her."

"Yeah, you."

"No. Somebody else. Anonymous. He sent her a poem. Beautiful stuff. She cried when she read it. She hid the letter, I'm not supposed to know, so don't tell her."

"Wow."

"He writes like real old school piropos. I mean if I was a woman and I got those letters I'd be wet."

"Well that's cause you're a classy lady," I say.

"Lissen, I'm gonna go home. I'll see you guys tomorrow."

As I see Hector walk out with a newfound determination to tap his wife I know that the collection of boleros was a godsend.

Victor, meanwhile, is enjoying the sex life of a porn star. Whereas before it was stand back and admire and sending them home before the dawn's early light, his comfort in being seen as less than perfect has filled up his hootchie mama dance card to the max, and it couldn't happen to a nicer teletubbie.

When we get to the theater, Joel is already there, so is Kearn. Fuck, why can't I hook these two guys up? They totally avoid each other all night. That's just not right. In my Shirley Temple Little Miss Fix It world they, of course, belong together. We take our seats. It's sold out! Which at twenty eight seats isn't too hard to do. But I know that robpup has performed for an audience of three so this is the big time for him. The play starts, great set by the by, and then robpup, at least I think it was robpup makes his entrance. The thing with a small house is that the actors are right in your face, and I swear I don't see robpup in Rob. He is menacing, he is heartbreaking, he is flawless. He is the actor he was born to be. Like, all of a sudden, he emerged. That's the word. Emerged. He is so brilliant people can't even blink. Not showy, not big, just fucking perfect. We all sense it. We all feel it. This is why people go to theater, for the hope of a miracle like this. My childhood friend has become an actor with a capital A.

At the after party, people are literally clawing at robpup. Joe Bear stands to the side, and I catch "the man" crying in pride. His boi, his pup is a helluva actor.

robpup and I hold hands and he just smiles at my speechlessness. So many shared memories and dreams between us. "You still going to dance class?" he asks.

"Yeah."

"Good. Sometimes it takes a long time for a dream to get here. You look at everybody and it looks like their dreams are on the express track and yours are on the local, but you know, if that's the case, you might as well enjoy the ride."

Oh, robpup, you are my God!

Dear Diary:

I'm officially a cater waiter! Oh, like you didn't see that coming. Joel is in constant demand, what DOES he do with those canapés one wonders, and after mucho begging on my part and a promise of no more meltdowns, he's gotten me some gigs. This on top of my steady eddie work at PB's means that for the first time Javier Rivera AKA Javi has a bank account of his very own! Azucar! I'm saving up for a share with the guys in the Grove. A room I'll probably have to share with somebody, but hey half a slice of heaven is better than none, and these guys, please girl, son familia. Might even convince Moms to make a day trip.

Sonia is still getting her anonymous love letters which is driving Hector to distraction maximus. He's actually reduced the days he goes out, but he still hits the Castle. Man, it must be hard to truly be a bisexual. He loves Sonia, I finally really see that, but he loves dick too. Balance, I tell him, it's all about balance. Or as Victor says, "Nene, get her a strap on, problem solved." But that's not our Hector. Shit, if he ever found out I was the one sending Sonia the letters he'd kill me...

Joel and me are working a gallery opening in Soho, and unlike before I'm front and center, out with the guests and my tray. I smile and feel zero shame. Nada. And yeah, some people remember me from the JasonandJavier era, but I'm not that guy anymore. It's weird, I'm the one who has to put them at ease. Like yeah, I will make eye contact with you and you can make eye contact back. This is how I make my money now. Con orgullo. I even get cruised a couple of times, which I'm told is how you know you're a successful cater waiter.

Now, what kind of event would it be if the current "it" couple didn't make an appearance? Ay loca, you know me so well. Yep, there in all their gory are Jason and Eric. And I don't flinch. Jason nods in my direction and I nod back with a smile. Eric, on the other hand bounds up to me, "Javi!" Ah, he's yet to retire that exclamation point. "You look so nice!"

"Take something, baby, you have to take something from the tray." Whoa, did I just call him baby?

He follows me on my round until Jason literally pulls him away. Of course someone took a photo to immortalize the moment. Me serving him. And Eric turns just at the right moment, like he had planned this photo op in his dreams. Que se va hacer? What can you do?

Joel makes sure I'm okay, which is super sweet but unnecessary. He waits until we're alone to whisper, "I'm kinda seeing somebody."

"Joel, you puta sucia, since when?"

"Few weeks."

"Tan secretive."

"I don't wanna rush it."

"You love him?"

Joel shrugs and says, "I've seen that don't necessarily mean anything, but yeah, I think so."

"Well, don't go by me, but take it easy, take your time." As Joel is about to head out with a new tray, I ask him the 64 billion dollar question. "He love you?"

"Better. He gets me."

The night and the wine go on, people are just not leaving. Except for Eric who apparently goes home alone in the car. What's up with that?

"Jason's hitting the chardonnay a little hard." Joel tells me.

Shit. He's not a drinker. When he does imbibe he goes one of two ways, he falls asleep or he gets angry. Pretty. As midnight approaches there are only a couple of stragglers left so I mosey up to Jason.

"Hey, were closing up shop. Where's the toddler? Past his bed time?"

"I'm buying something."

"Oh, okay."

"For you."

Awkward! "For Eric," I correct him.

And he leans into my face and says, "For you.," as if he were defying me. I take him and his white wine breath in.

"You sleep with Kearn?" Jason blurts out.

"Oh, so not your business," but then I can't help myself and add, "no."

"Knew it!" He proclaims a little too triumphantly. He moves suddenly, almost losing his balance and in the sweepstakes choice of grabbing on to me or the wall for balance, he picks the wall. Wise man.

"You're coming to the wedding." He says this as a statement, not a question.

I having been going back and forth on this and today's one of the uh uh days. "No." I answer. I turn to leave, then add, "You know, the money you were gonna spend on that painting for me, give it as a donation to the homeless."

"Don't tell me who to give charity to. I give to a ton of charities." He snaps.

"Fine." I raise my hands up in a you win gesture. He's right, Jason is an extremely generous and caring man. For a second Jason looks like he's about to cry. His eyes look haunted. I know those eyes.

"I want the painting." he says.

"Jason, go home. The painting will be here tomorrow."

"Yeah, the painting will….."

"That's what you want, the painting. The painting is for sale."

And I leave, I don't even change. Joel and I ride the subway back together. It's odd, while I remember some of what was said, what I really remember the most was what remained unsaid.

Dear Diary:
The Mentos commercial that is my life took a decided turn

to the "there just isn't enough alcohol to live through this." Jason's fumble at the gallery haunts me. I was done, I was moving on, okay I was trying to, but how can I heal in a city where Jason is just a 'fancy meeting you here' away. Ah, but when you arrive at this sub sub basement in your life - and by the by, some wild paisley curtains would totally rock this place - yes, once Hades is a flight UP from your current domicile, dearest of Diaries, it is your friends that will unlock the trap door sending you further into oblivion. Or more precisely, one friend. Let's give it up for the nearly dearly departed, Joel...

"Desgraciada! Have I got news for you! This will put a boner of a smile on your face."

Okay, I'm intrigued. So he continues.

"You know the Center for the Gay, Lesbian, Bisexual, Transgender, Questioning and MWSLM?"

"The one with the long sign?"

"Exactly, cabrona."

We are walking around the East Village in heavy parka winter coats. Put us in a fundoshi and we'd look like padded sumo wrestlers. Oh wait, redundant.

"What the hell is MWSLM?" I ask, trying to navigate through a corner snow drift. Ah, I love me some winter.

"Men who sleep with men, sangano."

Silly me, I thought certainly that would have been covered somewhere in that mile long sign at the building's entrance.

"Okay, so the Center needed a fund-raiser and I immediately thought of you and your rolodick of the super rich-"

"Sweet."

"Of course no one will return your calls, but you were the inspiration for my fund raising idea."

I'm aging just waiting for him to get to the point.

"We are going to do a one night revival of 'FUEGO!'"

I stop dead in my tracks.

"The owner of the rights of the show donated them."

"FUEGO," I repeat so softly there is no way Joel could hear me. Not that he'd stop, he's on a roll.

"And it'll be like a kinda staged reading, kinda concert version-"

I hit him. Hard. This is no love tap. I punch him on the arm as hard as I can, knocking him over.

"Cabron!" we BOTH say.

By the sheer force of my blow, and by the fact that we are both standing on ice, I join him on the snow covered ground where I'm sure we look like sea lions trying to hit each other through mittens.

"You crazy or something?!" Joel screams.

"FUEGO?! FUEGO! mother fucker!" I scream back as I hit him again.

"Ouch!"

Forget the fund-raiser, we coulda sold tickets to this little piece of street theater.

"Okay, wait! That hurt!" Joel says before finally pinning me down.

The slapstick portion of the show is now over, on to mime! I give Joel the finger, which through a mitten is an exercise in infutility.

"You got all that FUEGO! shit and that's why the show popped into my brain. They're inviting everybody in the original production to participate, so that means you too, loca boricua."

He gets off me and for a second we just sit there, breathing heavy and staring at each other. We both wanted to do the nasty right there but cooler heads and butts prevailed. We are both silent as we help each other up, trying to find some traction in the slushie street.

We walk silently for maybe like three blocks before I finally say, "Gracias, I think."

"De nalga," he replies.

Trudge, trudge, trudge.

Dear Diary:

The FUEGO! meeting has been postponed three times (maybe they should change the name to CENIZAS!) and I have used every delay to diet, exercise and drink far less than before. I've taken a picture of me from my "FUEGO!" days and have taped it to the fridge. That is the goal, baby. I will WILL my way back to the past. I want to walk into that meeting and wow them. And then I'll invite Jason to the show, let him see me and HAH! it's hasta la vista, baby...

I'm really buckling down on my dancing classes, too. Pushing myself past the "ow, it hurts" to "I can't feel my legs!" And unbeknownst to todo el mundo, I am going to do my signature move. Yes, wait for it, I am going to do my full airborne leap. Yep, I'm that guy. Oh yes. I learnt it once I can learnt it again. The first time I try it or attempt to try it, I freeze. I do the walk, get to the point where I should be airborne, but I choke; and not in a good way neither. And I never should have tried to get into my costume. After a couple of false starts I was finally able to squeeze myself into it. I looked in the mirror and realized I had beaten Sonia at her own muffin top game. No jodas. What the hell was I? A 26 inch waist or something? So, I didn't exactly approach my move with the confidence of a Rican Stallion. But I won't be dissuaded. I redouble my at home work outs and runs and scrounge together the money to rent space at my dance school. I was insane to try my move at home. I need the high ceilings (and mirrors! Hello gorgeous!) that dance studios provide. I surround myself with every mat I can find and juevos to the wall I fly! Except, opps, I didn't do it again. My body, in a particularly sadistic mood, lets me take the leap but the landing is a crash. I land HARD! on my side. Those mats are for shit. My crash landing is loud enough so that a young dancer pops his head in.

"Are you okay?" he asks, what to him must look like a senior citizen in a fetal position.

"Oh yeah," I whimper, trying to save some face.

But he runs out, screaming "Who knows the number for 911?!"

And laying there, in my pain, I laugh, hurting my ribs. Fuck.

Dear Diary:

Okay, the ribs are bruised but not broken, but tell that to the excruciating pain. The FUEGO! meeting is finally set in stone. A week from tomorrow. A week in which my damaged self keeps me from exercising and making me only want to eat comfort food. Moms obliges, the woman is deep frying water, and suddenly I am seven pounds heavier than when the FUEGO! rebirth first reared its ugly head. I'm not fat, but I'm not going to fit in those shorts without undergoing some MAJOR surgery...

The meeting itself is at the Center and after having agonized over an appropriately slimming outfit I arrive in basic black to a much smaller group than I expected. After those of us who showed up lie and tell each other that we haven't changed a bit, we realize we're it. No more FUEGO!ites. Esto fue lo que trajo el barco.

Cheo, the one surviving member of the creative team, arrives and he was at least smart enough and rich enough to have himself refreshed surgically. His face looks like Joan Rivers bungee jumping in a wind tunnel. "We've lost so many of our family," Cheo tears up, or tries to without the presence of tear ducts. "We're what's left."

We all look at each other and without having to say it, know what has thinned our musical theater herd in the last couple of decades. We go from "Gurl, you look good" to the Supremes "Someday We'll Be Together."

Cheo pretends to remember each of us as he goes around the room airkissing us and hugging us. He gets to me and squeals, "El backflip!"

"Actually," I try to correct him, "it was a front fl-"

"So you married rico, right? I should totally write a show just for you!"

Ye gods! He doesn't know I've been sent to the showers. "We broke up," I say, keeping it simple if not sweet.

"Oh." And he and his interest move on as I return to my role of background dancer. I pretend to read a burnt at the edges "No Smoking" sign until my awkwardness settles.

While this is going to be a one time only fund raising event Mr. Nipped and Tucked is treating it like "FUEGO!: the Second Coming!" He is trying desperately to infuse us with his enthusiasm and some, I notice, drink the kool aid. Mostly the ones like me, for who FUEGO! was their only Broadway credit. Jesus Maria y Jose, one of my fellow chorus boys even managed to squeeze himself into his original costume. Is that what I would have looked like? He bounces over to me, his over-hair-sprayed hair the only part of him that doesn't move.

"Javi!" he squeals. Oh good, we're about to bond.

"Remember me?!"

Barely, but of course I say, "Yeah, of course. You look great!" Sure it's a lie. YOU tell him the truth.

"I'm Ruben!!!! I haven't seen you since the show closed,

well not in person I mean. I'd see you all the time in the society pages, I was so proud of you!"

This?! is Ruben?, I think. "And I know you guys broke up, but I know in my heart of hearts that you are going to meet someone even better when we do FUEGO! again."

"It's just one night," I gently remind him.

"Oh no! We're going to be picked up and moved back to Broadway! You know, we should do some stretching exercises." And down he flops on the floor. He's weird but he's limber, I'll grant him that. I remain standing, a little self consciously at having this human pretzel at my feet.

"I do daily self affirmations and that's why I know that FUEGO! has reentered our lives to laden us with abundance!" Okay, the man said 'laden'. "I can't wait to see you do your airborne turn! You are gonna rock it!" I don't want to tell him that it might take a rocket just to get me off the ground. "That's the plan," I tell him. "I'm still working on it." "Oh no," he tells me, "you can do it. I know you can do it. You have to see yourself doing it." Now I suddenly don't want to leave his side but the meeting disbands after a final round of self masturbatory compliments. "You look fabulous!" "No, YOU look fabulous!" we leave with the agreement that a) we are all doing this for free, b) we will have exactly eight hours of rehearsal and c) most importantly this is not a backer's audition. We all nod solemnly at this but the room is heavy with the seductive aroma of possibility, even if it is ridiculous and unlikely. The Drill Sergeant, excuse me, stage manager, gets our info and reminds us costumes are our responsibility.

"Try to recreate your original look at much as possible but don't," and here he eyes Ruben, the oblivious contortionist still astretching at my feet, "get carried away."

I take the subway home and just like in A Letter to Three Wives, the train tracks seem to whispering 'what if...what if....what if....'

Dear Diary:

Okay, I have been working on my trick for a week and still cannot do it. The missing ingredient is fearlessness. Back then I either didn't know or didn't care that I could break irreplaceable parts of my body trying to master this foolishness. Now I'm very aware that I'm not a kid anymore, certainly not the kid who thought that maybe, just for a second, he could fly. I have to do this. There is no other option. My boys are going, even Hector, if for no other reason than just to hector me...

"Now, you all know we'll just have eight hours of rehearsal," I warn.

"You're gonna stink!," yep, Hector is rehearsing, too! Who knew.

The gauntlet she be thrown. My one bit in the show, the one thing that made me stand out and I can't do it. I feel a hollow predictability to it, this. Of course I can't do it. Why should I be surprised that I CAN'T do it.

The rehearsal and the show are scheduled for tomorrow. I crawl home from trying to recapture my past glory and get into bed. Parts of me hurt that I had forgotten existed. I lie in the darkness and make deals with God, something I haven't done since well, God knows when. "Please God, just let me do this flip and I'll 'insert Your request here'. Then I think, while in some things I have been insanely lucky, I can honestly say I have never gotten what I prayed for. Even if it was stupid stuff. No go. Do other people get their prayers answered? Cause I can't be the only one with a 'no fly zone' for prayers. So why ask God at all if His mind is already made up? It was my destiny to have everything that has happened to me and continues happening, happen. God is not gonna change His mind and I'm guessing He won't be micromanaged, but because I have run out of options, I am forced to pray again. Ask a heavenly Father, who while I still believe in Him, too many years of catholic school, saints and rosaries not to, I don't believe praying is gonna make any dif at all. The die is cast. We are all living out our predetermined life, so do I think the Big Guy is gonna veer? Stay the course! My free will, while a fashionable accessory don't you know, doesn't change a damn thing.

But I still light a candle to Saint Judas, the saint of impossible causes, the next morning and beg/pray for one more shot of flying. Because it was the only thing that I ever did that impressed people.

Dear Diary:
Tonight's the night. Help. S.O.S. Auxilio. Socorro...

Rehearsals begin at the crack of noon, because some of our merry little troupe are still equity members, if only the dues paying kind, we are allowed x number of hours to rehearse. Out of what was once a twenty member cast we are down to nine original cast members (original being the accepted word after the person who suggested 'old' was tarred and feathered). Being short 11, a bouncy, new and YOUNG group will arrive to join us in two hours. They will learn everything in half the time and look better doing it, so our director Kiki (yes Kiki) cracks the whip. We stretch, we vocalize. This is only supposed to be a glorified concert version with movement (who wrote that blurb) but we are, all of us, stupidly hopeful about it. I too have caught the FUEGO! fever of yore. What if, by some miracle (there I go again, praying to God, but who else have I got?) the show should get a full on revival? I would come full circle and have my first job again and get the magical chance to relive my life if not my youth. Okay, definitely not my youth. During our precarious run through, which thanks to tantrums and tears, none of them mine dear Diary, I am a professional, the newbies arrive just before my bit. I look out at them and it's like a sea of Erics. They all know each other and while they smile and make nice with us, it is the politeness of the young, who know we are anchors who are going to slow them down. We go back to the top of the show. They know all the songs, having studied the soundtrack, and the dance steps I struggled so hard to learn the first time out, they pick up by just standing behind us and imitating us. I take them in and then I look at us and feel, what? embarrassed for us?

The senior cast has squeezed themselves into Capezio dance wear that we have been holding onto for close to twenty years. We all look so dated. For us, this is a special occasion, for them it's a quickie job.

We again arrive at my point of take off and the only thing louder in my head than my prayer is my heart beating. Please! I have to be like a kite, I have to soar!!! I see myself, I'm doing the walk, going for my ta-da! moment, the one that defined me and my life and I fall. Fail. Fall. Fail. They are almost the same word. I am immediately helped up and after having relearned how to blush, I'm sure this one's a beaut. One of the younger dancers says, "I think you just need a step ball change before it and you'll be good." And of course, the mother fucker demonstrates.

Another dancer says, "Oh, you mean like this?" and another UFO is launched. Pretty soon it seems that every male under 25 is yo yoing before my eyes. Kiki loves it and picks Billy to do my step as I stand next to him. I say nothing. I think I sorta nodded, but I'm not sure. How can I say anything? I am no longer here. This is worse than Vavoom. This is me on the side of milk cartons. This is a total bon voyage to who I was with nothing to replace me with.

I can sense some of the others waiting to see which way the wind of my ego will blow. Cause child, I can tell you some of the guys here would have gone all Christian Bale on Kiki, but I know I can't do it, so I graciously/unconsciously take a step back just when I should be taking a step forward and let the youngster fly.

The day, the rest of it, moves quickly. It's too late to uninvite my boys, so I give Joel one job, uno. Contact them and tell them I am officially an extra in my life. I am wall-paper, they, the new boys, are screen savers. I think to tell my Moms not to bother coming but she's gone and had her hair did so that's outta the question. Because I am not doing the jump I refuse to wear the costume. Tank top, cut offs and high tops? Really? Not this little black duck. The boy closest to me and I switch clothes. I am stuck with a dull gray guayabera and jeans that are way too big while he is finally wearing pants that land on his waist. I could just wear what I wore to rehearsal, but this is somehow better. This completes the disappearance of Javier Rivera, nee Javi, nee gone gone so gone. Happy/Desperate hour cannot get here soon enough. I've gone from hoping for a packed house to an audience of a merciful few who will hopefully be generous enough of spirit to accept that the role of "airborne boy" usually played by yours truly has been handed off to Javi 2.0. And because I've disappeared I'm no longer there when we're backstage getting ready. Some of my contemporaries, the ones not sharing their rapidly dimming limelight with their younger counter parts are slathering on their make up with a trowel. I am bare faced. Not even eye brow pencil, which is just elemental good grooming. The one thing, the one thing I brought to the party is no longer mine to give. So I'm still here because...? Of my friends. My Moms. All of which will be out there expecting me to be the original me. I will use my time on stage as a wallflower to come up with a suitable story as to why I'm no longer allowed to play me.

Places, please. Death was never so polite.

We hit our places and the lights come up. The show is a mess, but it was always a mess, something I couldn't see back then. FUEGO!! was never a plot driven show - oh please! - a salsa club owner and a disco owner overcome their initial mistrust and create, wait for it, FUEGO!! No, it wasn't much in the way of theater, but it was my escape from years of bullying and teasing so the mother fucker always had a soft place in my heart. But now, seeing her as an aging hooker who's still trying to cadge a free drink at the bar, I can't help but feel sorry for her.

The creators of the show sit in the audience, laughing louder and longer than anybody else. I don't look out. I avoid all eye contact with, as Norma Desmond would put it, 'those people in the dark'. There are no Jason eyes out there to land in. Why bother?

Billy does his/my flip to gasps and a smattering of applause. Applause that once belonged to me. He gives me a 'we did it!' smile and I make a mental note to skin him alive and join AARP, in that order.

The rest of the show plods on. We sing, we dance, both to varying degrees of quality. I know I would care more if I were actually here. The show ends. We have one big cluster fuck of a curtain call to a standing O led by, surprise surprise! the director and then we are at liberty to mingle with our guests and accept their compliments on steriods.

"You were the best one up there!"

"Boy, you really have stage presence!" (hey, they're

reaching, okay?)

"Better luck next time, cuz!" I did mention Hector was coming, didn't I?

As Victor and Joel find silly things to compliment me on, robpup just holds my hand. It means the world to me. I search out my Moms and she is crying, crying okay.

"Ju look eso much like jour father in that guayabera."

My Moms didn't even notice I didn't do my signature move. All she noticed was that I reminded her of the man she loved/loves.

I head out with them, my crew, my entourage and there at the curb is the limo. I don't even have to check the plates, I know it's Jason. "Come on," says robpup, pulling me away from the mouth of a volcano, but I pull away, assure him I'll be okay and I'll catch up to them in a few. "Just take care of my Moms," I say. "Take care of you," he answers, and much against his better judgment leaves me.

I walk slowly to the limo. Eric may still be laughing, I'd hate to interrupt; but I get there and it's just Jason.

"Hey," I say.

"Hey," Jason says. We both see me look for Eric, we both don't acknowledge it.

"You didn't do the flip."

"His name is Billy. I can get you his number if you like." I see Jason flinch, just a little bit. "No, I…." he fumbles. Now I could get all angry at him, but why? Just to bring me back to the land of the living, but I can see that I've honestly hurt him. And I love him. Still.

"You. You didn't even look up much." Jason says, not looking up.

I am holding on to the side of the rolled down window for dear life. It's like I've aged overnight before his eyes.

"You didn't do the leap and you weren't wearing your shorts-"

I reach into the car to hold his hand, but he pulls back.

What is he afraid I'm gonna hit him? "I didn't do the leap and I didn't wear the shorts cause I'm old, Jason. Say it with me, Javi you be old."

He looks away. I think this truth hurts him more than it hurts me. I pull my hand back, wave and walk away. I don't turn around so I have no idea if he stayed looking after me or just left. And I finally got it, the reason I had to go to Jason and Eric's ceremony. I wasn't the one who had to let go, it was Jason. He will never fully move on until he lets go of the Javi that I once was. I'm not that boy anymore. It's time for Jason, not me, to say "adios."

Dear Diary:

Today we are gathered here together for Lorraine's wedding. Her eighth. Since Jason and me became a couple, oh three years ago, she has had seven, count 'em, seven husbands. God only knows how many marriages there were before I entered the scene. So far, she's had one each from our armed forces, an actor, a model and a waiter (and really, just one usually covers all three of those categories) and today's special who is old enough to be her son? grandson?

Lorraine's age was of an indeterminate amount and she'd sooner remarry an ex that give up her real age. But she was a "hopeless" romantic as she called herself, albeit one who invented the iron clad prenup. Although all of her formers left with lovely parting gifts she was not so "hopeless" as to give them one red cent more than she thought they deserved. Well, there was that one ex that got his own villa in la bella Italia, but he apparently had a tongue that could lick stamps from across the room...

We were standing around at the after party/before divorce

event and Jason went off to drop off our gift. He sadistically always gives her the same thing. The most exquisite, most expensive personalized stationary that he must know will have the shelf life of a gnat. Every one of Lorraine's wedding ceremonies was more elaborate than the one before it, so she was currently up to the Versailles level. He, the groom (and I came to see that learning their names was pointless) sat across the room, ignoring all women. Hey, this one was smart! and chatting up a politico. Lorraine sidled up to me.

"Boo," she said.

Oh.

"Billion for your thought," she joked. At least I thought she joked.

"Nice wedding," I smiled. She beamed through her bee stung lips. She was always happiest at her weddings or her divorces.

"Excuse me a moment," she said, and then moved her current husband from seat A to seat B, like maybe six inches. She kissed him, copped a feel, oh yeah, she's a hopeless romantic and returned to stand by me. Her view of him now unobstructed.

"He's brand new and I just have to look at him." She smiled, and then revealed perhaps a bit more of herself than she intended. "Why can't he just stay new? Is that too much to ask?"

"You don't stay new," I dared to venture.

"I don't have to. Neither does Jason, neither does Kearn. Oh, and neither do you." This last statement clearly an addendum. Then she really studied me for a second. "I'm going to give you the number of my surgeon. He's fabulous."

I was barely twenty three years old.

Bitch.

But the lesson had landed. Stay young! Stay shiny! Stay new! And above all don't change. Right now I was exactly who I'm supposed to be for the rest of my life. World without end, amen.

I close my old diary, and you know, it's the first time the past hasn't broken my heart. Some good memories, some bad, but none, no matter how hard I try, that I can recapture.

That was then, this is now.

It's early am and I'm getting ready for the car that will drive me up to the napalm nuptials. I'm going up solo, my boys will be coming early tomorrow, but tonight, tonight starts the official demise of all things JasonandJavier. I look in the mirror and see myself. And I kind of see my father's face, with a little mix of my mother's thrown in. I am shaving and have to keep the door open so the steam doesn't fog up the mirror. My bathroom is so small a broom would be insulted to call it their closet, and yet it's mine. I think to myself, I should get some colored tea lights in the dollar store to brighten the window shelf, and that's when it hits me, I finally think of this place as my home. Not as a stop gap on the way down from what was paradise, but my home. And that guy in the mirror, the me there, I kinda like him. No, no kinda about it. I like him. He's the me I haven't seen since in forever. Sonia interrupts my fan club meeting of one.

"Hey," and she catches herself before she says "loca," we've been kind of trucing it lately, "you got any coffee?"

She heads directly to the machine and wipes out what's left. She is wearing toreador pants and a halter, so I'm assuming she just dropped off the kids at school.

"There's a car waiting for you outside."

"I'm almost ready." I'm running around gathering stuff as Sonia shares my coffee with me.

"The boy's in the car."

Oh God, he's gonna ride up with me? "His name is Eric."

"His name is puta."

That's it, I'm switching to decaf.

"Why you goin'?" she asks, and I just sort of shrug.

"Maybe you dislike him cause he broke me and Jason up and you would hate anybody who broke up a couple."

"So you done fighting for Jason?"

I see in some strange way it unnerves her to think I've given up the ghost. It just reminds her she could never leave Hector.

"S'matter, you don't love him anymore?"

At that moment little Eric joins us, all smiles and light.

"Surprise!!!! Sorry, I just wanted to see if you needed any help with anything." He beams.

Sonia and he eyeball each other. He with his perpetual blinding grin, her with a coffee mug barely concealing her scowl. Ah, so introductions are in order.

"Sonia, this is Eric."

"Uh huh." And read into her response what you will.

"Eric, Sonia is sorta my sister in law." Me calling Sonia that visibly softens her.

"Wow," Eric says taking in all of the Sonia, "you could be a calendar girl in your outfit."

What can I say, Eric shoots and scores. He grabs one of my bags and exits to the car as I follow him out. Eric and me. How so very cozy.

Dear Diary:
Give me strength...

We're in Claryville. The place where Jason and me were supposed to become the old gay couple on the hill. But I've been 'ahem ahem' "recast." Jason finds every reason known to a (desperate?) man to touch Eric in front of me. His neck, his torso, his butt, it's like he's trying to read him in Braille. For what? My benefit? If he's trying to prove he can't keep his paws off him, mission accomplished. Yeah, I get it. He's brand new. Very lovely. Oh, and that new car smell! I don't care but I see he still wants me to care, cause what? it won't be a real blowout without a full out nervous breakdown from yours truly?

If Eric is nervous at having me around Jason, he doesn't show it. The tater tot even goes to bed early, leaving Jason and me sitting in front of the fire. On far sides of the same couch. We are nursing a brandy. "How are the dance classes going?"

"I'm not the worst one in the class anymore. And I'm not the oldest either."

"Cloris Leachman join the class?"

"Bitch." We laugh. "Thanks again for coming. It means the world to Eric." I shrug. "You seeing anybody?" I think of Junior, smile and say "No."

"I've made a lot of mistakes in my life," he says. Where is this coming from, I wonder. "Me too," I say.

"I'd hate the idea of one of us standing over the other one's casket and just being filled with remorse." He says staring at me.

"Maybe we should have had cognac." I say and Jason laughs. He gets my jokes. Still.

"You know, the fact that we broke up when we did meant I got to spend more time with my Pops, I probably saw him more this last year than the twenty years you and me were together. So something good came of it. And I have these friends who love me and I work, support myself. I wanna say also," and here my voice kinda cracked, "I'm sorry I let go of my dream, that wasn't your fault, that was mine." Jason grabs my foot, nods. This is what history feels like. "The way you behaved when my father died…" and I trail off. There are no words to tell him what his being there meant to me.

"I loved your father, very much." Jason says. Then he looks at me and adds, "To see you happy I would eat rocks."

I smile, "I could never get that one either."

"No, I get it. I would do the impossible, I would suffer to see you happy. That's what he meant."

Jason takes a mighty sip, "Okay, full disclosure, I'm on Viagra now."

"Okay, full disclosure right back at you, you were taking it during the last couple of years we were together."

And that's how the night goes. We laugh and talk and share. We take turns feeding the fire and when the wood is gone sit and stare at the embers. Sometimes the memory of something can be just as beautiful as the real thing. Then he says, and I know it comes from the heart, "Javi, I'm sorry." We sit, quietly, watching as the fire slowly dies out.

That night Jason and Eric have sex so loud that it could wake up the six feet under crowd. Plenty of "Oh Jason!" "Oh Eric!" just in case I had somehow developed temporary amnesia and forgotten just how madly in love these two little bunnies were. I'm surprised Jason hasn't parked them right outside my room. I fall asleep to the sounds of vintage Donna Summer love making and I don't dream a thing. Not a thing.

Dear Diary:

My boys arrived, and yes, I'm now including Hector among my boys (standards, where fore art thou) early next morning. All except Joel who has been MIA'ing it big time lately. Hector, robpup, Joe Bear and Allan Carr (I mean Victor) were freshly limoed and sloshed and all care and concern. They were truly a sight for this sore heart. I gave them the grand tour, as if I still co owned the place...

The day is a blur, a lot of smiling through tears and the like, you know, survival. I have to shoo my friends into enjoying the festivities. Party hearty! Free booze. Look, Victor, buffet bar! rob pup, he of the pastel leather dog collar, and who says you can't take a fetish too far, corners me and says, "Okay, what's up?"

"Nothing."

"You've been Miss Mannering it since we got here. Omigod, loca, you're going to kill Eric aren't you? Javi, you're here and that's wonderful, but come on, I've only been with Joe Bear for six months and if he left me I'd track him down and kill him."

"He would do the same for you."

"God willing. So how is it possible that you can be floating around here as if all were right with the world?"

"Let's dance."

And we do to Giselle's "Lo Quiero a Morir (I Love Him To Death-who is DJing this mother fucker?!) a salsa song born for us hip swinging latins, me and my oldest friend hit the dance floor. I look up and there's Jason on the balcony, smiling at us. Just like at the gay pride dance, only a few months ago, only a lifetime ago. I extend my arms out to him and invite him to join us. Jason's always been a tentative dancer. Shy at first, 'people are looking at me make a fool of myself', then really getting into it. He's on the cusp. One salsa step away from entrega total when Eric enters the balcony. I extend my arms to Eric who smiles broadly at me, but then shifts his death gaze to Jason. With the music and the distance there is no way I can tell what Eric is saying but it isn't pretty. Jason skulks back into the house while Eric stomps his feet and in TEARS heads off in the other direction. Oh dear Diary, pre wedding day jitters and Eric's losing

255

it. Fetus, I'm here to give the groom away, I'm no longer in the running. You've won.

Eric, dear sweet Eric, has somehow found a way to merge faun and pitbull into the same jittery package. Hang on to your seats, folks! Next mood change in fifteen seconds, that's fifteen seconds! The closer we get to the exorcism, uh wedding, the more Glenn Close he becomes. Why? I'm doing all the heavy lifting. All he has to do is nuzzle with Jason. But, see that's the thing. I don't think Jason's all of a sudden is so mad desperate to hang out with me as much as I think he doesn't want to be around Eric.

I know (trust me diary, after twenty years, boy do I know) how Jason is when he's angry or upset or confused. He disappears into himself. He vanishes right before your eyes. And that's what he's doing with Eric. Poof. Jason's gone. And Eric, child what is up with you?, Eric seems to delight in pushing Jason's buttons. Like he's testing him or something. So I run upstairs to comfort Eric who has vanished, and then return to defend Eric to Jason who just looks down and walks away. Hello? Am I the only sane one here. I go in search of Eric to soothe his shattered nerves, and search is the operative word here. This is the only "cottage" I know of that could benefit from a GPS. I hear Eric, before I see him. He is belting it out to the balcony in a nails on blackboard voice.

"Eric! My name is Eric!!!! It's not Javi, it's ERIC!!!!!!!!!!!! !!!!!!!!!!!!!!!!!!!" He screams at Karen, one of the maids, who is trying to disappear into herself. Eric knows I'm behind him from the look on Karen's face. He turns to face me.

"Honey, the staff just knew me for a long time, that's all. They're not trying to disrespect you." I say, looking at his face. This lovely face that for a second looks like an older, harder version of its cherubic owner. He dismisses Karen with a wave of his hand (oh, when did he learn to do that?)

and faces me.

"Jason called me Javi while we were-"

I cut him off, "I don't need the exact description of the act. You were in an intimate moment."

"No," he corrects me, "we were FUCKING and he calls me Javi."

So that's why he blew up at Jason.

"I'm sorry," I say. What the fuck am I apologizing for? And Eric doesn't say anything. Not a thing. He just walks away.

At the end of the day I am emotionally exhausted. Worse than physically tired, heart tired. Why do I still love Jason? That's the question that keeps me up at night, here in this guest bedroom with the most expensive bedding I've been in since I, we broke up. I'm back in the lap of luxury, temporarily, and the man who gave it all to me in the first place and then took it away is just down the hall with his future husband, and I still can't hate him. Nah. I can't hate Jason. And I've tried. Believe me. Every old corny love song I know plays like a loop in my brain, but the one that digs its groove into my soul is "Can't Help Lovin Dat Man Of Mine." Cause when you do, when you really do, and you can't lie to yourself about it anymore, there's a weird kind of peace in knowing the truth. Yeah. I love Jason. I will ALWAYS love Jason.

My boys join me in my bed for a slumber party/wake. "How you holding up, cuz," Hector asks, with something actually resembling concern. I shrug.

"Think we'll get a show tonight?" Joe Bear asks. He knows.

I nod, and almost as if cued by a porn autuer the "Oh Jason's" begin. Louder than last night, well he does have a packed house after all. Pero aguanta, there is no call and respond this time. The duet has become a solo. No "Oh Eric's" only "Oh Jason's" with muffled "ssshhh's" where Jason's verse should be. Oh, now he's embarrassed? A perverse side of me wants to scream out "Sing out Louise, sing out!" but I fight it. Good night, Jason. Good night, Eric. Good night, John Boy.

Dear Diary:
So we're down to the wire. In two days Jason will take Eric in wedded bliss, only it's been anything but blissful, more like blistick. Eric's on edge. Jason seems to be avoiding him like the plague and yesterday I saw why…

The blow up. The guests had been taken on a tour and we, Jason, Eric and myself, were having a small late lunch when he threw a plate full of salad across the room, the tantrum of a two year old. Only this brat was 21 years old and his name was Eric.

"Croutons?! Croutons are carbs! Why is everybody against me in this house?!"

Gee bridezilla, no idea.

"Just eat around them," said Jason, with a patience that had most definitely seen better days. And that's when the plate went airborne.

Connie the maid, tight lipped and muttering something under her breath in a Slavic language, bends down to clean the salad autopsy but Jason stops her. Turning to Eric he says three little words that are definitely not I love you. "Clean that up." There are only three of us at lunch, but by Jason's tone I can tell he wouldn't have cared had we been dead center of Times Square during rush hour.

"Clean that up." It's his all bets are off, hell to the no voice. Eric apparently has never heard this voice before. He rises, crying so hard he's hiccuping, and he yanks at the table cloth, only it's not the grand gesture he had hoped for, more half assed. Only the wine glasses are upended, and the centerpiece. Eric, covered in shame, runs upstairs bawling like a baby. Jason doesn't move, he turns to Connie and says, "Another bottle." I make to go after Eric, but he stops me. "Don't. He has to learn."

And I snap, "Like I had to learn?"

"No. You were never rude." We continue eating in silence for a while until Jason blurts out, "He's very beautiful. Eric is very beautiful."

Yeah, he is. Does the man expect me to gift him with an argument. "He's gorgeous, duly noted."

"He's just a little nervous."

"Of course," I say.

Jason looks at me as if he expected something more from me. What? I gave at the office.

"Just don't judge him too harshly, that would be unfair of you."

I'm at the fucking wedding, cabron, I think to myself. I left selflessness a couple of area codes ago. He nods, my silence somewhat satisfying him. Some of his friends join us, and it's strike the sets, kill the lights. Thank God that tasteless little scene is over. Jason's friends are here! A stag party!!! All is right with the world.

That night the toasts are never ending. Not fast and furious, more like slow and deadly. Oh, they start out great, very "Jason you is the man" (well, said in the gay fabulous language of his friends). A few comments about him finally finding true love that have Eric beaming and me statuelike. And then, things slowly take a turn from the civil (union) to the coldblooded "where's your sense of humor?." It seems that all of Jason's 'friends' have the bad taste to tell him what I couldn't.

"Don't marry him, adopt him!"

Guffaw.

"Did you get a senior citizen discount on the ring?"

Raucous laughter.

"At least you'll be dead by the time this one's warranty runs out."

(Really? A friend just said that? Really?)

Jason's laugh is as hollow as Eric's is full. He doesn't see what I see. That the man we love is so very afraid. For a moment, Jason looks at me, we lock eyes and I know he needs my help, so fuck it, I step up to the plate for Jason. My Jason, at least for this one last moment.

"Jason and Eric, I can't explain love, no surprise there, huh."

(Mere titters. Tough room.)

"But real love, is timeless, so here's to you both. …That's all I got. To Jason and Eric." I toast. robpup's hand is at the small of my back, propping me up cause that's what hermanos do, you know. And the poison finally dissipates in the room.

I go to bed but don't sleep a wink. Not at all. At five am I sneak out to the kitchen for my café con leche with hopefully a very strong shot of bourbon in it. I know I look a wreck, no sleep, stress, I could pack my Gucci bags into the bags under my eyes and still have room for my carry on items; but at least I'll be alone.

I spoke too soon. Jason's already in the kitchen when I get there. Lost in thought. I look at him , all rumpled in his bathrobe and inwardly swoon. "Today's the big day, huh?" I state the obvious.

Jason points to the coffee pot. "Freshly made. And you know where the bourbon is." I want to say something, but I can't. I came down here to be alone. We ignore each other. Then he drops, "…I'm not stupid. This is a mistake." I can only guess someone else has been at the bourbon in a big way this morning.

He grabs me and he kisses me, wait, is this the mistake part?

"Your boy is upstairs," I tell him.

"You're my boy."

And then I say something I never ever said to Jason. "No. I'm not that boy anymore. I'm older. We both are. Jason, you let go of Phillip cause he got old and you dropped kicked me the moment you could download my upgrade. You don't wanna grow old with me. You don't wanna grow old, period. And I can't stop aging. I could be everything you wanted except new."

I probably would have hurt him less had I hit him, cause saying it out loud, shit, him hearing ME say it, kinda scared him. The mask was dropped, if for just a moment and he did the only thing he could do. He walked out and left me with custody of our truth. We, and it was fucking plural, had gotten older. Among all our friends that was the one thing that was never discussed. We were rich. We simply didn't age. We didn't. We didn't.

I followed Jason out to the hallway, who looked like I had pimp slapped him or something. "Eric," he finally said, "is different."

"Is he Dorian Gay?"

"Not funny."

"Not meant to be. He's not gonna make you younger. He can't."

"….maybe I just love him more than I loved you." I hope he regretted saying it, I regretted hearing it. Jason turns and leaves. Jason is gone. I stand there, heartbroken that time hadn't stood still for us.

Dear Diary:

Okay. What did I think was gonna happen? Age before beauty is not the world JasonandJavier ever lived in. So I mechanically got ready for the wedding. I joined my boys who huddled around me, like my own little team of kick ass Cristinas...

Victor gives me the biggest sunglasses known to man and my sleep deprived and tearing up eyes disappear behind them. I pose for group photos, remind myself to breathe and circulate. I could make a break for it, but really, to where? I have to be here for our end, just as Jason will be.

We are being summoned to take our seats, and which fucking side am I supposed to sit on? Bride/Groom/Living Dead? I look up and see Kearn arriving, not with the cash register trying to pass himself off as a dental hygienist, but with Joel. And they are holding hands! For the first, and I'm sure the last time today, I smile.

"Pendeja, you couldn't tell?" Joel teases.

"Sssh. We're keeping it on the underbelly," Kearn says.

"Downlow, papi."

"Same thing."

Joel is beaming. "He gets me." And right there, they kiss. Ah. Kearn knocks a solid one from his flask and so does Joel. At the moment there is a gong, gee just like the Met, alerting us to take our seats in the tent. I grab the flask from Kearn and help myself to a mouthful of salvation. Except-

"What the fuck is this!?" I scream and spit simultaneously.

"Gin with piss," Kearn says, most reasonably.

"It's my piss," Joel brags.

After my uncouth imitation of a lawn sprinkler I follow the third gong and my boys into the big top (no jokes, please). There is the general abuzzing that occurs at all these events and I zone it out the best I can. This will be it. The bitter(est) end. Ever after in 5...4...3...2...1 ?

Okay, someone's planning to make a Vegas size entrance. 5...4...3...2

One of Jason's assistants comes in and curtly and efficiently dismisses us. The wedding is off.

Almost against their will every mother fucking pair of eyes finds itselfs drifting in my direction. I want to scream out "Ididn'tdonuthin!" but instead just sit there as sphinxlike as possible, internally thanking Victor for the use of the Jackie O's.

As people leave, you can tell they no longer know which way the all important wind is blowing. I mean, it's not like Jason has come downstairs and swept me in his arms or nothing, but you can tell by the manicured and pampered faces that I am suddenly back in the game. Thus.

"Javi, dear, won't you ride back with us?"

Someone else whispers "I knew it," and discreetly touches my arm, bestowing me with a secret nod that could never be traced back to him.

Lorraine gives me the smallest of smiles and a little wink, she snaps her diamonded fingers and hubby number you're guess is as good as mine, falls in step behind her as they leave.

I hear "Maybe Eric will go back to hustling. He is a one trick pony." Followed by a guffaw. The Macgaybeth witch now stands before me, and oozing charm brazenly says, "Javi, you and Jason have got to come up to the shore. I won't accept no for an answer!"

Which elicits from me, "Oh, sorry, but I hope to get a half share on Cherry Grove, which by the by I'll be sharing with my downlow cousin here; but if I can tear myself away from that new shipment of anal pleasure beads, gurl they glow in the dark! I'll be sure to call you."

Joe Bear bursts out laughing and I think I actually made the old cuz blush.

I don't dare turn around. I don't dare turn around. I don't dare turn around. Eyes forward, I get in the car, I don't need to wait. Jason is not coming for me. The ride back to the city is quiet, then giddy, then quiet. The boys all have themselves tremendous gift bags. (No seriously, who did Eric hire to do their shopping?!) and while I was gonna leave mine, Victor commandeers it. "For Sonia." Which leads to a fight with Hector which is a virtual blow by blow (absolutely no irony here, but believe me, plenty of tongue in someone's cheek, clearly Victor and Hector have hooked up) of the Hector and Sonia mating last summer on the roof.

Last summer. When I thought I was gonna die. But I surprised myself. I didn't. Thanks to my boys and you, my dear Diary.

Three months later

Dear Diary:
We are scheduled to hit Cherry Grove tomorrow!!!! Yay!!!
So we are meeting at the Castle. Kearn will be joining us. Yes,
he and Joel are still a couple. Amazement all around. Kearn
even bought a mansion (I'm not gonna call THAT a cottage)
for Joel on the Grove but Joel just said, "ay papi, it's too soon."
Maybe he doesn't want to fall into the trap I did. Maybe, no
maybes about it, he's just smarter than I was...

It's 4:30, the meeting's not till 5 but as per usual I'd rather be here than just about anywhere. No, not even drinking that much, just sitting here. Chilling. Until an ice floe this way comes. Jason.

I see him in the backsplash before I turn around. He's never been here before and he looks out of place and nervous. And beautiful. I'm sorry, diary, he does. He always will to me. He sees me and walks towards me, as every ending to every romantic comedy I've ever seen plays in my brain.

Without even turning around I say, "Well, don't just hover. Sit."

He doesn't.

Little by little the bar noise typical of this joint begins to die down. Prompted in no small part by Victor, who upon turning around and catching sight of Jason gasps audibly, drops a bottle of domestic vodka and crosses himself. "Ay virgen!" It seems me and Jason are about to play the last scene of our telenovela to a very hushed (sssh, callate loca!) house.

"Can we go outside?" Jason asks.

"No," I answer. This is met by appreciative nods. After all, the entire bar can't fit in the back of the limo. Not that they wouldn't try.

"I wanted to come here for a long time, I just had to be by myself for a while," Jason tells me.

"Where's Eric?" Let's cut to the chase here.

"In Miami with a lovely condo."

"And you just dumped him?"

Jason, of course, has no answer.

"I did tell you I was sorry, didn't I?"

And I cut him a look that makes him forget that we are currently, I'm sure, being filmed by every iphone in the place. I'm half surprised that a baby pink spotlight (gay bar, remember? there IS no other color) hasn't found it's way to us.

"I am sorry, Javi. Javier. I am more sorry than you will ever know." And I look down, cause words are useless here. He sits. The room leans in. The bar phone rings and is promptly disconnected.

"...When they were toasting me at the house."

"Roasting," I correct him.

"Even after what I did to you, you had my back. Still."

"Well," I say, half looking up, "I once had your front, too." And I say it so casually the total inappropriateness of it doesn't land until Jason is laughing so hard he is crying.

"Oh Javi," he says, smiling all the way down to my soul, "I've missed you so much."

He takes my hand, then looks at it. "You have calluses."

"Yeah, I do. I didn't before, but I do now. My hands are older. I mop floors. Like my Pops."

And he takes my hand and kisses it. "I like this hand." he says. "You still love me?" he whispers. And the room, which was quiet before now takes on the stillness of outer space.

My boys enter now, loud, but quickly struck dumb by what they see. And hear. Jason, Mr. Wilcox, a man of indescribable wealth and means drops down to one knee.

"Will you marry me?"

And I want to say "Yes!" More than anything, yes is the word I want flying from my lips, but I am silent. Jason takes out a ring, inscribed inside it reads "Javi te amo."

And I know the script, I know my part here is to I hold on to Jason as tight as I can. To hold on to him forever. Te amo. My line is "Yes!" It's just one word. Why can't I say my line?

"We'll get your things, forget them, I'll get you brand new everything, and we'll go back to the triplex, or do you want a townhouse, whatever you want. Say it and it's yours." Clearly for Jason, this is a done deal, but as for me....

I look at him, and I go back into his eyes, back where I once felt so safe and loved, but that was then, and now, well now is now.

"....No," I say in a voice I don't know but must be mine, almost like I'm hearing myself from far away. "This is not because I'm angry, I'm not, not anymore and it's not to get back at you. I swear. There's a part of me that's always gonna love you but you threw me away, you did, and I didn't think I could survive, but I have. The Javi you're proposing to now is not the same one you met a hundred years ago. I'm older, wiser, stupider, and you, ...you gotta earn me now."

robpub is the first one. He begins to applaud and my boys join him. Of course I want to be with Jason, but for the first time I think I'm just as worth loving as he is.

And Jason being Jason he makes the kind of exit I always wanted to make but never could, his dignity intact, even as Lorena hisses "toma cabron!" Everyone laughs it up in the bar, but I see Jason's shoulders hunch as he gets to the door and dart out after him, as the bar begins to gossip and rewrite what they just witnessed.

Jason is standing by the limo, his back to me, his shoulders heaving as he cries. Having hurt him gives me no joy. I go to touch his shoulder but catch myself and fold my arms in front of me.

"Jason."

"Tell me," he finally says, "what I can do to make it up to you."

"You can be my friend."

And without looking at me, he nods.

Dear Diary:

At a certain point I had it all and I was careless. Yes I was. My friends thought I had abandoned them, and I had. My parents thought I ignored them, and I did. And Jason thought I had taken him for granted, and that was true too. And of course you, when was the last time I had even talked to you? But, the person I most took for granted, the one I just would push to the side cause he'll always be there, so what's the rush, was me. I was so busy trying to be the person I was supposed to be, the one that went with this lifestyle that I totally lost the me of me. The me that makes me special. I'm still taking my dance classes, religiously, four times a week. Dance classes are all the same, you stretch, you go from corner to corner and then you're put into little groups and learn a combination. There are two lines to every group, front and back. I always go into the second group, back row. Really trying, but not confident yet to be in the front. Until the other day, when Kenny, the dance teacher, took me by the hand and leading me to the front, said, "You're good enough to be in the front now." And for the first time, I believed it...

Jason comes to the Red Castle from time to time. He knows he can usually find me there. That's like home to me. We talk, and sometimes he gets a little mushy, but too much has happened for me to be with him again, maybe ever. The trust he broke, that just doesn't grow back. I was always so grateful that he picked me I never thought that, hey, he should be grateful I picked him, too. At the end of the night, Jason will get in his limo and leave, hoping to pick up someone to share his paradise with him, if for just one night. Me, I'm holding out for someone who deserves me. Maybe it will be Jason, maybe not. I'm not the god from Mount Gay Olympus, even though I had all the accouterments. I'm just a demigod, but for the people who love me, that's more than enough.

The end

For more of my writing check out my plays:

Unmerciful Good Fortune

Diosa

Clean

Trafficking in Broken Hearts

Barefoot Boy With Shoes On

Icarus

Floorshow: Doña Sol and her Trained Dog

The Road

Edwin Sánchez: The Short Plays

All are available at BroadwayPublishing.com.

CPSIA information can be obtained at www.ICGtesting.com
Printed in the USA
LVOW12s0235110615

442046LV00001B/97/P